A Page from My Life

A Page from My Life

A SELECTION OF STORIES FROM
RAY D'ARCY SHOW
LISTENERS

HarperCollins*Ireland*

HarperCollins*Ireland*
The Watermarque Building
Ringsend Road
Dublin DO4 K7N3
Ireland

a division of
HarperCollins*Publishers*
1 London Bridge Street
London SE1 9GF
UK

www.harpercollins.co.uk

First published by HarperCollins*Ireland* in 2020

5 7 9 10 8 6

A catalogue record of this book is available from the British Library

HB ISBN 978-0-00-844792-2

This book is a mixed offering of short stories and memoir:
part fiction and non-fiction. Where references are made to real people,
events, organisations, institutions or locations this is intended only
to provide a sense of authenticity and may be used fictitiously
or may have been changed.
Opinions and views expressed by characters or authors
do not necessarily reflect those of the publisher.

Printed and bound in Great Britain by CPI Group (UK) Ltd, Croydon

MIX
Paper from
responsible sources
FSC
www.fsc.org   **FSC** C007454

This book is produced from independently certified FSC™ paper
to ensure responsible forest management.

For more information visit: www.harpercollins.co.uk/green

Contents

Life

Laughter

Lockdown

Love

Little Ones

Loss

FOREWORD

I have to confess to being more than a little self-conscious writing this foreword. Why wouldn't I be, here, in this book, in the company of so many great writers. We asked the listeners to the *Ray D'Arcy Show* to be honest, creative, funny, engaging and evocative in their writing. We asked them to try and make us laugh, make us cry and make us think. We never imagined we would get the quantity and quality of entries that we did for *A Page from My Life*.

Well here's the good news they delivered in 'lurry loads' as they say in Kildare. There are moving descriptions of loss. There are laugh-out-loud scenes. There are beautiful descriptions of loving moments and cherished memories. There are dogs, birds, babies, goats, aunties, uncles, brothers, sisters, and more. All life is here.

I truly hope you enjoy the collection of pages from our listeners' lives. Thanks to everybody who shared their stories with us, and congratulations to the writers herein, who in most cases are being published for the first time, which is hugely exciting. I'm confident we will be hearing from a number of these writers again. Everybody on the *Ray D'Arcy Show* is so proud of this book. Thank you so much for buying it and supporting LauraLynn.

– Ray D'Arcy

THE LAURALYNN STORY

by Jane McKenna

A Legacy of Choice and Kindness

Magical, a dream come true – that's how I felt as President McAleese cut the ribbon on that beautiful sunny day in September 2011 to officially open Laura-Lynn House.

I was nervous as the crowd gathered; I could feel butterflies in my tummy. Thoughts of making my speech a little daunting, but I knew my girls would be with me, guiding and helping me as they always do.

The journey to this sunny day was a long and painful one.

My husband, Brendan, and I lost our two beautiful daughters in 1999 and 2001. Our little Laura (4) died after her third and final heart surgery, while on the same day, her sister Lynn (13) was diagnosed with leukaemia. Lynn sadly left us just 20 months later.

We were living every parent's worst nightmare, but our strength to carry on came from the courage Lynn had in her last weeks. At 15, knowing she was dying, she 'lived' every moment and left us the most precious memories and encouragement not just to 'carry on', but to 'live'. She had courage, strength, wisdom and acceptance beyond her tender years.

Lynn's last and greatest wish was to die peacefully at home, which she thankfully got. Her final wish is what set me on the road to this day.

Stood beside Mary McAleese and our patron, Miriam O'Callaghan – by pure chance, all of us dressed in red – as we officially opened the state's first Children's Hospice. The hospice is a legacy, a gift from our two angels to the children and families in Ireland who need hospice and palliative care.

When the event was over and the crowds had left, I had an overwhelming sense of elation that we had achieved this wonderful goal for all the families who would benefit from the care and comfort for themselves and their precious little ones. From my research, I knew that LauraLynn would give families a choice as to how to spend their precious time with their children.

Later that evening, we had a small private celebration with family and close friends. As Laura and Lynn's mum, I felt so proud of our beautiful girls and their legacy.

LauraLynn will be celebrating our 10th anniversary on 27th September 2021. I get goosebumps just thinking of this milestone: a decade of children's hospice and palliative care in Ireland. What an achievement, and a testament to all involved in LauraLynn.

My hope for the next decade is that LauraLynn House will continue to be a 'home from home' for many families forevermore, and that our support can be rolled out nationwide. I also hope we continue to hold on to the kindness and generosity of the amazing people of Ireland, without whom LauraLynn House would simply not exist.

That night, as I hung up my red jacket, I went to bed with a heart filled with joy.

But most of all, as I reflect back on that sunny day, I am proud of our precious girls, our wonderful hospice and its role in Ireland. I know they would be too.

The future is surely bright.

My HEARTFELT THANKS to one and all from both myself & Brendan.

– Jane McKenna
Founder, LauraLynn House

A WORD FROM THE JUDGES

Most writers I know cycle through varying levels of self-esteem. This means that we are supremely confident that we will indeed win the *Ray D'Arcy Show* writing competition one minute and then swamped by regret the second we press the 'send' button. It is a difficult thing to commit private moments to paper, and almost a form of torture to submit those raw memories to a forum of so-called experts who have never walked in our shoes and could not possibly know how we feel.

This is what the competition demanded of people; choose a memory, describe it as best you can and then, somehow, make the judges feel a level of empathy, using only letters on a page. All I knew going into this competition is that it would be easier to be a judge than a competitor. In one way I was right because many of the entrants managed to mine their own emotions so expertly that I wasn't sure I would have made top ten as a writer, never mind win. But being a judge was also tough because we had to pick a winner from this bunch of literary equivalents of hearts-on-sleeves.

I can honestly say that this was the best crop of submissions I have ever had the privilege of reading, and I look forward to browsing this volume with nothing on my mind but admiration.

— *Eoin Colfer*

I always knew the people of Ireland would have great stories in them, if they were given just a bit of a dig. Getting to read a *little* snippet of a tiny fraction of those stories as a judge for *A Page From My Life* turned out to be an honour I wasn't really prepared for.

They were funny, they were devastating, they were wide-ranging. They reminded me of my childhood, they made me appreciate my parents' childhoods, and they made me think about what's really important in life at a time when life itself feels a bit like a simulation. These 500-word autobiographical snapshots left me desperate to know what came before the first sentence and after the last, but they're also so satisfying as the shortest of short stories. I'm so glad that this selection is being shared and appreciated.

While judging this competition I thought about what I'd write my 500 words on. Maybe the time the cat was sliced into neat pieces by a combine harvester. Maybe that summer I spent in New York when the Twin Towers fell. Or maybe, as the beautiful winning entry shows, I could have kept it as simple and as dazzling as being nine on a wall on Wednesday afternoon.

– Emer McLysaght

All of us have stories to tell, and yet so many of our stories go untold.

Perhaps we think that our stories will not interest other people, or that we don't have the right words, or that we will embarrass ourselves. Perhaps we think that we should stay quiet about certain things, and so we hold them, and carry them, silent inside us.

What kind of courage does it take to break that silence?

The answer to that question is found in these pages. When each of these authors decided to send their stories out into the world – a page from their life – they found a way to stop for a moment, to look at their lives, and to listen to the voice inside that says, 'this thing that happened to you, it is important.'

All of us have stories to tell.

Let's tell them.

– Emilie Pine

The stories in this anthology live in the blurry borderlands between memory and memoir, between events and subjective impressions of events, between cold recall and joyful recounting, and each one represents a significant achievement on the part of its creator.

To take a blank page and fill it with words that become living images in the reader's eye, sounds in the reader's ear, and resolve into a perfectly formed slice of the life of another living being is an admirable feat: to compress this effort into 500 words requires great skill and economy and judgement.

I love that this book exists and that so many people have been given a chance to share their stories, funny, sad, surprising, inspiring, always fascinating, with a large and appreciative audience, and that so many words that might otherwise have been left unspoken or unheard will live forever now between its covers, waiting to be discovered, over and over again.

– *Donal Ryan*

Life

Carrying the Tree

BY AOIFE MHIC MHATHÚNA

She said we should go and choose the Christmas tree and I wondered how on earth that was going to happen. His car was gone from the driveway, sold or given away. People had offered to teach her to drive, but we all knew that was never going to happen. She said she was too old to learn something new, but that wasn't it, not really. She was always a walker, a cyclist, and slow and deliberate at both. It must have been a week before that first Christmas. We never bought one earlier than that because my mother didn't even really like Christmas trees anyway. She campaigned each year for a painted branch instead – anything to avoid watching something slowly die in the corner of the sitting room.

She said we would have no trouble getting the tree home. It wasn't far, and it wouldn't be too heavy, and we could carry it between the three of us. It sounded tragic. All I could think of was some kind of scene from *Little House on the Prairie*, except it wouldn't be all pastoral and snowy with the bonnets and the aprons and the braids. It would just be sad in the suburban Irish drizzle, with the tree too heavy and my mother trying to jolly us along and no one really wanting to do it in the first place. I imagined someone from school driving past us and pitying me. I hated the thought of that.

3

Being pitied and feeling 'less', somehow. I said nothing, of course. I didn't slam a door or refuse to go, or tell her she was ruining my life like I would have in another teenage life. Another teenage life in which I might stay out too late and drink too much and dye my hair purple. I couldn't say anything to upset her, because if she fell apart, then what would happen? This family was just too small. There were too few of us for one to crumble, especially her. My brother said nothing either. Perhaps he didn't care, or just thought the same as me. Don't make her cry. Don't break this fragile thing that is life now. She's been through enough.

So, we walked down to the village and picked a tree. I don't remember what it was like, but it wasn't too big, and she was right that we could carry it. She was always right about things like that – how heavy something was, or how to fit a big awkward thing through a doorway, or how to dig a pond or how to make a crib out of cardboard and bits of straw. Who knows what we talked about going home but we laughed trudging up Temple Hill. Even at the time I remember thinking she was brave and mighty, and when I think of her now it's 'gallant' I'd use. We three could carry the tree.

Victoria and Tracey

BY DANIEL COLLUM

I wasn't supposed to be in Central London that day. My wife thought I was en route to a conference in Stockholm; my colleagues thought I was in Malaga with my family. The plan was to take the District Line to Victoria Station. From there, I would take the train to Kent, where I would meet Tracey. I hid behind a broadsheet almost the entire journey, terrified I'd run in to someone I knew.

I took a furtive glance over my paper on the approach to Victoria Station. There was a man standing in front of my seat – he was tall, overweight, and unfashionably dressed in loose jeans and a red Puffa jacket. His name was Alex Pritchard. He was 32 years old (though he looked older), had recently been laid off from his construction job, and he had a newborn baby and a wife. Nothing about Alex's appearance was remarkable. In the ordinary run of things I would have forgotten his face almost immediately. But, as if the heat and pressure of the explosion had seared his image into my brain, I'll always remember his face.

I recall nothing of the blast itself except an initial white flash. Anything I know now I've gleaned from the news coverage that ensued. At 09:34, a home-made device consisting of eight satchels of triacetone triperoxide concealed in a brown Samsonite suitcase detonated in the third carriage of the westbound District Line. The blast sent a shockwave through the adjacent carriages and derailed the train. Alex, who was unfortunate enough to be standing only three feet from the bomb, was instantly shorn into pieces by the shrapnel projected by the blast. I was shielded primarily by the woman sitting next to me at the time. She happened to lean forward at the moment of detonation, shielding me entirely from the main force of the explosion. Her name was Laura Carr. She was 24, had moved to London only a month prior, and was one of the last victims identified, all of her distinguishing features obliterated in an instant.

My memories of the following days are elliptical. The interior of an ambulance, various figures in scrubs speaking to me in words I couldn't parse. My earliest lucid recollection was on 11 August, three days after the explosion. I awoke in a hospital bed; early evening light was coming through the window and a scrolling news feed was playing on a muted TV in the corner: 'LONDON TUBE BOMBING. 22 CONFIRMED DEAD. SUSPECTS CAPTURED ON CCTV...' I glanced over to my right; my wife was sitting in the corner. I tried to say something, but the words came out as an indistinct garble. She came to the side of the bed and grabbed my hand. 'Andrew, can you hear me?' I nodded. She massaged my hand and nodded back silently for a moment. 'Andrew,' she said finally. 'Why are you not in Stockholm? And who is Tracey?'

Not for Moving
BY AL MULCAHY

It was as I was moving about among the slippery rocks on the shore of a secluded cove at the foot of a high cliff near Kilkee on the west coast of Clare that it began to rain. I had been busily engaged in searching for floats of any kind that had been blown ashore, as they made useful markers for my lobster pots. Fortunately I had a plentiful supply recovered before the rain commenced. While most of the flotsam would be at or above the high-water mark, occasionally a float could be found jammed between rocks further down. As I was preparing to leave the cove, dragging my booty behind me, I happened to spy a shiny seven-inch aluminium float jammed in a cleft in a rocky outcrop. Dropping down on my knees, I reached in and set about recovering it, shoving the middle finger of my right hand through the lug and giving it a hefty tug. Despite a few desperate attempts I was soon obliged to admit defeat; this particular float was not for moving. On attempting to remove my finger, I panicked when I realised that it had become so swollen that I was unable to free it. The tide was on the rise, and I became stomach-churningly aware that barring the timely intervention of the Norse god Odin, who obligingly stopped the tide for Tony Curtis, I was on schedule for a watery end.

Pulling hard enough to break off my finger came to nought; the excruciating pain rendered me a slobbering wimp. I lay thus for the better part of half an hour, and it was only when I felt the chilling effect of the rising water about me that I decided that a spell of constructive and rapid thinking was needed. Emulating MacGyver, I glanced about me and, miracle of miracles, what did I see but a handy-sized loose piece of rock. After a number of serious thwacks by using my free left hand, the errant float came free and before you could say 'sound Ballyvaughan', I was painfully making my way up the side of the cove. Painfully, as the aluminium float, still attached to my now badly swollen and decidedly purple finger, kept striking against any protuberance that presented itself.

My joy on eventually reaching my Austin Cambridge was somewhat dampened when I realised its keys were in my right trouser pocket. Five minutes later, and much to the bewilderment of a passing lady motorist, I managed to extricate them. I then drove to Tommy Lynch's, where he skilfully, but painfully, removed the errant float with bolt cutters.

First Date

BY ANONYMOUS

I haven't been on a date in . . . Jesus, when was the last time? I shifted my ex-husband at a house party; that couldn't have been considered a date. It was more like a drunken hooley, bodies everywhere. I hadn't been out with a man since we broke up. Why the hell did I think this would be a good idea? It was all me. I asked my friend to give me this guy's number and I texted him. At the time I felt compelled to put myself out there. I pointed the gun and I pulled the trigger.

Right, stop panicking. He's probably just as nervous as you are, I told myself. I was nervous to the point of vomiting every time I thought about walking in to the restaurant where he had suggested we meet. I had to walk in there alone. Bare. Me. Like Julia Roberts in *Notting Hill*. Standing in front of a boy, asking him to like her. I wanted him to like me. I needed the validation. I know you shouldn't. You should validate yourself. Everyone knows that. You hear the self-help gurus on the radio saying that we are enough. Well, unfortunately in the case of my marriage, which lay in smithereens on the floor, I clearly wasn't.

I checked myself in the mirror one last time. I looked alright, nice even. The dress was good. Feminine and floaty. The shoes looked a bit funny. There was something not right about them. They seemed a little bit too chunky for the dress. But I could walk in them, and they had sturdy heels that would ensure I stayed upright for the entire date. I declined the offer of a glass of wine to steady my nerves. I hadn't been able to eat all day and pouring a glass of red into an empty stomach would end in disaster. It had before. Not just the once, either.

I couldn't talk in the car. I honestly can't remember being as nervous before in my life. Even my Leaving Cert didn't instil such a degree of fear in me. We were there. 'Enjoy yourself,' my sister said. 'He'll love you. Sure, what's not to love?'

Fuck. 'Thanks. Which door do I go in?' I asked. Why did one establishment need such a vast array of entrances? She pointed me to the one on the left. I got out and my legs felt like jelly. I stood outside for a second with my hand on the door to steady myself. My heart was pounding and I watched her pull away from the kerb. I wanted to flag her down, go back home with her, back to my comfort zone. But I was here now. The pull of what and who lay on the other side made me turn back around and push the door open. I looked down at my ugly shoes and watched them take me inside to the bar. To hope. To possibility. To him.

Outburst

BY OLIVIA COOGAN

He walked up to the makeshift stage, cane in one hand, the other arm supported by a young fresh-faced graduate. An old black man, bent with age, arthritic fingers clasping his notes. On his head, a straw boater. Around his neck hung turquoise beads, and on every finger turquoise rings shone as they caught the last of the spring sun inviting itself in through the domed windows.

'This poem is about the political situation in Northern Ireland. I was there once a long time ago.' A shout came from the audience. 'There are Irish here! I hope you know what you're talking about.' A hushed silence descended as everybody looked around to see who the heckler was. To my utter amazement all eyes settled on me, but I hadn't said a word. Or had I? Such thoughts danced about in my head, but I would never give them a voice. It looked as if I had. I turned to my sister Val for support, but she looked away, embarrassed, distancing herself. I felt like a ventriloquist's dummy, but I didn't feel guilty, only self-righteous. The preceding poet had duped us all. I was determined not to be taken in again.

He spoke with dignity, his velvet voice like a hug soothing the crowd. Candles flickered in wine bottles, and as darkness crept into the room, he was silhouetted

11

against the white wall behind him. When he finished, it was to thunderous applause. We all spilled into the adjoining bar. Immediately I went to seek out the poet. He was seated; head bowed, and cradling a glass of whiskey. I did think his poem was moving, and was eager to tell him so. Sensing my presence he lifted his head. 'I was going to say a few words in Gaelic – I had written them down phonetically, see here?' He pushed the pages towards me. 'After your outburst I lost my nerve.' His body slumped, eyes now vacant where earlier there had been the hint of devilment. A cowed dog came to mind.

I slithered away and joined a table where my sister and others were talking about the works of James Joyce. Of course they were. What else would you discuss following a poetry reading in Greenwich Village! Nobody asked me my opinion, although I had read *A Portrait of the Artist as a Young Man* and half of *Ulysses*. I did endeavour to worm my way into the debate, but I didn't have the currency, which was a degree in English Literature, to warrant the attention of the group. Now it was my turn to feel embarrassed.

Some hours later as we made our way back to the hotel, guilt washed over me and I held it on to it tightly like rosary beads clutched to my heart.

Many years have passed, and I often thought to write to that old man and apologise. I never did.

Victim of Circumstance

BY JOEY STENSON

I don't remember feeling much, other than a profound efflux of adrenaline when I got that phone call. It just left me in a state of celerity.

I wanted to sort out work, it felt important that I did, probably a way of deflecting. That was as far as my realm of emotions went.

It was like a switch was flicked. In the space of a three-minute conversation, my life in that part of the world took on a distinct irrelevance.

About 6:30am on our side, I had just left our squat, one-bed apartment and was on my way to work in Fremantle, Western Australia. Billy Joel was on the radio, 'My Life'. It was only this morning, eight years later, that three words in that song resonated with me as I listened to it again, this time actually hearing the lyrics: 'victim of circumstance'.

Little or no traffic heading south on Sterling Highway. I arrived on site before anyone else. I hadn't really paused for thought or absorbed much of the three-minute conversation I had with my sister 15,000 kilometres away, I just kind of put it in the top drawer for the moment. To be honest, most of what would happen over the next fortnight or so would be stowed away in that drawer too.

I must have phoned my boss a dozen times, no answer. Typical, such a busy man. I would never get to say good-bye to him the way I wanted. I dropped off some tools at the job. I had them from the previous day's toil in the back of the Nissan patrol we had recently purchased, on finance. Loved that jeep. Luckily, we had already gotten the chance to take it into the bush, got the wheels dirty. We had plans for it, turn it into a real off-roader. Maybe fit a fridge in the back, and a roof rack for the surf boards.

A lot of that day is a blur, like a war veteran writing his memoirs years after the event, things are hazy. But some things stand out. Like the lady on the other end of the phone in a Qantas office somewhere wishing me the best and offering a prayer when I requested two one-way tickets on the next available flight to Ireland, one for my partner Caroline, the other for myself. That lady never really enquired as to the nature of our travel. She just assumed, I suppose.

Or when I got back to the apartment, trying to decide which belongings to squeeze into the one battered ruck-sack I had purchased in Capel Camping and left home with, 17 months before. Most of our effects also became 'victims of circumstance'.

I'd been back home the previous Christmas. Flying visit, via San Francisco. Surprised everyone. How grateful I am for that trip. Little did I know then, how life would drastically change in just over six months' time...

The Clinic Visit

BY SUSAN CARRY

October 2006 and I'm in the clinic at Our Lady of Lourdes Hospital in Drogheda, waiting for a colposcopy. It's a big day for me; as a very celibate single mother, my female bits haven't been exposed in the presence of another human being for a long time. I looked at the other women waiting. Were they here for the same thing? Were they like me? Did their last smear test need further investigation? Did their sister die at 30 from cancer? And their mother?

The door opens and the nurse calls me in. I'm tempted to ask her if she has a Dyson to break through the cobwebs that form my chastity belt, but she has a very professional and serious demeanour, so I don't.

In the room, there's diagnostic equipment, a bed with a monitor at its head and the consultant. He explains the procedure, tells me not to worry and I strip and lie on the bed. Nurse Serious Head helps put my legs into the dreaded stirrups and my dignity says goodbye and leaves. I lie there, staring at the ceiling, trying to imagine that I'm on a beach in the Seychelles. My imagination is not good enough, and, instead, I imagine that the doctor is putting on a miner's lamp to hack his way through to his destination.

As the procedure starts, the monitor beside my head

blips into life and there it is: my cervix in 32-inch Technicolor. Of course, I'd googled what was going to happen, and what an abnormal cervix could look like, so I stayed glued to the screen, second-guessing everything I saw. And as I lay there and as the procedure continued, the atmosphere in the room changed. Was I imagining it? I looked at Nurse Serious Head, but she wouldn't make eye contact. Suddenly there was a tangible gravity and tension in the room. And silence. Finally, the doctor said he was finished, and I could get dressed.

Fully clothed now, I gathered my belongings as the doctor explained that he would see me for the results in two weeks' time. My head was telling me not to ask, just leave, say nothing, but I couldn't resist and said, 'Did it look OK?' He looked me in the eyes and said, 'It didn't look normal,' and those four words heralded the start of my fight with cervical cancer.

A Red-letter Day for the Red Rabbit

BY KATE MURPHY

can't remember what the row was about now, but I do recall every detail as it unfolded. The usual exchanges, insults, threats and shouting. A quick retreat. Door banging, kicking and objects breaking. I sat silently and fearfully in the kitchen of my small terraced cottage. Alone with this huge young monster. If I didn't move, maybe he might not attack me. Or maybe this might not be real.

The insults became louder, and there was a sudden crash in the hallway outside the kitchen. 'You are just a fucking slut!' my 19-year-old son screamed close to my face. He retreated to his bedroom. Loud music filled the house.

Eventually, I went to investigate the damage. I was horrified when I saw what had been flung up the hall. I didn't know whether to laugh or cry. I kept staring at it. Oh my God! What glared up at me was my red rabbit vibrator, top off and batteries slung all over the floor.

This was a divorce present from one of my friends after 26 years of my very emotionally abusive and lonely marriage. It was her second vibrator gift to me. The first one was like a lipstick holder. It had taken me quite a while to actually pluck up the courage to hold it in my hand. I had carried it around in my cosmetic bag for months. When I finally did turn it on, I had such a wondrous experience that it had very quickly become my new best friend.

Unfortunately, this wasn't good enough for my friend, who wanted me to progress on to the next stage. I could hardly breathe when I saw the size of the new rabbit. For the life of me I really could not figure out how the 'ears', as she described them, could help as well. And it was red as well. I had hidden this new member of my family away in my wardrobe, but was now staring at it in my hall.

As I saw it, I had two options. Lie down and take all this abuse from my son, or get up and stand up to it. It had taken me a long time to finally stand up to my husband, but I had done it. I was now ten years divorced and reclaiming my own life again. That included my sexual expression. Sexuality is what made me feel alive again, and I was having some fun. Older people with wrinkles and 'unbeautiful' bodies can still feel pleasure.

I put my new rabbit friend together again and placed it proudly in the middle of the worktop in the kitchen. I was going to use this opportunity to confront my son and explain that I was no longer accepting his abusive behaviour towards me; I would offer him some more help and support if he needed. I was no longer going to hide myself or make excuses. The rabbit had brought the light back into my life and let me see the way I wanted to live it. Again.

Making My Mark

BY LOUISE MCCARTHY

I was new to the city. Yet another bright-eyed twenty-something with a degree in my back pocket and a desire to make a mark on the world. I was one of those souls who had a little too much trust in humanity. I knew that coming to Dublin I would have to wise up. People got mugged here. They may want you for money, for your worldly possessions, for your body.

I felt relatively safe along the leafy avenues between home and work. Cycling everywhere, bike accidents and bike theft were my only threats. Still, this trepidation mostly arose when I trekked outside the familiar.

One late summer evening while still a newcomer, I finally got a taste of the city's meaner side. Some friends from college were in town and wanted to catch up before a gig. I planned to meet them on Dame Street over drinks, share my tales of the Big Smoke and then carry on my way.

Having never parked my bike anywhere central before, I thought it wise to lock it alongside others on a busy laneway for passive surveillance. The lane was stepped with a handrail in the middle, so I secured it there and was on my way. The previous year, in a bout of bad luck, my bike had been stolen, and then two weeks later, the wheels from another bike I'd borrowed. This racer was the replacement bike, and I was determined to mind it; in fact, I'd had the front wheel replaced days earlier.

After parting from my friends, I made my way back towards my bike. Along the way, I spied the unusual sight of a man at a bus stop holding a new-looking bike wheel. Alarm bells went off. I darted to the laneway, but even at a distance, I could see my bike falling forwards. I knew he had my new wheel. I could not get done over again. Typically, I'd run from confrontation, but at that moment something swelled within me.

Back I went. 'Sorry, but that's my bike wheel!' I said.

He denied it, so I persisted. No longer pleading, blunt accusation now. His voice became aggressive, cursing at me. I grabbed on to the wheel, back and forth we went in a tussle. Next thing I knew, his bus had pulled up and the driver was trying to diffuse things from his cabin, siding with me, but this guy was on the verge of hitting me. I let go, hands in the air.

Reeling and shook, with my heart still pounding, I wandered back to my racer, unable to process what had just happened. Rounding all the other bikes, I stopped. Stood at a tilt between two steps, there was my trusty bike, a wheel on each step, both perfectly intact, looking good as ever.

That poor man. I was making my mark on the city alright.

LaMonte Armstrong

BY ALICIA HAYES

I watched the surrounds whip by from the passenger seat. The fields were mostly yellowed and dry. Not like the emerald lushness of home. Wisps of heat rose off the tarmac as we drove, the tyres whooshing rhythmically. We were headed to Greene Correctional Institution, North Carolina, to visit a man named LaMonte Armstrong. Greene Correctional Institution, and specifically its death row, had been his home for the last 17 years.

Tereasa chatted through the details of the case with me. She knew every one by heart.

In 1989 Ms Ernestine Compton was strangled with an electrical extension cord in her home. Her murder was unsolved for almost seven years until, seemingly out of the blue, LaMonte Armstrong was arrested and convicted of her murder. He had always maintained his innocence.

There had been no forensic evidence. The case against Armstrong rested solely on the evidence of man named Charles Blackwell. The police had offered a Crime Stoppers' reward of $5,000 for help in solving the murder of Ms Compton. Blackwell, for reasons best known to himself, called the crime stoppers line and gave the name of LaMonte Armstrong. Though Blackwell later recanted his evidence, Armstrong was convicted. With all avenues of appeal exhausted, he reached out to Tereasa at the Duke Wrongful Convictions Clinic, based in Duke University in North Carolina. The Clinic is part of a wider network of Innocence Projects, all of which work to exonerate the wrongfully convicted. Today, Tereasa and I travelled together to see LaMonte.

Greene Correctional Institution is literally in the middle of nowhere. It sits within a vast expanse of scorched fields. As we finally drew near, the building loomed before us, large and grey. It had wire fencing running the entire perimeter, and over a small exercise yard. It looked like a giant chicken coop.

As we stepped out of the car, the dense heat of the North Carolina summer washed over me. I could feel the beads of sweat already forming at my temples. It is hard to describe the heat of North Carolina but it feels oppressive. Heavy on the lungs. I had spent the last few months darting from one air-conditioned place to another. And so we darted from the car to the reception area of Greene Correctional Institution.

I was nervous. I could feel my heart knocking loudly on the inside of my chest. We took off our belts and boots and passed through the X-ray machines, leaving our cell phones and car keys behind in a locker. We signed in. I passed my Irish passport through the Perspex window. I expected a reaction of some kind. Being Irish usually sent the Yanks into a spin about their mother's grandfather who married someone from Cavan. This particular woman clearly had no interest in any long-lost Irish relatives. She pushed back my passport without even meeting my eyes. And so, we were in.

Tereasa and I followed another guard into the prison as he led us to the attorney's room. Everything was green – industrial green: the walls, the floors, the window bars. When we reached the little room there were seats for us, and one for LaMonte on the other side of some Perspex glass. The guard shut the door with a clang, and we waited for LaMonte to join us.

I Had Never Seen My Mother Run

BY SIOBHAN FLYNN

I t was the sight of my mother running that struck terror into me.

In all my short life – despite her constant busyness – I had never seen my mother actually run. Yet suddenly there she was, in the middle of a late July afternoon, still wearing her apron and house-shoes, charging across the yard and down towards the lane.

'Mammy!' My voice puttered out, feebly.

Alarmed, I half-rose, and sank back down on the grass. I was barefoot, having painstakingly walked from the back doorstep to the small lawn, as we called it, to avoid smudging the glitter nail polish that I had applied to my toe nails.

Next to me, blank-eyed and stiff-limbed, on an old baby-blanket, my dolls were assembled for a picnic of flowers and soil I had prepared. Colette, my old rag doll, tipped over, and I just left her, inert, with her yellow hair trailing in a mess of mud.

My mother had vanished down the lane. In my memory of that day, a red-and-white-check tea-towel fluttered from her hand as she raced past, but in fact the tea-towel was found later, flung, crumpled on the kitchen draining board.

At no point had she glanced across in my direction, or attempted any gesture of explanation, or reassurance.

Earlier in the day, my father had gone to mend fences with his brother Patsy on his small farm out the mountain road, taking Rex with him. Rex was eight, just a year younger than I was; I loved him dearly, but he was my father's dog. The rest of us had to make do with the leavings of the slavish devotion he directed mostly towards his beloved master. With his dense black coat and solemn eyes, he travelled perched upright in the front passenger seat of the van, erect and sombre as an undertaker's assistant.

Transfixed, I stared at the spot in the lane where I had last seen my mother – beneath the canopy of horse chestnut, a dapple of sun and shade, a tangle of ivy and fern – willing her swift return. Carefully, I negotiated the sharp stones and rough gravel of the yard, back towards the open kitchen door. I was alone now, unable to recall an occasion when I had been alone in the house before, and reluctant to walk into the empty kitchen, from where my mother had so inexplicably fled.

I stood and listened to the silence, my ears straining, my bare legs and arms prickling with gooseflesh. What I expected to hear, I wasn't sure; the drone of my father's van; the efficient tap of my mother's footsteps; anything that might offer reassurance.

The Bensons' house was three fields away from ours. We would hear, occasionally, if the wind was from the west, ribald shouts, or bursts of raucous outdoor activity. But that afternoon there was only the soughing of a light breeze in the uppermost leaves of the horse chestnuts, which were already touched by the first signs of autumn.

The Line

BY CATHERINE BURKE

Five down, six across. I start to count the tiles, to verify my calculations. But some of the squares lie beyond my line of vision, so I give up and assume there are 30. Instead I close my eyes and start to hum. Not a melodic tune or even a recognisable one – except to me. 'Are you OK?' a voice asks, less concerned and more quizzical in tone.

'Yep,' I reply, eyes still closed, 'just going to my happy place.'

The voice laughs. But I am not in my happy place. I am actually trying visualisation, willing my body to relax and to open itself up to this. I am not in my happy place. I'm not sure I even know where or what my happy place is. Just thinking about it makes me anxious, and that elusive utopia slips further and further away, more intangible than ever. How can I not know my happy place? It isn't supposed to be a trick question. Where do you feel happiest? Answers come to me: on a remote beach; with my lover; cuddling my baby boy . . . but they are not mine. I use them, of course, in those self-help classes – can't be the girl who has no happy place.

I feel a warm trickle on my arm and instinctively open my eyes and glance down. Blood, viscous and vibrant, is pouring along my forearm. Carol is trying to shift the plastic underneath my arm while maintaining her progress with the needle. We both hope that she won't have to withdraw and try again. But after a few more tense minutes of trying to thread the line, it is clear that it will go no further. The hot shower, my visualisations, my distinctive humming, Carol's experience, and dogged determination have all failed.

'I can't go any further,' she sighs. 'The valves won't give way.' She slowly retracts the line and removes the needle. Never one to convey her thoughts through a facial expression, Carol sets about efficiently mopping blood from the various surfaces and says we will try again later. 'Drink plenty water' she calls over her shoulder as she leaves the room.

I exhale, and as I do, my shoulders drop and my body uncoils its tension. Damn it. Obviously not as relaxed as I thought. So much for PMA and the power of mind over body. Load of bollocks. I stare at the jug of water on the tray in front of me. Full to the brim, mini icebergs causing trickles of condensation on the outer plastic. It sits there, proud in its solitude, facing me down like a formidable opponent. We need that IV line for the antibiotics. But by now, my veins are those of an addict, albeit without the highs. The familiar feeling of rising anger evaporates as quickly as it surfaces, crowded out by the equally familiar sense that this is my fault – a weakness of body matched by a weakness of mind.

Not All Superheroes Wear Capes

BY ENDA MCEVOY

My life didn't flash before me. Not that I remember anyway. Maybe that was a sign the situation wasn't as grave as it initially appeared, but that would only be seen with hindsight. I can vividly recall the smell. His smell. The stench of chronic addiction oozing from every pore and orifice. His frame, his fidgeting, and the fact my back was against a wall with a knife pressed against my neck meant that flight wasn't an option. It would have to be fight; and only at the right moment.

So here I was; alone on a dark, deserted, dingy street, suffocating in the stale night heat, in an unfamiliar city thousands of miles from home with an undecided fate. Did he want my wallet? Did he want something else? Something more?

I had left Dodger Stadium amidst the reassuring safety of the vast crowd when the concert had finished. At some point the crowd went one direction and I another as I attempted to navigate the way back to my downtown hotel along a route that had seemed straightforward in brilliant sunshine only hours earlier.

29

'What's your hurry, man?' he sneered, his eyes darting up and down the abandoned street as he exerted a little more pressure on the tip of the blade. Despite the faint, panicked and largely incoherent response that sprang from my parched throat, he was able to discern from my accent that I wasn't native.

'Where you from, man?' he asked with a mildly curious expression. But before I could muster an answer he grimaced as he struggled to get a grip on whatever concoction was coursing through his veins. He growled as its potency momentarily overpowered him, forcing him to roll backwards slightly on his heels. Attempting to regain his balance, he applied greater force on the blade which was now piercing my skin. I prayed.

Time froze. The sudden light was dazzling, so much so that it made me squint. I could barely see the outline of a torso clothed in white. The City of Angels had sent one of their very own to me. Its appearance distracted my assailant and forced him to look over his shoulder. This gave me the opportunity to push away from him. With that, he scurried back into the seedy shadows just as swiftly as he had emerged from them.

Not all superheroes wear capes and not all angels have wings.

The security guard and his flashlight escorted me to a main thoroughfare. After profusely thanking him for the thousandth time, I never forgot what he said before we parted.

'You were damn lucky a false alarm sounded on that side of the building when it did, buddy. Otherwise...' His voice trailed off before he finished the sentence. He didn't need to. I knew what he meant.

Are our lives determined by the chaotic randomness of a wrong turn or a faulty alarm sensor? Or is there something greater involved? Maybe it's just easier to think the latter.

Photo

BY JOHN GEOGHEGAN

Whitney Houston nailed it: 'Give me one moment in time...' Our moment is a framed photo in our living room. This is the 20th anniversary of my wife's epiphany.

'Why don't we get a family portrait? You know, a good one.' This instinct for posterity was not so spontaneous, but instigated by one of her friends who had the job done a week earlier.

'Well, I don't know,' I said feebly, feeling like I was in a dentist's chair. In my wife's mind, we were scrubbed up, groomed and smiling like cats at a creamery.

'Who does them, anyway?' I feigned interest.

'Luckily, I have his number: a lad called Harry. He has a studio, but he said he can call out to the house.'

'He said?' I asked, knowing the countdown had started.

'Yes. He's free on Thursday. He'll be here at seven. It gives us two days.'

That evening at the family dinner I did the manly thing and let the children know. 'Your mother has hired a photographer to take a family portrait next Thursday – that right, dear?' A hundred questions came at once as I gave my undivided attention to the shepherd's pie steaming in front of me. I heard snippets of *what to wear*, *won't be here*, and *yippie* from the youngest. Eventually they too realised all resistance was futile.

'Right.' My wife's tone sounded an octave higher than usual, more akin to a military commander. I recognised it as a weapon I had succumbed to years earlier.

'He'll be here at seven. Get ready after school: cleaned, showered, hair done and your best clothes on.'

'Which ones is that?' my son, aged ten, enquired and was ignored.

'Your dad and I will be getting our glad rags on as well.'

'What are they?' my youngest, aged six, asked, again ignored.

Thursday arrived. I was home as the children arrived from school. My wife was showered and preened, ready to pose as we were ushered to be buffed and ready. Our clothes were laid out for us like jerseys before a cup final match. All we had to do was tog out.

By 6:30 we were ready, giggling at each other, stiff as mannequins afraid to crease anything.

'He's here,' my daughter shouted.

Harry entered, hauling his camera, tripod, lights and backdrops. He sat us at different angles, testing the light as we were ordered to smile by my wife, who was flirting with this young lad flicking his hair and guiding us with a chorus of 'OK, OK, yes, just a little more, yes.' Lights flashed, poses froze, and that was that.

A week later the photos arrived. Delight, embarrassment, blushing and more *Oh my God*s than you would hear of a Sunday service echoed with skittish excitement. Interest waned as the novelty faded, the main print interred in a frame and hung on the wall.

Today it hangs frozen like Dorian Gray, cleaned once a month.

Ticking the Boxes

BY TIMARA LAWLESS

She couldn't believe her luck when she was called so fast and ushered gently from the waiting area. 'This way, please.'

'Oh sorry, last time it was that way...'

'No, through here, please.'

'...not that I come here a lot or anything... oh God,' she joked nervously.

'Very good.'

Institutional hues dulled the room, with its empty desk, swivel chair, plastic seats and couch. 'If you wait in here, Dr Mahon will be along shortly.'

'Great, thank you. Here's my ticket, Nurse.'

'Hold on to that, you'll be needing it later. Can I get you water or anything?'

'No, I'm fine thanks.'

'Sorry for keeping you, mmm... Tammy.'

'Yes, that's OK. I didn't expect to be seen so early.'

'Good. Let me see, mmm... Lawless. Tammy Lawless?' she said, looking through a file.

'*C'est moi.*'

'Date of birth?'

'Eleventh of the third.'

'Year?'

'Sorry, I never reveal my age. 63… the year that is, 1963. Not that I'm 63.'

'Hee hee, wouldn't want that now, would we?' she said. 'That makes you 52, yes?'

'Afraid so.'

'You certainly don't look it.'

'Thank you.'

'So, I'm Dr Mahon. I'd like to run through your registration form, before you get to clinic, OK?'

'Yes.'

'First, are you in a relationship?'

'No.'

'Have you had sexual intercourse since… you know?'

'No.'

'And the last time you did, prior to…?

'With my ex.'

'Male?'

'Dee. No, female.'

'Same-sex relationship?'

'Guess so. Seven years.'

'When did you break up…? Sorry to ask.'

'It's alright, I don't mind. A year and seven months.'

'Thank you.'

'…eleven days, sixteen hours…'

'I'm sorry, it must be difficult.'

'Yeah, I'm okay… it's just…'

'Do you need a tissue?'

'I'm grand…thanks.'

'You know, it takes a long time, bereavement.'

'Bereavement?'

'Yes, losing someone close, you experience many of the same emotions. They aren't dead, but we've lost them nonetheless.'

'Seems like yesterday.'

'It can help us cope with loss, allow us to process, to give ourselves permission to grieve...' Dr Mahon continued.

'Oh God, I'm sorry. You're not here for this. You're not a therapist.' Tears rolled unnoticed down her face.

'Sorry, weren't you told? I'm a psychiatrist.'

'What? No. Why...?'

'You should've been informed beforehand, Tammy. I'm sorry.'

'This is still the Guide Clinic, though?'

'Yes.'

'I guess I'm here to tick the boxes, like. To get tested...?'

'Well, no... but we do need to check with you about what happened. How you're coping, and to ascertain if, in addition to STI checks, we need extra tests to gather relevant samples and swabs – you know, for potential evidence.'

'What extra tests? I just... want to make sure I didn't get any infections...'

'I understand, Tammy, but when someone is sexually assaulted–' Dr Mahon began.

'What...?'

'...raped.'

'But I wasn't raped.'

'You did write on your registration form that the reason you're attending the clinic today was to be tested for sexually transmitted infections, as you had "non-consensual sex".'

'Yes...'

'Non-consensual sex is rape.'

'Oh...'

Snake Stopover

BY MARGARET FLANAGAN

Leaving grey buildings under grey skies, we hit the jungles of Mozambique. Staying at a country lodge made perfect sense, as the journey was too long for both of us, and the Mozambique border can be sheer bedlam at Christmas. We purchased supplies at a market on the way, including a deliciously scented bottle of lemongrass oil. The label read, 'Good with all snake dishes'.

On arriving at our country lodge we went for a stroll with Ross in his buggy. The frangipani smells were dizzying. Bougainvillea blossoms lined our pathway like a welcoming carpet. A balmy breeze fluttered my curls. I knew I was in Africa, especially as the mosquitos feasted on my soft skin, though the persistent rustling under rows of tangled trees left me a bit on edge.

Not being one of those nature buffs who impulsively leaps on anything that moves in the jungle and holds it up for viewing while it hisses, spits and wriggles, as shadows jumped, so did I. I prefer to make a quick exit, so with faster steps we hightailed it back to our thatched rondavel, tip-toeing through the leaves to be safe from any slithering wildlife.

I settled Ross on the bed beside me. At last, I thought, my favourite time of the day had arrived, as velvety red wine tumbled into my not-too-miniature goblet.

Stretching out, I was snug and cosy. I read Dervla Murphy's book, thinking, 'This is the life.'

I heard rustling sounds by the bathroom. A bottle fell on the tiles, making a loud noise. I glimpsed movement from the corner of my eye; I froze solid as I saw a long snake slithering towards my bed. I hate snakes. His head was held up high, with serious dark eyes looking over the bed as if he knew where he was going to sleep for the evening. He was gliding closer by the second. He slithered with such speed there was no time to think. Holding tightly onto my goblet, of course, I flung Dervla's book at him. I did not miss. He got such a fright he curled and coiled, then reluctantly slid away from us.

I gathered Ross up in my arms, and collected my passport and car keys. I decided to squeeze out the window to make a hasty exit, as I did not want to meet that slippery reptile again. I stiffened on the window sill at the sight of flowering cacti between me and my car. I'm no David Attenborough, but I did know that snakes love this sweet cactus plant. It's their favourite. The chances of a snake being looped around a plant here were high. I spied a box; a game of 'snakes and ladders' – of course! I was able to reach it. I threw it on the cactus, alerting snakes of our imminent landing. No doubt fear motivates, as I performed my best Olympian jump ever, well clear of cacti and snakes.

Far from Home
BY CLAIRE LYNCH

The cold of the floor tiles brings momentary relief to my burning cheek. 'I'll just rest for a second,' I think, my eyelids slowly drooping, until a sudden noise behind my ear sends me jolting upright again. A large yellow-and-brown speckled lizard scuttles by where my head has just been. I watch, propped up on an elbow, as he makes his way along the edge of the wall and disappears through the broken grate that half covers the drain in the corner.

My face is wet with sweat and my bones are heavy. I am too tired to keep my eyes open, yet too scared to let them close. I feel like the blood has been drained out of me. I feel like a car with a flat battery. I have nothing left in me to give to this night. It must be nearly light now.

I wonder what time it is, as the now familiar sensation rushes over me once more. The heave starts deep inside me and moves like a wave. It's all I can do to roll over and assume the position. Summoning what little energy I have, I drag myself onto my hands and knees, head hanging limply from my sunburnt neck. My muscles start to spasm. The bile comes hot and fast and is a vicious shade of green. Acidic and sharp, it burns my throat and tongue, forcing a convulsion from coughing that shoots pain the length of my rattling body.

I know what's coming next, so I begin to inch towards the mucky, cracked toilet bowl.

As I drag myself across the floor, I look away, trying to ignore the stench emanating from my destination. Searching desperately for signs of daylight, I glimpse the dark African night through the bars on the window. It is pitch black and endless, and the noise is relentless. It is nothing like it seems in the films. I swear I can hear children crying. I worry about them until I convince myself I must be hallucinating. I will later know it is the sound of hyenas circling nearby.

I make it to the toilet and sit a while – it is as comfortable a place as any. Something bright catches my eye and I spy my long-emptied little bottle of hand sanitiser, discarded on the floor a few feet from where I am perched. I stretch out my hand but cannot reach. I'm overwhelmed with a sudden loneliness. It stares back at me like a ghost from a past life. Just six days ago I had packed it into my bumbag in the comfort of my childhood bedroom, eight thousand miles from here. Now it's like the pink and blue of the label are sneering at me.

My tears form little pools of red as they mingle with the dust on the floor. 'Oh, what have you done, you silly girl?'

Some Days Are Made for Bovril

BY LISA HOWLEY

The hooter sounded. I slid into the inky black water, shivering with a combination of cold and anticipation. It was still dark and murky outside and the wind was blowing directly into my face. This was it – the culmination of years of training, planning and many sleepless nights. My opportunity had finally arrived. I was about to embark on my lifelong dream.

It had all started with an ad on television for Bovril when I was about ten – some 20-odd years ago. Something about it captivated me immediately. It was a grainy black and white clip with a tinge of the greenish hue that night-vision goggles give off. The ad depicted a grease-clad heavyset female swimmer climbing out of the ocean onto a rocky outcrop and accepting a steaming cup with both hands. A threadbare white towel was thrown loosely across her shoulders and she had big circular rings around her eyes from her goggles. The caption read: 'Alison Streeter, Channel Swimmer, Drinks Bovril'. I remember turning to my dad at that moment and saying, 'I'm going to do that someday.'

When I look back now, the audacity of that statement was beyond belief. While I was an average club swimmer, at that stage I had barely ever been swimming in the sea – other than playing in the waves in Brittas Bay during the long hot summers we had when we were kids. I had no idea what swimming the Channel even meant – I didn't even know where it was back then!

The night before the swim was due to take place the weather was horrendous – I sat up in bed all night watching the most amazing electrical storm I had ever witnessed. The wind was howling and the rain was pelting against the wooden window frames of the Dover guest house where we were staying. When I say we, I should introduce you to my team. There was my sister Elaine, and my friends Jenny from Jersey and Eoin from Dublin, both of whom were successful solo Channel swimmers. All three would be accompanying me on my boat, which would be piloted by the renowned Mike Oram. I had spoken to Mike earlier that evening to get the 'green light' for the attempt the following day; we were to start at 4:45 a.m. and we had to meet at the marina in Dover at 3:30 a.m.

Rather than make me nervous, the storm raging outside filled me with relief. I was convinced that Mike would call us very early in the morning to say the forecast had got it wrong and that the swim would have to be postponed. It sounds strange to say that I was relieved, but I was so incredibly nervous that I would have grabbed any excuse with both hands for the swim not to go ahead that day. I couldn't explain it, but I was convinced I needed another day to prepare, just one more day....

Ribena with Ryan

BY HOLLIE HANNON

If my life resembled a book, it would more than likely be this: a dog-eared paperback, crumpled pages and the accidental ink-spill here and there.

Let me take you back to 2014. Life was good then. I was in fifth class, I had gotten my pink braces fitted and I had just won the Sligo Spelling Bee final. My 12-year-old self, you could say, had peaked.

Luckily for my family, the run-up to the semi-final was going to be broadcast on RTÉ. I do adore my family, but we can only be described as a hot mess. Minus the hot.

The camera crew arrived to the house to film some clips and ask me what my hobbies were.

'Um,' I said nervously, hitching my glasses up my nose. 'I don't really have any hobbies. I like to read. But there's six in my family, and we're all kinds of crazy.' I said that with such an air of confidence, as if every Friday night we gathered around the kitchen table playing beer pong.

When the show was broadcast, that statement was followed with a slow pan of my sitting room, showing us all nestled in different corners reading books.

My teachers, relatives and friends were also interviewed for inclusion in the show. They all sang my praises. It seemed to be written in stone that I would win the Spelling Bee.

Finally the big day rolled around and the homemade flags were flying high. My father and I were interviewed just before lift-off.

'How are you feeling today?' the man behind the camera smiled.

'Oh, she's gonna win it. We're certain. Come on now, Hollie, we're going in,' my dad said firmly, giving me a slight push in the door.

The next thing I knew I was staring at Ryan Tubridy – and most importantly, the trophy, taunting me.

'Right, guys, we're going to move on to the first round. You're gonna get asked a word, you'll spell it, and if it's wrong you're out. Alright?'

We nodded.

'Hollie, you're up first. Your word is "blackcurrant".'

My sister relaxed behind me.

'Ah, she's sound. That's eeeasy. A *baby* could spell that.'

I opened my mouth. It was my time to shine.

But in my moment of panic my mind went completely blank.

Blackcurrant? What's a blackcurrant? Is it a fruit or vegetable? How many k's and c's?

Ryan's face began to morph into a blackcurrant.

Suddenly all I could think about was Ribena.

'Blackcurrant,' I gabbled.

'B. L. A. C. K. U. R. R. A. N. T.'

Blackurrant.

Their faces died.

Slowly, my soul died.

Sniggers from the three other contestants beside me.

Ryan's forced smile.

'Aw, I'm sorry, Hollie, but that's incorrect! You missed out on the c! A horrible, nasty word to trip up on. Go and give your family a hug.'

Yeah, we all know what he really meant, though. *Bye, loser.*

I got up and sank back into the seat beside my sister. Her face resembled a question mark.

'How did you *do* that?'

And to this day, readers, I still don't have an answer.

So, I hope you enjoyed this page from my life.

And at least if nothing comes from this, I can say my original claim to fame was the RTÉ Spelling Bee documentary – now on a CD, banished to my attic.

Belonging

BY MAURA BROSNAN

February 2005

I stood in the doorway and looked at him for a while. I knew from his profile he was smiling. He was always smiling. It was his resting face. My whole life's memories were wrapped up in his. My dad. I adored him, and he, me. Was I really about to do this to him? Ask of him the impossible?

I was vaguely aware of John and the children in the background, chatting and laughing easily with Mum. Mum and I had a great relationship, based on love and loyalty. Emotional conversation never came easily to Mum; that's just the way it was, she was, but that never mattered. She left that to Dad, and he was always more than willing to take up the mantle. No one could ever fill my mother's shoes – but perhaps could walk alongside. But should they?

I sat on the edge of our old but loved couch. He turned then and saw me.

'Ah, there you are, girleen. How are you?' Words stuck in my throat for a while and would not come. He knew what I wanted to talk about and he was easing that path for me.

'I'm scared, Dad,' was all I could manage to utter.

I couldn't tell him that I was worried: what if I fell in love with her? Would I love him less?

His beautiful, wise and crinkly eyes met mine for the longest time. Tears rounded and swam at their edges, but never fell.

'Dad, I don't know. Am I doing the right thing? Should I go through with this?' I asked. I knew whatever he told me to do, I would do. My father was to me the wisest person I had ever known, full of kindness and knowledge. His hands, so giant, dwarfed mine when he held them in his. They could knock the strongest man in one blow, but they were hands not meant for violence, but love and warmth – the same warmth that enveloped me my entire 29 years.

He leaned forward, supported by his walking stick. He's aged, I thought, but still not quite looking all of his 79 years. I could feel the heat from the stove rising on my face, the clock ticking in the background, seeming louder than it was. He became serious then and said, 'You must do this, my girl. You must do the right thing, and meet the woman who gave you life. But know whatever happens, after tomorrow you will always be my little girl who I adore.'

Less than 24 hours later, I sat alone waiting in the HSE Adoption Service in Cork. I smoothed out the non-existent creases on my carefully chosen trousers. I longed for a cigarette, and my mouth was dry. I looked at the ridiculously expensive Burberry handbag and my cheeks burned with embarrassment that the bag cost more than my week's wages. Was I that desperate to impress? I must have been. I thought of nothing, only my parents and my brother – how much I loved them and hoped not for the first time that I was doing the right thing. How my parents fought so hard in 1970s Ireland to have a family, a fight they won, but the prize was ours.

I got up to leave, convinced there was no way I could go through with this. As I rose, the door opened. My social worker standing there asked gently, 'Are you ready, Maura? Are you ready to meet your birth mother?'

Silent Phones

BY NUALA SMITH

Christmas Eve 1972, I'd done my last trip as cabin crew and made my way to the house I shared in Dundrum. All in darkness. Jackie'd gone home days ago. I'd no idea when Steve might come – or even if. In the fridge I'd half a bottle of milk and two apples.

It was after eight when I heard his car. I rushed to the door, couldn't wait to hug him. He looked shattered. 'Hold on, Freddy, I've not much time.' He removed my arms, steered me into the sitting room.

'Pack a bag, get over to the Montrose. Now.' He'd join me there as soon as he could. A job on in Newry. Routine. Nothing to worry about. 'Only sixty miles.' He peeled off £200 from a wad in his breast pocket. 'Chin up, Freddy. Sooner I'm off, sooner I'm back!' With a quick kiss, he was gone.

I couldn't wait to get out of the house. Neighbouring houses had Christmas trees, car doors banging, visitors coming and going.

Sleet fell as the Montrose loomed up, all lights and red ribbons, people tugging cases from the carpark. Revolving doors spilled us into a Christmas buzz where waiters and porters dodged each other. I joined the queue at reception.

'Mr Harrington's booking? A double?' She scanned her list.

'Yes, Madam. 120, second floor.' I nodded that yes, Steve would check in later. Flicking her eye over me, she handed me the key.

Our lifeline now, the room had a phone. I put away my things, sat on the bed to wait. How many times I checked that phone. Normal dial tone. Twice I rang reception, asking if there were any messages for me. No, none. Around 1 a.m. I got into bed and tried to sleep.

Christmas morning, I'm awake in the dark. No messages, no calls. My anxiety soaring. Nothing on the TV news. At eight, a brief bulletin because of the day. There'd been hopes of a Christmas cease-fire, but so far, nothing more. Footage of the Queen and her family heading to church in Sandringham.

The day wears on with the TV chattering to itself. I'm hungry. Around one, I ring down.

'No room service today, Madame. Sorry. We've 200 Christmas lunches. Fully booked, I'm afraid. No, nothing… sorry.' Now she's saying if I'd like to come down in a couple of hours, she'll see what she can do.

Even up here I can smell roasting turkey. Terrified to leave the phone, hunger drives me down. Reception rings the kitchen. Waiting, I can see into the dining room: packed, paper hats, shrieking children, laughing dads pursuing toddlers.

A boy arrives, proffering a tray with a ham sandwich on white sliced pan and a slopped cup of tea. I take it, thank him, head back to the room.

As evening turns to night, Morecambe and Wise

seem to be dancing away what's left of hope. Round 12, I get into bed again. No messages, no calls, nothing. Oh God, please…

Freefall

BY AISLING CARMODY

The 26 August 2007: a day that changed the path of my life as I knew it. We had reached the final zipline – 'Freefall' – and I was relieved it was nearly over. 'There's a bit more to this one. It's the fastest of the ziplines,' explained the guide, 'hence the name. It'll feel like you're flying. Each of you will have a parachute-type mechanism attached, so when you let go of the trolley, put both your arms on either side of you and lean forward. It will slow you down and make the experience more enjoyable.' I was struck by the terrain under this final zipline: tree stumps just below the platform from which we were to launch, boulders at the far side, and then the forest's mossy ground in the middle.

I had only booked the ziplining trip that morning after my friends had booked the day before. 'It'll be a once-in-a-lifetime experience,' and as it was near the end of my summer living and working abroad, I eventually plucked up the courage. I had been feeling very unsure and was never really the 'rollercoaster' type. Come the last zipline, I was looking forward to being done with the whole experience. I had nearly turned back at the second, as I was completely petrified; you couldn't see the ground, we were up so high. In hindsight, why didn't I turn back...?

For each of the ziplines two people would go at the one time, parallel and side-by-side. On the second line, one of the two guides had stayed back with me until the rest had gone ahead. I can't remember his name, but he was a really cool, carefree kind of guy. He calmed me down and reassured me that it was going to be OK. And it had been, once I reached the other side.

Given it was the final line, I struck up a bit more courage and decided to go in the middle of the group. I remember seeing one of the girls who went before me launch from the platform as we had been instructed, giving an excited whoop. This was going to be OK, I thought, and regardless, we were nearly finished!

As with each zipline, I asked whether I was tied alright with all of the different attachments, and got the nod from the guide to launch. The last thing I remember was looking over at the girl who was going at the same time as me. As I launched from the platform, something did not feel right. We had been told to let go straight away so we could slow down and enjoy the scenery from a height, but I knew something was wrong. 'Just let go, Aisling,' I thought, 'and it'll be OK.' Next came a feeling of falling followed by darkness. I remember some flashes of faces and cautions of 'Keep still and don't move'. Everything hurt...

Happy on the Fence

BY EMAN AHMED

There have been many stories about the Irish mammy, flashbacks to the wooden spoon (typical weapon of choice), prayers to St Anthony and potatoes in variant forms. Despite having an Irish mammy of my own, some quintessential Irish lingo remains rather foreign to me, like the mysterious 'hot press', which I still struggle to locate.

The issue here is that I am a half-caste: Irish, but not quite Irish enough; and Arab, but not Arab enough. I lie somewhere in the in-between, not really knowing whether I should indulge in a cheeky potato, or a bowl of rice – and potato-rice wouldn't tickle anyone's fancy.

I only realised my rather odd disposition when I was eight. Sitting in class, rummaging through my bag trying to find my homework, my automatic response was to say a prayer to St Anthony, which I did so under my breath. My fellow peers jolted their heads towards me and looked at me, disconcertingly... I suppose St Anthony has no place in an Islamic Studies lesson, surrounded by Ahmeds and Fatimas. I cough, correcting myself: 'Ah, Alhamdulillah, I found my work!' – but I don't think they bought it.

Everyone has a place they call home, and some may say I am lucky enough to have two. They're very different homes: one wet, with great craic; and the other rather humid, with camels. Once again, the wet-camel combination is not a desirable one. You can expect the unexpected with a half-caste like me: thick, dark hair, olive skin, and a very distinctive nose, but once I open my mouth, 'Sameera' gets replaced by 'Saoirse'. The raised eyebrows and head scratches come with intense interrogation: 'Oh, you don't look very Irish'; 'What fake tan do you use?'; 'OMG, you're so good at accents. What other ones can you do?'

This is me, what you see is not what you get, and sometimes what you get changes. Some days I wake up more Irish than Arab, and others I forget the Irish side altogether. People may say I'm having an identity crisis, on the fence about who I want to be.

But I'm quite happy on this little fence of mine, picking the best parts of both sides, creating a tanned, witty, rice-eating, Guinness-drinking, camel-riding girl who will happily jig her way to the mosque. Being caught between two worlds does not make me feel lonely or unwanted, as there are many half-castes like myself. Although we may not have the same experiences or be from the same places, we find comfort in the shared feeling of 'otherness' and 'difference', making home the in-between.

Holy-head

BY AISLING CULLEN

Beneath us, water lapping against steel, the Irish Sea gurgled with apprehension, like my stomach. I felt as though we were encapsulated in a matryoshka doll of transportation, and thought how peculiar it was to be in a car while on a ferry.

We left our belongings safely in the hull and climbed sets of stairs up to the lounge areas, taking in the dated chairs and coffee-stained tables propped against fogged windows, condensation blurring Dublin's grimy port. The weather was typical; the grey and white clouds blooming over the sea, misty rain and salt spray indiscernible from one another. We had to drive because the insurance company wouldn't cover her to fly after the surgery – it would be too much of a risk with the cabin pressure on the way home. I had imagined the scene; Sinead with her head bruised and bandaged, a piñata about to pop, brain matter scattered over the Ryanair seats instead of lost travel sweets. This was our alternative route; we would drive to Great Ormond Street Hospital and return on the ferry after The Operation.

I wandered to the deck at the stern to break up the journey and watched the trail of swirling white foam behind us. This gushing pathway from Ireland, a seam splitting the sea as we chugged slowly towards Holyhead and Sinead's fate.

Every night before the surgery, my mother withdrew from a box of stiff tissue paper and silk, the cloud-white skull cap of Pope John Paul II ('a first-class relic', she informed me). She had managed to borrow it from a well-connected doctor and had taken up a nightly rite of passage. She would place it on my sister's head; Sinead sitting still as a stunned animal before sacrifice, and we'd pray fervently from a dog-eared blessing card. We were told there was a 40 per cent chance that the operation would successfully leave her seizure-free, and my mother was determined to better the odds by any means or miracle. What were the odds that when they opened her crown, my little doll of a sister, they would reveal another girl underneath? After 11 years of heavy medication, 16 tablets a day of Epilim and Topamax and God knows what, she was already dampened and doped up. She turned 13 and this was presented as an alternative route. They could remove part of her frontal lobe and cut away the nocuous epileptic knot, but there was a risk posed to neurological pathways in the process. Would they tear the tenuous threads of language, memory or personality? Would she be a different person when this all unravelled and they stitched her back up?

From the Pier at Portmagee

BY MICHELLE WALSH

From the pier at Portmagee, I see the tip of Skellig Michael push through the surging waves like a shark fin. Little Skellig trails in its wake, its shape flatter and less menacing.

The waves swell, then pound against the rock, sending spray into the sky like confetti. It is possible the waves originated as far away as Newfoundland and rolled, over days and weeks, along the seabed, scooping sand and shells into their curling forms until they completed their crossing of the North Atlantic, charging to the surface to break over the Skellig rocks in front of my eyes.

As the sun sets, the rock turns black, its hulking silhouette reminiscent of an iceberg that dislodged itself from its frozen roots and, like the waves, travelled far from home.

Tomorrow I will take a boat and my belongings and go to live on that triangular rock for the summer. There is no running water, no electricity, a single gas ring for cooking, a solar-powered toilet, and an instruction to pack bread mix in the event of being stranded by an Atlantic storm.

I am worried about two things – the sea crossing and my hair. Skellig Michael lies eight miles off the mainland. It looks close enough to swim to, but the boat journey has a reputation for causing severe sea sickness. My long, thick hair takes two days to dry without a hairdryer. It is a time before dry shampoo. I pack multiple hairbands and a hat.

The monks in the sixth century transformed Skellig Michael from a barren rock into a cathedral of prayer. Its triangular shape lends a gothic air to the vertical, black cliffs that rise like the high, imposing outer walls of Notre Dame that tower over the tourists. Ribbons of stone flutter down three sides of the island, some in better condition than others.

The seabirds are the choir. Their cries are natural songs of praise. The cliffs are a gallery of sounds, a natural orchestra. The plaintive cries of the kittiwakes, that onomatopoeic bird, crying *kittiwake, kittiwake,* reverberate into the air. The seagulls squawk, their *caw-caw* sounds harsh against the wind. Guillemots laugh, shoulder to shoulder on tiny ledges of rock that jut from the cliff face. They are the avian equivalent of high-rise apartment dwellers sitting on their balconies at the same time.

These are the sounds that greet me as we draw alongside the pier at the east landing. There is a smell of fish, seaweed and salt in the air. I taste it on my tongue as I heave a sigh of relief at putting my feet on solid ground.

We walk the stony path on an incline to the Porta-kabins. Seabirds clot the sky, wheeling and screeching through the air, back and forth from their precipitous nests. They have a magnificent view, I think, as I look outwards, nothing but endless ocean stretching towards the horizon, dark blue meeting light blue at the hem of the sky.

Like Many Others

That day had started like many others. I had awoken again in my sleeping bag in a doorway of a shop in Dublin city centre. It was early – I would guess it was roughly between six and seven o'clock. I sat listening to the traffic passing up and down, the patter of people's feet passing by and muffled conversations of people I guess were either coming or going from work. I got up and got on with my usual situation of hiding my sleeping bag nearby and heading out to get my fix for the day. I had a horrible addiction at the time, which was heroin. It had brought me to some terrible places, and that day would be no different; I just never knew what was going to happen or where I would end up each day.

I managed to get my fix that day. I remember it was a nice evening when I got back to where I was sleeping that night. I had been sleeping rough around the city centre for roughly a year at the time, but that night was rougher than most. I had fallen asleep at God knows what hour. I was physically, mentally and spiritually drained from all that had gone on with my addiction and situation. I awoke in the early hours of the morning, roughly about 3 o'clock, to what I thought was lashings of rain. When I peeled back my sleeping bag and turned my head, I realised it was some bloke urinating on me. Today from time to time I can still get that smell, which brings me back to that moment.

I remember the feelings that I went through at that time. I felt so weak and absolutely worthless, and not having the courage and strength to jump up and confront the person still eats away at me today. Instead I cowered away again back into my bag until the person had left. There was tears streaming down my face from the worthlessness I felt at the whole situation. I ended up walking up towards James's Street and found myself at a set of apartments where the gate was open, so I wandered in. I found myself sitting in between two industrial bins, which were tied together with a blue rope.

It was a decision made in a split second, but it was the accumulation of all that had went on in the build-up to that moment. I untied the rope from the bins and climbed up to a rail outside the top apartment. While tying the rope and getting it ready for that awful moment, all that was going through my head was the feeling of worthlessness and how this world would be much better off without me. The tears were rolling down my face but the decision was made without any thought for anyone other than myself, and getting away from the hurt and pain I felt or had caused others. I put the rope around my neck, and dropped.

by Philip Ormond, a person of gratitude, a proud father of two beautiful girls, and now a frontline worker using my past to – hopefully – benefit others.

Zoom

BY ORNA SHERRY

Sitting side by side on a hospital trolley covered in a cobalt-blue disposable sheet, my head whipped to the left, his to the right, to stare into each other's eyes. Never had I looked this way into another's eyes. It was more of a 'ZOOM', deep into his soul and his into mine. The love, the years and the life ZOOMED within me in that flash, like the whoosh from *Back to the Future*. I pictured him, standing at my front door, in his John Major glasses and patterned jumper, smiling his happiness at me. Me in Levi's, size eight then. I knew at that moment, that he was the one. Another ZOOM! Quick-stepping down the Victorian church tiles, our wide-open smiles and our eyes upward, towards the soft, pastel confetti falling like snowflakes onto our hair.

'Brain tumours?' I said.

'Yes, two of them: here and here,' said Priya, the petite doctor, pointing to her own head. 'I'm so sorry.' Her words ZOOMED through my body, causing a giant heartbeat to reverberate inside me. A tsunami of a heartbeat. It was painful, I remember. I could feel some tears, but they were just automatic, like a hiccup after sipping 7 Up. I should have felt the sorrow, but the heartbeat was too big to allow that in, for now.

I had a feeling, to be honest, when we arrived by

ambulance to Beaumont, that this wasn't a stroke. After the CT scan had taken place, we were being avoided by the same doctor, diverting her eyes each time she passed us. She did eventually find the courage to tell us. I wish it had just been that stroke.

'No, it can't be!' I pleaded.

'We'll admit him now, and he'll be seen by oncology tomorrow.' Priya was braver now that the news had been broken, the evil gift delivered. Her face kind, but assertive.

Another ZOOM! 'Quick, it's getting away!', I yelled at him, while cowering from the big spider on the bedroom carpet. Calmly, eye-rolling at me, 'It's OK, the monster is gone,' he laughed, tossing the beast out the window.

Boarding the plane in Spain to come home a few hours before, I knew he wasn't himself. 'My sinuses,' he said. The migraine was back, and he was dragging his foot while walking. On we limped, to Arrivals, planning to get him to hospital. That plan was axed after he collapsed. I can still hear him telling the paramedics that he was fine, just dehydrated from the flight.

I had to pull in on the way home, on the M50. Another ZOOM! To an unwanted destination on my itinerary. Standing, sorrow-sodden, in the cemetery, husbandless, feeling the hard leather of my best handbag in my petrified grip and the insecurity of my highest heels.

Today I zoomed again, three years of radiation and chemotherapy later, on my laptop with some pals, waving back at me. He peeped his head in, grinning, 'Gin and tonic, love?'

Laughter

Darby's Daughter

BY DECLAN O'CONNELL

On a torrential Sunday in September 1982, around 5 p.m., Séamus Darby entered the annals of Irish sporting folklore and broke my eight-year-old heart. Almost everyone recalls the Offaly substitute's contentious last-gasp winner to deny the legendary Kerry football team the elusive five-in-a-row. What's forgotten is the media controversy that I caused sometime later over said goal.

That evening, armed with the sense of injustice only an eight-year-old can possess, I stormed into the drizzle and gloom of the back lawn, replaying the game from throw-in to whistle. Time to right some wrongs.

I was Jack O'Shea. I was Brendan Lowry. I was the guile of Mikey Sheehy, the velvet of Matt Connor. I was every player. I was the ref and the crowd. I was Mícheál Ó hEithir. And near the end, I was Offaly manager, Eugene McGee, telling Séamus Darby to sit back down – not today, son. Darby stayed on the bench and Kerry completed the five-in-a-row. Revenge. Sorry Séamus. That's business.

The world of an eight-year-old moves fast. Some weeks later, and Darbygate is a fading memory. At home, Radio 2 children's show *Poparama* is playing on the wireless. Ruth Buchanan – of Shane Ross fame – says

67

Mícheál Ó hEithir is going to be taking questions. Just ring in.

Dial the number. Kerry calling. Sure enough, on the first attempt, *drrr drrr* – I'm in. Before I know it, I'm in line to talk to the iconic Mícheál Ó hEithir live on national radio!

'What do you want to ask him?' asks the researcher.

'What's his most memorable football match,' says I.

'Sorry,' says she, 'somebody already has that one.'

'Hurling match so,' I say, disgusted, the sense of injustice building again. Kerry fella asking about hurling – the shame of it!

All the while, the family is huddled around the radio, my sister's tape recorder ready to chronicle this historic moment.

'Now we have Declan from Kerry,' says Ruth.

'What's your most memorable hurling match?'

Off goes Mícheál, his unique tones describing some ancient final played in a thunderstorm. I've pretty much zoned out, but as Mícheál finishes, he asks cheekily, 'Why didn't Kerry win the five-in-a-row?'

Red. Rag. Bull.

'Because Tommy Doyle was pushed by Séamus Darby!' A lifetime (or weeks) of hurt healed by this outburst. Gotcha, Darby! You're outed, boy. It's over for you. I was quickly bundled off the air, and as we listened back to the recording, all seemed well with the world. The whistleblower had blown. Sam was coming home.

As *Poparama* played on, Ruth's voice drifted from the corner of the kitchen.

'Now we have Naomi from Offaly. What's your que–'

'MY DADDY DID NOT PUSH TOMMY DOYLE!'

It was Séamus Darby's daughter, incensed at my claim on the national airwaves, and ringing in to defend her dad's honour; another last-minute intervention, you might say, by another Darby. With *Poparama* offering me no right of reply, she'd had the last word on it, same as her father had in Croke Park.

1982 was a year to forget in the Kingdom.

Christmas Cheer

BY CATHERINE LAHIFF

It was the last Friday night before Christmas, one of the busiest nights in London's social calendar. I had arranged to meet my nephew and niece for dinner. They had both come to the city to work earlier in the year so this would be their first experience of Christmas in London. We met at the restaurant, had a nice meal and a pleasant evening catching up with each other, the atmosphere was festive and everyone around was in high spirits.

My nephew had told us that as he had been running late, he had driven up from south London rather than take the train. He said he had been lucky to find parking somewhere in Leicester Square. I thought no more about it, and after leaving the restaurant we wandered around town, admiring the beautiful lights and decorations and savouring the seasonal atmosphere. Music was playing and the place was packed with party revellers. London at Christmas time is magical.

As we headed back to Leicester Square, my nephew turned towards the small, exclusive city car park. My mouth hung open.

'You mean you parked HERE?!'

'Yes, it was all I could find!'

As we walked into the foyer, I looked around and

stifled a giggle. The three of us looked at each other and burst out laughing. Picture the scene: the place was full of the well-heeled of London, all dressed to the nines in evening or cocktail attire, having just been to dinner or the theatre. It was a valet parking garage. The smartly dressed young valets approached each customer, took their car keys and asked for the vehicle registration. Off they went eagerly to collect the vehicles. It was clear they loved their jobs, which allowed them a few minutes to drive the cars of their dreams. Down the ramp came shiny BMWs, Mercs, Jags and sports cars of all types to be reunited with their glamorous owners. Then it was our turn; we could not stop laughing in anticipation of what was to come. People turned to look at us, wondering what on earth was so funny. We didn't appear drunk, this middle-aged woman in her elegant business suit and high heels and the two 20-somethings. Soon they would find out. Down the ramp trundled my nephew's battered white work van (he is an electrician). Now the other customers got the joke and to their credit they entered into the spirit of the moment. Everyone cheered as the red-faced valet handed Ronan his keys, while Síle and I in our skirts and heels tried to climb in with as much dignity as we could muster.

I think it made everyone's night. It certainly made ours.

What Else Could It Eat?

BY CLAIRE WALSH

It started with an innocent curiosity. What was it? Why did it have that shiny appendage? Why did it make that noise? At first, I hid behind the bathroom door, unable to look directly at it, for fear that it might be looking right back at me. The path was a clear, straight line from the bathroom door and yet I took my time making the journey. Over weeks I tiptoed past the sink and felt the cold of the tiles on my feet, each day getting closer and closer until I found myself face to face with my own glassy reflection.

My features were distorted in the white ceramic surface and my head poked slightly above the top but, I could be sure, that was me. Once I had breached the distance barrier and approached the beast there was no stopping me. I peered into the bowl, my mind swimming with endless possibilities, and was utterly disappointed to be met with some bleak – and slightly blue? – water. Perhaps I had got it wrong. Was this some variation of the sink or the bath? No, surely not. I knew I had seen it in action, I had heard the rumbling and the sloshing. The sound had emanated from the bathroom for as long as I could remember, and now I was going to figure out what it was.

I decided to take action. I reached out and up,

extending my arm to its full length and grabbed the shiny handle, large in size when compared with my hand. I pushed it down and heard the familiar rumbling sound, accompanied by the swirling water getting higher and higher. In an instant it was all over and the noise died out. I was left standing, frozen in position, completely in awe of its power. I couldn't believe what I had just witnessed. How had I only become aware of the white, shiny, magical machine that had apparently been under or rather at level with my nose this whole time?

After a few successful attempts I grew braver. I threw a white tissue into the bowl and – to my amazement – it disappeared. With a rumble the tissue paper had been swallowed, and so I was left to wonder... what else could it eat?

At first, I started small: a tissue; a ball of tissue; a cotton ball; a tea light; a cotton swab! Over time, more and more of the common bathroom items found their way down the drainpipe and my power was only growing.

I had become well acquainted with my new friend and I knew the bond would only grow stronger. It was at that exact moment that I realised, on Monday morning, as I reluctantly awaited my first day of pre-school; I knew just the place for the car keys.

Circle of Life
BY SEÁN LARNEY

The sweat was rolling down my neck, the droplets teasing my spine as they slowly descended. Despite the heat of a high 20s summer day, all of us were shrouded in our funereal finery, none comfortably, listening to the crackling tannoy service, unsure how much responsibility lay with the microphone and how much the ancient priest. Personally, I felt a slight jealousy as I looked over at Mum in her suitably formal dress that nevertheless allowed freedom of the shoulders. These were turning a soft pink that would later necessitate a trip to the chemist for a bottle of Nivea Aftersun, where she would agonise at the counter over whether or not we had a half bottle left at home from last summer.

I looked down at the grave in front of me. It had been cleaned recently; weeded, resoiled, old flowers replaced with younger models. I knew, because Mum left a note on the fridge last week: 'Gone to fix up Grandad's grave. Mass of the Graves next week. Lasagne in the fridge. Don't eat it all!'

Looking at the flowers, it struck me that two circles of life were taking place concentrically here, never to meet, the old replaced by the young, a ritual ubiquitous to all species. Mysterious, but beautiful, in a way.

'Jesus, I'm roasting in this, aren't you?' My brother was shuffling next to me, trying to shrug off his black suit jacket without Mum noticing. He leaned in and whispered right into my ear, his warm breath tickling my eardrum.

'Have you got some water?' I leaned away, shaking my heads giving him a warning glance that took Mum in as well. I'd just seen her head turn towards us slightly in the manner of a lynx when tracking the progress of prey. I didn't want to take a bullet here.

'I'm definitely not getting buried when I die,' he went on, not picking up on my subtle hints at all. 'Cremation all the way. What about you, Dad?'

'Christ no, the heat of it,' said Dad, from my other side. 'You can just put me out in the green bin when the time comes.'

This was too much for me. I could feel the laugh bubbling outwards from my chest into my lungs, and then it was out and my shoulders were shaking as I tried to muffle my mirth in my jacket sleeve. Other bereaved families were standing around us, the more pious glaring with the superiority of ones that have observed proper etiquette. I risked a glance over at Mum, and she didn't look happy, but there was the ghost of a smile that she was trying to hide under righteous anger. With a Herculean effort, I straightened my face as the priest told us to go in peace. I held my breath as she leaned over to Dad, looking exasperated.

'How many times, John? The green bin is for recyclables. The brown is for compost!'

Kissing Cousins

BY EDDIE KELLIHER

H ellos and goodbyes. Why are they so hard?

Not the emotion of a reunion or anguish of a separation – what I mean is *physical* etiquette. I've always struggled with these situations.

The perfect storm happened to me one day, many years ago, as I was visiting some cousins in Australia. I can guarantee that as I recall this day in *my* life, you will cringe into your socks *for me*.

Backpacking in Australia with my girlfriend, my father burdened me with the task of making sure I visit his brother in Brisbane. I made the phone call and he invited us to his house for dinner.

Upon arriving we were greeted by a slew of cousins that had been corralled to meet the never-before-seen Irish. I did well. My girlfriend looked at me proudly as I greeted them appropriately and made small talk like an expert.

We had a good time! No awkwardness. No gaffes.

Two of my cousins, Emma and Ashling agreed to drop us back to our hostel. We smoothly said our good-byes to everyone else. I breathed a sigh of relief. I had not embarrassed the Irish Kellihers in front of the Australian Kellihers. Success.

And then it happened. Forgive the following detail, but it exists to explain my humiliation.

My girlfriend and I slid sideways out from the back seat. I left first. I turned to see my girlfriend, still in the car.

'Goodbye!' she said, and squeezed between the driver and passenger seats.

She hugged Ashling and gave her a kiss on the cheek. This was a disaster. I had planned a wave or fancy salute to add some humour. Now the pressure was on me to do something similar. 'Just do the same,' I thought. I planned to return to the car with the objective of landing a cheek kiss.

My girlfriend left. I slid back into the car and awkwardly leaned in between the seats. My lips geared up for the cheek peck. But in front of my face, my cousin's hand was extended for a cordial handshake.

And this was the moment when my brain farted.

For some reason – I shall never truly know why – but for some reason, the following seemed to be the most sensible course of action: I grabbed her right hand with my left hand and pulled it. Her hand was now facing up. I leaned down and planted a big smooch right in the centre of her palm.

Please stop reading so you can do that to yourself. Grab your right hand with the other and kiss the centre of your hand. Now imagine doing that when you say goodbye to someone.

Then, imagine doing it to someone you *just met*.

As I slid out of the back seat of the car, away from her confused expression, it hit me, what I had just done.

I had just kissed the palm of my cousin's hand.

I had just *kissed* **the palm** of my *cousin's* hand.

77

I Think I'll Write for the Fox

BY BERNADETTE CARROLL

'I think I'll write for the fox,' my mother would say when one of our hens got old and stopped laying. What use was a hen if she couldn't produce eggs? A waste of layer's mash!

Still, deep down, my mother was fond of her brood. We had Rhode Island Reds and Brown Leghorns, names I found hilarious. One of them was missing for two days and my mother was fretting about her, searching the fields and the ditches. She found her closer to home, trapped behind a sheet of galvanised metal in one of the sheds. Staggering and disorientated, the hen was immediately approached by our rooster, who had his wicked way with her there and then. My mother was horrified. 'It wasn't THAT she wanted after being stuck for two days!' she told me.

She was funny without meaning to be. One time we were shopping and wanted to get something to eat. I tried to open the door of a café but it was jammed. She said to me quite seriously, 'Maybe they're closed for lunch!'

She had a sweet tooth and found it hard to resist temptation. My father was strict about not starting on the pudding until Christmas Day but my mother found a way round it. She used to cut slices from the bottom, so the pudding kept its shape... it just got a little lower every day!

She was matter of fact about death, if it wasn't an untimely event. When her cousin died, her words of comfort to his daughter were 'He's not the first Farrelly to die, and he won't be the last!'

When her sister passed on, she peered into the coffin and declared, 'She told me I could have that cardigan!'

When it came to her own illness, and she knew time was running out, she said to me by way of consolation, 'Sure, you'll forget about me in six months!'

The day I called the ambulance, Father Sheerin called to the house while we were waiting. As he gave her the Last Rites she said to him, 'I'm not too bad, I just have to get some phlegm off my chest.' He said to her, 'It's the only thing you have to get off your chest, Anna.'

As she was being helped into the ambulance and we were preparing to follow it she said, 'See you later, alligator,' and managed a smile. Maybe she was thinking back to her dancehall days.

No Michael Nouri

BY ÁINE RING

'm loving my job as the only girl working at an engineering company in Cork. Those were the days of
cheques and snail mail, of big perms and shoulder
pads. My favourite movie at that time was *Flashdance*,
which was about a girl who loves to dance part-time
while working as a welder in an engineering company,
where she falls in love with her boss, played by Michael
Nouri. Now come on – how sexy was that? And there was
I, surrounded by all these handsome muscular guys,
welding. I had my very own *Flashdance* set and fancied
myself as Alex the dancer. All I needed was the music.
But would I fall for my boss? Ahem. No. I was only 20
and single, and he was, well… oldish, and married. He
wasn't attractive – or not to me anyway.

How shall I describe him? He was no Michael Nouri.
That bar is very high, and let's face it, no one could hold
a candle to him. My boss had the unfortunate habit of
moving erratically about the room while he was talking,
jumping from foot to foot, his wobbly, gangly legs going
all over the place.

I was at the train station waiting to board for the
20-minute journey to work when suddenly I get a
doubling-over pain in my abdomen. I think it's my usual
irritable bowel and decide to board the train anyway.

There it is, my first mistake of the day. As soon as I board, I have to run to the loo and find that I can't flush it until the train starts to move – it would have emptied its contents and mine onto the track in the station if I had. 'Oh my God!' I begin to sweat. 'Will the train ever move?' I needed to go again and the loo was almost full. There's a knock on the door. It's one of the welders, wondering if I'm OK. These toilets are not soundproof, which makes my bowel even more nervous, and before I know it I have to go again. The train moves, and thank God for that. I go to flush the toilet, and the handle almost breaks in my hand with the urgency of the flush.

I go back into the carriage, where all my welder buddies look up. I try desperately to draw attention away from what just happened, and decide to talk about our boss. That was my fatal mistake. I was asked what did I think of him. 'He's very erotic,' I replied in my most impressive accent.

'We wouldn't know about that,' they say, falling around laughing.

'I meant *erratic*!' I say helplessly, but they drown me out as they sing the soundtrack from *Flashdance*. The toilet beckons me once again.

The Aldi Excursion

BY DAMIEN B. DONNELLY

We're going to Aldi tomorrow, me and The Mother. She started making a list last Sunday! She's never been before. The excitement is bouncing through the freshly aired house (we open the windows at 11 a.m. and close them at 3 p.m. before the cold air gets in). She's preparing like it's a first date! She's looked in the wardrobe twice for what to wear. Her sister wears those jeans with the stretch in them; the ones with the extra bit of comfort. Her other sister only does Marks. 'An excursion,' she's calling it!

'They've a lovely price on their beans, not the baked kind, the foreign ones. I know you like your pulses,' she says. I giggle – anything with a pulse always has potential! 'I hope they've a good date on them,' she remarks. 'Make sure there's a good date on them' is her staple supermarket comment.

She's arranged a pickup for afterwards and notified everyone in the family by phone the exact details of where and when, in case we don't return. The plan is to go mid-afternoon, everything is planned midafternoon, giving a good two to three hours beforehand to get ready and the whole evening then to recover and call everyone to tell them about the day, whether there's been an excursion or not, mainly not, but the phone calls still go out and come in:

'Did you do the washing? I did! You did? I did! Do you see the rain? I did! You did? I did!'

She did!

'Will I be able to bring me own shopping bags?' she asks me.

'Will they take me card?' she wants to know. 'Me credit card? I've never been before,' she tells me and she's off, calling up the sisters and cousins just to double-check.

'You have your passport?' I ask, and she looks at me and thinks, but eventually catches up.

Last night she was on the phone to The Mary from Tipperary. For 35 minutes. The Mary took her through the proposed visit; ran along the layout, each aisle, the best route, the spots to rest; she read her the offers of the week – even though they were the offers for last week! Less plotting and planning goes into a bank robbery.

Then came the rundown on the wine. Now, I'm not bigging myself up here, but it felt a little off-centre to hear someone in Tipperary call The Mother in Dublin to suggest what wine The Son – me – would like. I say it felt a little off-centre because, of course, between the three of us – The Mother, The Mary and myself – there's only one of us who ran a bar, in Paris, in France, where they made some of The Wine. And I can give you two hints: it wasn't The Mother or The Mary!

Oh God! Roll on The Excursion. Aldi: we're on the way, and you've been warned!

The Day the Lotto was Won and Lost

BY VERENA CUNNINGHAM

I t was 1990, I was 11 years old and that Saturday began like any other. An Irish music lesson in St Michael's Hall, followed by a visit to Mollie's sweet shop with our hard-earned pocket money for our weekly treat. Mollie would wait patiently while we pondered what combination of lollies and penny sweets would yield best value for money, then load her paper cones with that week's choices. If we had been frugal, we could afford a visit to McCauley's newsagents for the *Beano* and *Bunty*, one of each for my sister and me. Sometimes we helped Mum with the weekly shop, but more often than not we sat in the car reading our comics, getting giddy on Black Jacks and Fruit Salads and destroying our teeth in the process.

Last on the Saturday 'To-Do' list was a pitstop to Hannigan's, the local lucky lotto merchant, for the usual ticket purchase and fleeting fantasy that today would be the day when all six of our birthday numbers were chosen.

Later on, as 8 p.m. approached, my mother was still in the bathroom bathing my two much-younger sisters. A yell came from down the hallway for one of us to watch the lotto draw and record the winning numbers. I duly obliged, fetched a pen and paper, and hatched a plan to enliven a relatively dull Saturday evening. At this point I must confess that I was the ringleader, my sister, younger than me by a year, merely my accomplice. I tore the paper in two while she skulked into the kitchen and retrieved that precious lotto ticket from my mother's handbag. I took down the winning combination on the first piece of paper, which I pocketed; then on the second, my mother's chosen six, jumbled to add authenticity to the deception, which I casually tossed on the kitchen table.

When the girls emerged gleaming from our steamy aubergine bathroom, Mum disappeared into the kitchen. 'Did you get the numbers for me?' came a shout through the hatch.

'Yep, they're on the table there.' My sister and I exchanged a duplicitous look. The kitchen grew eerily quiet before the screams started. I felt a flutter of panic.

'Oh my God... girls... the numbers... I think we've... come and check this... I don't believe it... we've... we've won the lotto... WE'VE WON THE LOTTO!' I scrambled to my feet. The woman was on the verge of a heart attack. I raced into the kitchen, pulling that first piece of paper from my pocket. She was shaking.

'No! No! We haven't. We haven't. It was just a joke... those aren't the real numbers...' And I watched as my mother's face went from heady elation to utter deflation in a matter of seconds. I apologised profusely, and made tea and added sugar to help her recover from the shock.

Thirty years on, my mother still plays every Saturday and dreams of a lotto windfall. But that day in 1990, when the lotto was won and lost in our house, has never been forgotten.

The Opener

BY GARY MARTIN

'You know, Hitler was a great man.'

My heart sinks. I give a nervous smile. Don't panic! Maybe it's the opening line of a great joke. But now I notice swastika tattoos creeping up over the hardened knuckles of the huge hands clinging to the steering wheel as the horizon hurtles towards us. I turn slowly in the passenger seat to look at him. His tightly shorn head blends into the distorted backdrop of fenced fields blurring into one another, giving me a nauseating helter-skelter feeling. But this isn't the adrenaline-fuelled fun and friendly banter I've become accustomed to in Aotearoa, the 'land of the long white cloud' as the Maori named it, or New Zealand on modern maps. I reckon he's a modernist when it comes to cartography.

He turns and smiles at me. A silver glint of demented dentistry. My heart hammers and I hope he returns his gaze to the road that's rising up to meet us at a rate that mimics my pulse. How do I get out of this car? It's a metallic fusion welded tight from the sparks of a union of *Mad Max* and the *Dukes of Hazzard*. Behind my delicate torso, with a seeming gravitational pull on my spine, is a Jenga gym of weights and bar bells that blocks the view to where I have come from, a long way away.

Six months ago I departed Dublin, bidding a fond farewell to the Emerald Isle. A shy culchie lad who thought he'd be back home early, wouldn't last the summer, confidence and self-esteem the short nooses that bound me to home. Four friends together, we took the bold step onto that plane and towards the future. They were waved off by family. I was alone. I continued to be pulled along on the coat tails of their confidence and positivity.

I'd kept the trip a secret for as long as possible, until unintentionally the postman let it slip. But I was committed at that stage. The inevitable tide of negativity dished out at home washed over me, leaving its detritus, but I was still standing, ready to step into a new future. I'll prove them wrong.

Now, here I sat alone beside a man who looked unhinged. The long-lost love child of an unholy union between Jack from *The Shining* and Tom, the psychotic village-idiot friend of *Father Ted*. Had I just stepped into the opening scene of a hitchhiking horror or a cult Kiwi comedy?

The demonic engine revved its retort as we accelerated towards a corner on the road ahead. Was Charon about to chauffeur me across the Styx to Hades with a metal disc in my mouth? Or would I return home to regale all with a tall tale, the prodigal son returning from his epic Odyssey?

The long white clouds flew by. No one was laughing.

The Gherkin Episode

BY PAUL KEOGH

The machinery revved up and the line of glass gherkin jars started to rattle loudly along the conveyor belt system again. I reach my arms across the track and claw my fingers into the spices heaped atop the metal tray. Looking like a lunatic, I'm back frantically picking up and dropping the spices into the jars, filling two at a time as the jars whiz by under my arms. The stench of the spices travelling up my nose is already making me nauseous again. Yep, still hate this job.

As the jars pass me by, they take a quick right turn, travelling under the multiple chutes where the gherkins are sliding down and dropping into the jars. The pumps then start to fill the jars to the brim with vinegar, and they scuttle left and out of my line of sight where the lids are about to be robotically twisted on top. I anxiously wait for the jars to come back into my line of sight.

'You think this worked...?' I'm starting to ask to myself.

Just twenty minutes ago as everyone had left the factory floor for break, making sure no-one was watching, I'd walked over to the lid machine. Pulling out my handy red Swiss Army knife, I loosened a handful of screws ever so slightly on the robotic lid device.

The jars now come back into view: I can see no

lids attached. 'Oh my God, you're kidding me! This plan *actually worked.*' I can see the lids flying through the air, almost hitting the lovely old Turkish lady who is monitoring the gherkin chutes. A constant stream of lids is clattering all over the ground. The vibration of the track is causing the vinegar to swoosh out over the tops of the jars onto the floor.

There is confusion written all over John and Joe's faces as the train of lidless jars bears down on them. This is the end of the track. With neither of them removing the sloshing jars, the jars have no place to go. They start popping up over the railings and crashing down on the concrete floor. Jars are smashing all over, and all the while the lids are still flying through the air.

I'm smiling now, taking in all the chaos.

Shouts of 'stop' in German – '*Halt! Halt! Halt!*' Someone finally finds the red 'Halt' button and everything suddenly goes quiet.

The supervisors ask everyone on the floor to head outside while they sort it out. I glance back and see a bunch of mechanics yelling and puzzling over the lid system.

Outside everyone relaxes sitting around the edge of the plaza. I take out my packet of Marlboros, light up a cigarette, inhale and smile at this small moment of pleasure and extended rest I seem to have brought secretly to everyone. I lean my head back against the wall.

A shadow of a figure suddenly covers the blue sky.

'*Bitte*, Herr Keogh. May we have a word?'

Poultry-geist

BY HELEN KELLY

It was a week before Christmas when it was delivered. Mam won it at bingo. She had been so excited. A regular bingo-goer, she was often lucky, winning anything from a few bob to a box of biscuits. At festival times, she upped her game in pursuit of the big prizes. Winning the turkey was like winning the lottery – until it arrived.

The turkey was delivered complete with his head and feet; a beard of feathers covered his breast. Mam was horrified. A discussion ensued as to how the damn turkey was going to be made oven-ready. Having endured the birth of nine children, Mam refused to stick her hand up a turkey's arse; it was a step too far. Nan thought the local butcher might do us a favour. My offer to dissect the bird was met with scepticism: what would a 14-year-old know about gutting a bird? Explaining I had already dissected a worm and a cow's heart in biology convinced them.

Strung up by his feet on the back of the kitchen door, Nan covered the head in a plastic bag to stop the bulging eyes and bloody throat scaring the youngsters. I called him Tony, after the first boy who had kissed me. I'd pluck Tony's feathers and prod the younger ones with the tips, telling them their pillows were made from turkeys of Christmases past.

On the Saturday, Tony was taken out the back, where his head, neck and feet were removed with the hatchet. Back inside, I chatted to Tony as I ripped his guts out with my bare hands. The heart, kidneys and liver, along with the neck, later made the gravy. Once plucked, the wings were clipped and tied and he was left outside in a bucket of salted water. In the evening the kitchen sink became a Turkish bath where Tony would be safe from night prowlers.

At night I frightened my sisters with stories about Tony the Poultry-geist. I told them how a tear fell from Tony's eye as he was beheaded; how his beak had opened in a gasp as his feet were hacked off. I described his last meal still trapped in his gullet, never digested. My prop, Tony's foot with the three toes, added to my fun. I had secretly wrapped one in kitchen paper and hidden it. I would pull on the sinew connected to the front toe and make him walk, sending the smallies cowering under the covers.

The game was up when Mam, suspecting fowl play, uncovered the source of the lingering smell. Tony's foot was now shrivelled and slimy, the skin green, his toes blackened. The pungent smell was sickening. I threw the foot on the hot coals of the open fire. As it sizzled and crackled, I whispered to the girls, 'Watch for the blue flame, it's his ghost.' For the last time, the foot flexed, clenched, and a blue flame shot up the chimney. The sisters screamed.

A Wee Problem

BY JIM GRAY

Three young nurses arrived in my room. It was showtime.

I had discovered during recovery from surgery to repair a ruptured kneecap that an inability to piddle is one of the more embarrassing after-effects of anaesthetic. 'How are the waterworks?' the younger nurses would enquire in accents borrowed from county council workers, while the line of questioning from the senior staffers would assume the more formal, 'Have you passed urine yet?'

By day two, and still not a trickle, I detected a more serious approach. The dreaded question was posed more frequently, and the negative answer induced a worrying response. Now, the nursing trio carted me the short distance from my bed to a small bathroom, where they carefully manoeuvred me atop a lavatory bowl. There I perched in glorious ignominy as they surveyed the grotesque scenario.

From where I sat, it appeared as if one blue uniform was supporting three pretty heads. The three-headed uniform had an idea. They decided that turning a wash-basin tap to full blast might provide the appropriate encouragement. The water gushed forth with the velocity of a fireman's hose on Halloween night. The trio trooped away, their faces contorted by the effort to suppress riotous laughter.

Alone with the cascading taps, I endeavoured to perform. I prayed and pushed, squatted and squeezed. Childbirth would have been easier. But nothing happened. In my mind I should have been singing 'Raindrops Keep Falling on my Head' or 'Yellow River', but all I could think of was 'It Never Rains in Bloody Southern California.'

The Three Degrees returned to learn the bad news. 'Well,' their spokeswoman announced quite calmly, 'you'll have to be catheterised. We just run a tube through your penis, into the bladder, drain it into a bag, and all done. No hassle.'

My injured leg, encased in a cement-like tube and motionless for nearly 36 hours, now began to wobble like an overflowing bowl of jelly. Giant beads of sweat dripped from every pore. The blood drained so fast from my shivering body that my complexion now resembled the colour of the plaster on my leg. An observant nurse was quick to spot I wasn't in lotto-winning mood.

'It's a bit intrusive alright,' she conceded. INTRUSIVE? Nosey or noisy neighbours – that's intrusive. A swaggering drunk barging unwanted into a private conversation – that's intrusive. But they were preparing to use my frizzled, frightened little willie as a London Underground line.

'Give me five more minutes,' I begged, frantically. They disappeared, linking each other for fear they would collapse in uncontrollable mirth.

No sooner had they gone than I felt the first faint trickle, then a steady stream, and soon a healthy flow. Fear, the world's most reliable diuretic, had done the trick. I was peeing like a baby and grinning like one too when they returned.

And that night, as I drifted off to blissful sleep, I bargained one more favour from the Almighty: 'Please God, don't let me pee the bed.'

Franny

BY DONNA MARIE WOODS

Sundays in our house were special; long lie-ins, lazy breakfasts, late Mass, and fun-filled family afternoons. I remember them vividly and with great fondness, but one sticks out in my mind: the day it all changed!

That particular Sunday we all woke up a little late for some strange reason, and it was a bit of a rush to make it on time for the 12:30 Mass in the Cathedral. Before we left, my sister noticed that our pet goat, Franny, was missing, and mother decided we would look for her after Mass. So the seven of us piled into the Toyota Corolla estate the two 'little ones' in the boot as usual, the three 'big ones' in the back seat, and Mum and Dad in the front. Being one of the 'little ones', I can honestly say that I never experienced the luxury of a seat until I was in my mid-20s, but that's a whole other story. I can still feel the indent in my skull from being bashed against the roof over every bump. That was part and parcel of being a 'little one' back then!

We arrived just in time for Mass. This was an important one; it was the month's memory Mass for our dear friend Ambrose Walsh. Ambrose owned a newsagent on Dominick Street in Mullingar, two doors down from our shop. He was a character, and a good friend of my parents. We were marched up the aisle to take 'our' seat in the third row. Father Moore was saying the Mass and it was a solemn, sad occasion.

Midway through the sermon I noticed the mother's shoulders shaking. My mother had a contagious laugh, and she was doing her best not to explode. I looked over to the right, only to see Franny walking up the aisle. She then proceeded up onto the altar, stood in front of the pulpit, looked Father Moore straight in the eye and went, 'Mahaaaaaaaaaaaah.'

At that moment we were all willing to disown her, but no, not my father; he got up and went up onto the altar, took Franny by the horns, and escorted her out into the sacristy! She sat between us in the boot on the way home.

Over 40 years on I'm still baffled as to how a goat negotiated the five kilometres into town that day. What's even more mysterious is the fact that she went into Ambrose's newsagents on the way up to Mass and scared the bejesus out of the girls working there beforehand. Was it the work of a local prankster, or simply Ambrose having a laugh? I'm not sure I'll ever solve that mystery, but I've always been convinced it was the latter!

That was the last time we went to Mass in the Cathedral, and the end of my Sunday lie-ins; after that, Mass in Walshestown was at 9 a.m.!

When the Chips Are Down

BY ROSALEEN DALTON

Chipper chips were always my favourite. On a day out to buy my Communion dress, we stopped by a café and I, of course, ordered my treasured treat, while my grandmother had soup and my mother had a sandwich and tea. While they were chatting away, I decided to put some salt on my chips. Not paying attention, I accidentally poured sugar all over them. I was stunned, and jumped from my seat roaring and making a big fuss. I was very firmly told to sit down and be quiet.

My grandmother, not wanting to waste the chips, started to blow the sugar off. I could see from where I was sitting, that droplets from her mouth were dive-bombing into my plate, not to mention that these droplets were living with the same pair of dentures for years. The same dentures that were thrown in the bin by mistake, only to be retrieved, washed and deposited straight back into their place of dwelling. Years of tea stains clung to every nook and cranny such that most of their white colour had disappeared, making them appear like beach pebbles after the tide had gone out.

I decided there and then that I wasn't touching those chips, with sugar and droplets attached to them, even if she did manage to get all the sugar off. Meanwhile my starving stomach thought my mouth had gone on strike.

'There,' my grandmother said, 'all the sugar is gone, eat up.'

Eat up! Was she going insane?, I thought. Who in their right mind would put one of those contaminated chips into their mouth, now stone-cold, saliva-soaked and semi-sweet? Taking a deep breath, I shouted across the table that I wasn't going to eat them now or ever, and demanded a new plate of chips. We now had a non-paying audience watching this midday theatrical event.

With that little outburst, I was ejected from my seat by my grandmother, marched into the toilet and told in no uncertain terms that I was to walk back to my seat, eat the chips, and sit there until she and my mother had finished their snack. I was getting nothing else to eat. She saw nothing wrong with the plate of chips. In Africa, there were little children starving. They would eat the chips and be glad of them, she said.

I was marched back to the table to start the agonising task of picking out the chips that had escaped most of the sugar and saliva avalanche, a task that no child should have to complete just after having bought their First Holy Communion clothes.

We left the café with my mother complaining that I should watch what I was doing in future; my grandmother had been kind enough to treat me to a snack, she said, and I should apologise to her for my behaviour. After all, she was old and should be respected. A lesson duly learned.

Yes, Drill Sergeant

BY NUALA MCGARRY

One, two, three, four. All present and accounted for.
Dressed, fed, packed and belted up. Children, check. Schoolbags, check. Coffee in travel mug, check. Engine start. We begin our first trip of the day, a rainy day like any other, a stressed mother like any other. We made it out the door on time and without Drill Sergeant Mammy making an appearance. Success. However, a simple fact is often overlooked: getting to this point is nothing short of a massive military operation.

A career aptitude test, taken in my teenagerhood, suggested either the armed forces or teaching, the second being the obvious choice for one who detests guns. Maybe I chose incorrectly, as the military precision necessary for successful mothering comes as second nature, more so than any other element, and I often yearn for the strict discipline of the military forces.

Soldiers are selfless, apparently mothers are selfless too. Would I call myself selfless? No, certainly not. As every mother does, I fulfil their needs, and their needs are many. Yet I dream of alone-time, time away from mothering, away from demands, away from being the Big Boss. Even soldiers get leave from soldiering.

However, a member of any military force is voluntarily selfless by their very promise to put their life in

99

jeopardy. Is motherhood voluntary selflessness too, or a genetic desire to create someone, offspring, little versions of the makers, who will, in time, try every angle to become the rulers of the roost? Would officers in an army or navy accept such dissension in the ranks – and from new recruits?

That methodical attitude to carry out orders with a clear line of command – each understanding their place in the chain and the necessity for each link to work for the whole to function – is to be lauded. There is a semblance of this in school – not enough for my liking, but enough for the whole to function smoothly. Without this chain, life would be chaos.

Years of teaching prepared me for different stages of development, appropriate punishments, learning through love. Mothering is all this, tenfold, though I tend to veer more towards routine than nurture. The regularity of school routine, detested by so many, invigorates me, gives my day purpose, structure, a straight line to follow. The most successful schools are the ones with the strictest principals, the toughest leaders. As well as alone-time, I also dream of the day that my commands will be obeyed, without hesitation and to the letter, as any good soldier would do.

Principal doesn't seem far enough of a career aspiration for me now. 'Brigadier General' has a nice ring to it.

The words, 'Mammy, can I have…?' draw me back into reality. If they could reply to my answer with, 'Yes, Drill Sergeant,' life would be a whole lot easier – I live in hope – but alas, it is never their response. Dissension in the ranks once again.

Maybe I should have joined the army.

Superwoman Learns a Listening Lesson

BY ANNE DAVEY

Being a superwoman is not all that it's cracked up to be. Women have been duped, I thought, as I tried to wrestle the lunchbox into the school bag and put a wash on at the same time. I shouted at Ciara to hurry up and finish her cereal while I finished blow-drying my hair.

We were running late as we got in the car, and I was distracted with thoughts of the presentation ahead of me. Was the concept going to be strong enough to win the account? I vaguely heard Ciara say, 'But Mummy!' and before she could finish her sentence, I stopped her with, 'How many times have I told you? Pack your bag the night before. Get your clothes ready. Be organised!' I kept the rant up as I strapped her in, and didn't give the poor child a chance to complete her thought. The mummy in me did think, 'She's only just turned five...' but superwoman squashed it in an instant.

We were stopped at traffic lights and I was fumbling in my handbag for some lippy while I continued to lecture Ciara on the benefits of being organised. I found what I was looking for and proceeded to put it towards my mouth when I noticed the guy in the car next to me staring at me. 'What's his problem?' I thought, and was even more surprised when I saw him grin widely. I followed his line of sight and thought, 'Oh shit. Could this day get any worse?' I was holding a Tampax. A tornado of thoughts hit: 'That's up there on my top ten list of embarrassing moments. Why do lipstick and Tampax have to be the exact same circumference? Would the studio have the graphics ready? The bottom of women's handbags are a minefield. Did I take a dinner out of the freezer?'

I could see yer man's shoulders heaving with laughter as he drove off and thought, 'I'm going to be the water-cooler story today.' At least I wasn't going to need blusher. I was pink with embarrassment.

We finally got to the school. It felt like the end of the day and not the beginning, my energy levels were so low. Ciara, poor pet, kept trying, and as I got out of the driver's seat to open the back door she finally got it all out: 'But Mummy! I've no knickers on.'

The Snail

BY MARY KILKENNY

It was the summer of '82, and all my friends were talking about French kissing. I had no idea what they were talking about, but I went along with everyone else – sure, I didn't want to look stupid. I told them I knew all about it; I was practically an expert. If I had only known.

A boy a street away asked me out. He was very popular and he'd had a lot of girlfriends, including some of my own friends. It was decided that we would meet up on Friday after tea. I spent ages deciding what to wear, and even thought about putting on some of my mother's lipstick, but the colour was awful, so no.

I left the house at 5:55 to go on my big date, butterflies in my stomach and wondering if he would even turn up. After all, I wasn't much to look at: mousey brown hair and a face full of freckles. As I turned the corner, there he was. We stood awkwardly looking at one another. Then he said, 'Will we take a walk?' So off we went. No holding hands, just strolling beside each other.

He broke the silence by asking me about my friend Mandy. She was one of my closest friends. Blonde, blue-eyed and a bust I longed to have myself. I was happy to chat about Mandy; at least the conversation was flowing. Did she have a boyfriend? What's her favourite sport? What's her favourite colour? I really must have been stupid.

We sat down on a wall just out of town. It was a warm, balmy evening, and the smell of cut grass wafted in the air with the birds singing. Before I knew it he had his arm over my shoulder. I felt uneasy – don't know why, but I did.

He bent down to kiss me and my breath was taken away. Not by the kiss but by what he was doing to me. Images of seilidí (snails) or bogeys came into my head. He had his tongue in my mouth! It felt sloppy and slimy, it was disgusting. Spit was dribbling down my chin. All I knew was I wanted it to stop. I thought snails lived in a shell, but he had one in his mouth, oh Mother, save me! I pushed him away and told him I had to go home, as I forgot my Aunt Mary was calling for a visit and my mother would be cross with me if I missed her.

I now know why he had a lot of girlfriends: no one would go back for that a second time.

The Day I Learned to Drive

BY PATRICK LEE

I had been offered a job as a sales representative with a company car, something I had always dreamed of. The problem was I didn't know how to drive. When I explained my predicament to the company, they said that they would give me three months to get my driving licence. The pressure was on, and it was time for action. I set myself up with driving lessons but, after six of them, it was clear that without a car to practise in, they wouldn't be of much use. So, for the first time ever, I turned to Da for help, and he agreed to take me out in his car that very day.

Our drive was intense from the second we left the curb; Da was obviously regretting his decision to take me out. Every time I changed gear, I could hear him mutter to himself in frustration. When he wasn't telling me to keep up with the traffic, it was 'slow down, you're going too fast'. As we were approaching the gates of Phoenix Park, Da suddenly shouted in a total panic, 'For feck sake, slow down, you'll take the fecking gates off the pillars! Jesus Christ, slow down!' This completely distracted me, and I must have put my foot on the accelerator because we went through the gates like Stirling

Moss. Shock doesn't adequately describe the state we were both in, but at least the pillars were still intact.

From that moment on, Da cursed and complained all the way. 'What are you trying to do, put the gear stick through the fecking windscreen?' he shouted, as I struggled to change gear to the sound of a screeching gearbox. He pleaded with me to surrender the car to him. But I kept going, determined to make the most of this opportunity. Da then suggested we proceed to some minor roads. Before we knew it, we were lost in the Dublin Mountains, navigating dirt tracks only suitable for one car at a time, fenced in by a bog on either side. For fear of meeting an oncoming car, I sped up, and my Da went ballistic again. 'Can you not read the feckin' signposts? You're going the wrong way!' I hadn't the nerve to tell him I hadn't even seen the signposts. 'Stop the feckin' car!' he demanded. 'No, I'm not stopping! You promised!' Da and I had never exchanged so many words, and they were mostly his.

When we eventually found our way home, it was four hours later. We were both shattered, and the look of relief on Da's face said it all. Despite the heart-stopping experience and vitriolic diatribe, I had cracked it. I could drive. As I got out of the car, I turned to my da and jokingly said, 'Jesus, Da, that was great! We should do it again tomorrow.' Without a moment's hesitation, he replied, 'Not in a million years, son!'

In the Spotlight

BY EILEEN EAGERS

It was 4 May 1996. The shortening rays of sun were streaming through the car window as we traversed the windy roads from Wexford. The children were quiet now as they'd been outside the whole day playing with their cousins – the swings, the slide, and tig, up and down the concrete driveway. They were looking forward to visiting their grandma and grandpa on the way home, recharging their batteries for the next adventure.

We pulled into the driveway and they jerked awake. They ran inside to Grandma's with a new spurt of energy, straight to the kitchen to scavenge for available sweets or biscuits. Once they found them they were happily in front of the TV; *Kenny Live* was the staple TV programme on a Saturday night, Pat Kenny the host of the Bank Holiday weekend chat show. The programme couldn't be heard by anyone as the children had their own chat show going on, swapping stories and adventures of the earlier part of the day.

The highlight of the show was the winning of a car by a competition entrant, and Grandpa said, 'Sshh, till we hear who won!' Aileen O'Meara from RTÉ usually arrives out to the winner's house with the cameras to surprise the winner. The children turned quieter as Grandpa turned up the volume.

Pat Kenny announced, 'And we will now see who won the car...' The television turned dark, and suddenly there were big spotlights on the screen showing a house. At the same time we could see spotlights arriving at the sitting-room window. We looked out in amazement. Then the knock came to the front door, with the realisation of what was beginning to unfold.

I answered the door and Aileen said, 'Is Eileen here?'

'I'm Eileen,' I said, hardly able to stand.

The next sentence I barely heard: 'Congratulations, Eileen! You've won a brand-new Toyota!'

I was shell-shocked.

All the family came out from inside. My husband had arrived from our home, which is about five miles over the road. The TV cameras and vans had been set up there all evening. As night-time approached, it dawned on me that I was not at my own home. The television cameras and the prize had to be set up outside my parents' house; they had lain in hiding for a couple of hours to surprise me.

I now know what it's like to be a celebrity. Cameras flashed, and everyone was hugging me and shaking hands. Pat Kenny said, 'Congratulations, and safe driving!' The television cameras dispersed and the spotlights went out. Everywhere went dark, but the fun was just beginning. We had a big party that went on for the whole weekend. The local radio and newspaper came out to Carlow's newfound celebrity and her new car. It was a weekend I will never forget.

A Rush to Judgement

BY JOAN GRENNAN

My first name mightn't be Brigid, but the original
Brigid never had the bother with rushes that I
had. In a state of near-total absorption didn't
I just hear it: kids, adults, birds of the air, animals of the
fields, all latched onto my flippin' surname.

In an overcrowded classroom in the early days of
my education, little penetrated my consciousness. But
playtime – yikes! Unsupervised for all of 30 minutes,
and with feck-all diversion, kids just loved to bully and
taunt each other to their hearts' content. An unrelenting chorus of 'Bush! Rush! Thrush!' would ring around
my ears, in around the gravestones right next door,
through the cement supports of the bunker-like shelter, up by the turf shed and down towards the outdoor
privy.

In the roll-book I would be forever Siobhán Ni
Luachra; Irish, as it happens, for 'the rushes in the
fields'. We were submerged in rushes where I lived. The
cattle would graze among them, and never touch the
rushes, which had squatters' rights; stuck up all over in
big clumps, they defied everyone.

And it's home time now; there is the retired headmaster of another school, leaning over his garden gate;
furtively I inch past him – the evil goblin. 'Green grow

109

the rushes, o!' he calls out gleefully. In time I learn it's merely the title of a song, and a film.

In time I learn even more. Yet another headmaster was intrigued by the name. A past pupil recalled him peering out his classroom window and, catching sight of us lot, the tardy Rushes edging closer down the main street of the village, dolefully he remarked, he remarks 'Ta na Ruisigh ag teacht' (the Russians/Rushes are coming). That was the 50s, characterised by terrifying concerns about dying, and going to Hell, and the imminent arrival of the Russians.

My own father, Bill of the Rushes; now he was a well-behaved man. He knew only one bad word. The word was 'bugger', and he applied it to anything and everything in the universe: 'the buggers of sheep needin' shearing'; 'the buggers of hens, dirty things'; 'the bugger of a dog tormenting the poor things'; 'the bugger of a cow, always finding the only gap in the hedge'; 'the buggers of herrings' on a Friday. And always, of course, there were 'the buggers of Russians, up to no good ever'. And Khrushchev – well, he was just the biggest bugger of all.

The rest of us, we just fretted; never any the wiser about how many Novenas, Masses, First Fridays, indulgences and Rosaries were needed to convert all the Russians, for conversion was the dream in an age of innocence.

What Moves You

BY MICHELLE NÍ SHIÚRDAIN

'So with Bernie stepping down as treasurer, we're going to need a new volunteer to fill that position.' The air stilled in the cold, dimly lit kitchen of the community hall. The small particles of dust that created a thin film on the worn oilcloth of the trestle table were closely scrutinised by all 12 of us. We were a motley crew, ranging in age from 30 to 75. Paddy, our chairperson and eldest member, scanned the table, mentally sizing us all up.

The Knockshannon Community Group had recently got its biggest shake-up in decades when the perpetual heartfelt request for new members was suddenly answered. Government funding for rural Ireland meant that there was a real chance Knockshannon could get a playground, and the harassed parents in the area suddenly found the time to tear themselves away from their stoves to join the Community Group in the hope of having somewhere to offload their offspring for free while they caught up on local gossip with the neighbours. The existing members were somewhat stunned and, if truth be told, a bit disgruntled as well. They had derived a certain pleasure out of deriding 'the young people' (30 is young to pensioners). The 'young people's' self-centredness and lack of interest in community values were confirmed by their lack of involvement in community initiatives. To be proven wrong was a little disconcerting, as if the world they knew had tilted a little on its axis. However, from the young people's perspective, joining the group and taking on a designated role were two very different types of commitment.

The silence continued until Jenny, in her attempt to stifle a sneeze, let out a strangled 'ah-yee' sound. Her panic-stricken eyes met mine. I struggled to conceal my smirk. Whoever said these things were boring? Jenny lived in her overdraft and was the proud owner of two maxed-out credit cards used to fund her Asos addiction and penchant for ditching her three children and booking last-minute city breaks with her husband if her younger sister made the mistake of letting slip she wasn't going out at the weekend. We'd probably end up in some sort of charity tribunal for excessive spending if Jenny became treasurer, but we would all be impeccably dressed on the steps of the courthouse, courtesy of the community hall cheque book.

'Sorry, Jenny, were you volunteering?' I bit the inside of my cheeks to keep a straight face. Paddy didn't sound overly enthusiastic. Letting the young ones join was one thing; giving them control of the purse strings was another thing entirely. Jenny's mouth opened and closed, goldfish-style. 'Or were you making a nomination?' Paddy asked hopefully. Suddenly the mouth closed, and a mischievous sparkle lit up her eyes. My heart sank. I knew what was coming.

'I'd like to nominate Niamh', she replied in her best pillar-of-the-community voice. I squirmed as all 11 sets of eyes swung to me. 'OK,' said Paddy uncertainly.

'The nomination would have to be seconded if Niamh was happy to accept it.' How on earth was I going to get out of this?

My Own Personal Gag Reel

BY IRENE FALVEY

What do most people conjure up from the labyrinths of the mind for their biographies? I'd hazard a guess that most contain highs and lows, not insignificant Tuesday afternoons. The highs that feel so precious and unbelievable that you want to memorialise their sunshine in the written word, where it can exist forever. Or the lows that caused so much havoc you never imagined that you'd escape them; that you could reduce them down into something as trivial as words on a page.

What is achieved by this? You probably realise that the highs fade, that eventually human nature will kick in and you'll burst your own happiness bubble. The lows that caused so much pain will seem glossed over, that suffering now irrelevant. Perhaps the true biography is the diary, the capturer of all the details and emotions of your life as they take place. Could the diary be a biography in real time? A thought to ponder.

Like anyone else, I speculated on my highs and lows; little snippets of happiness flooded my memory, but it wasn't long until my thoughts were darkened by the nightmares of the past that my brain managed to regurgitate from the depths. Biographies are about life, which may take you on a journey into that oh-so-dangerous Pandora's box. What is the point of this all – Life? Does the relentless dishwashing, alarm-setting and getting back on the horse again and again and again really matter? Here is a life, and here is what I have done, and who cares?

But I choose not to let this Pandora's box defeat me. While it might be a trite phrase, it can be an effective existential crisis solvent; I choose to laugh, not weep. Let's just say that if my life were a film, I already know the basics, the love interests, the defining moments and decisions, the achievements and the failures. I don't need to re-watch it.

What I think is really important above all else is to laugh at it all. Guys, all I want to remember is my own personal gag reel; those little golden nuggets that even in their brevity outshine the rest. I want to laugh at my own ignorance, naivety, pretensions, drunken foolishness and the embarrassments that do eventually become hilarious anecdotes. I want to laugh at the fact that I once sneezed and farted at the same time in history class; that I used to be such a hoarder I kept the milk bottle-top because it had 'emotional significance'; and that it took me a seriously long time to come around to the fact that evolution is real. All funny, I grant you, but not laugh-out-loud funny.

What's really funny are all the times that I didn't believe that I was smart enough, thin enough, funny enough, interesting enough, creative enough, talented enough, lucky enough. That's the real joke of my life. LOL.

Lockdown

Feck the Bees

BY NOELENE NASH

Feck the bees. Another night of broken sleep leads to this. Feck the bees. Outside where everything is thought, fought, settled or forgotten, on my knees, I determine to dig out every single dandelion from the lawn while I can. The sun is slow to warm as I gather what I need. The water fountain but a mere trickle. I sink the black trowel in and give it a bitter twist, wrenching the roots out altogether. '"Weeds" they call them, but great food for the bees!' they say. Feck the bees. Pissy-beds in my day and on a good day magic wishes. I think on those wishes with each bend, my spine scraping as I rise and fall again and again. This is a special kind of torture, taking from another.

I wonder at the world as I pull at the roots and fling a plant into my red bucket. This world. The smallness of it. The sameness of it. The sore hum around it. Then I hear them inside. The working man, the exam student, the college girl. All home. All busy, busy, moving around, making tea again, raiding the fridge, having long showers, using 40 towels, leaving a mess. My old garden shoes, twice glued, drag across the grass as I reach out to catch a half-blown head of wishes. I stop myself from scattering the rest and dunk it in under the pile for fear of any floating away and spreading ideas.

Feck the bees. The silver birch darkens the green as I pull myself along, feeling the weight of the load trailing behind. Raised voices, *dig*, a slammed door, *twist*, my name called, *pull*. Ignored.

I move to the other side of the lawn. I feel the heat on my back now. Kneeling, weeding, feck the bees, gouging, tearing, feck the bees. Leaving nothing behind. I am forced to stop and stretch against the agony. I see in my blistered palm stuck wishes. Silent white whispers tickling my skin. I cast a shadow to brush them into the others but hesitate. Then I hear him laugh, I hear the other start a meeting, and I hear her sing through the open windows. The scale of notes carries like wordless seeds over the mossy lawn. I rest and raise my head slowly to breathe it all in. Cupping my palm, I blow the last of the wishes into the blue sky. Let them fly where they will. Almost there, almost gone.

Rhythm

BY FIONA FERGUSON

My small boy brings me flowers from our backyard. He has learned to hold the buttercups under my chin to see if the reflected light will tell him if I like butter. He confirms I do.

It's April 2020. Lockdown. Interminable hours in a day. Tears come periodically, feeling like grief although I haven't lost anyone. Just normality. Connection. A sense of safety. My husband is a farmer, gone during daylight hours while I am home with our three children. The small boy, one year old, and his two big sisters, six and eight.

The girls are inside, couch-bound, screen time rules relaxed to compensate for the loss of friends. I bring the small boy up for his nap, he drops to sleep easily, still in my arms. The human contact a comfort for me as much as him. I put him into his cot and creep downstairs. A few stolen moments before I tackle the home-schooling with his sisters. As I make a cup of coffee, I see a butterfly in the backyard through our kitchen window and venture outside to try and capture it on my phone. I play a game of catch, trying not to cast a shadow as it flits around the garden.

A female Orange Tip butterfly. I have seen plenty of males, which live up to their names, fluttering about, but this is the first female, white with grey tips. Eventually I drop to my knees and commando crawl towards her as she rests on a thistle. She works her wings but keeps them largely closed, so I can see the shimmering silver-veined backs. I am close enough to see the furry body, large eyes, delicate antennae – beautiful and otherworldly.

The dog bounds over, hugely excited by its human's strange behaviour, and the butterfly is gone. I lie in the grass for a while, the sun warming me. 10.30 a.m. I hear bees but don't see them. There is a patch of nettles nearby, brambles over the ditch. I see hoverflies land to rest in the sun from their territorial humming.

I start to feel damp from the grass and go inside. There is a sudden ruckus. A small bird stuck in the kitchen. Panicky fluttering at the window. The dog excited. I call to the girls, 'Would you like to see the bird before I let it out?'

They don't move from the couch, calling, 'We can see it.'

I sigh and shoo the dog out of the kitchen. I talk to the little frightened bird panting on the windowsill. I open the windows and it finds its way out. It flies straight across the garden to the shelter of the back hedge. Normality restored, completely unaffected by humankind's current crisis.

Like the small boy, it lives for the moment – eat when hungry, rest when tired, contentment when all is well. A rhythm life falls into in the absence of a structure imposed from the outside. A rhythm we had forgotten.

Maria

BY DAVID RALPH

My heart fluttered seeing the name flash on my phone. 'Kind of surprised to hear from you,' I said, hoping my voice wasn't betraying me.

We hadn't spoken in almost a year. I'll never forget it. Her last words before hanging up were, *Don't call again*, anger and disappointment and tears in her voice. 'Just seeing if you're OK. With this virus and all that.'

'I took to the hills. I'm home in Tipperary.'

'I'm home in Sligo too. Got out of Dublin.' Dublin. Our old life in Dublin. Our old house in Dublin. That night we spoke about the pandemic, how everything seemed suddenly more complex but simpler too, the strange sense of clarity amid the uncertainty.

That night, in my boyhood bedroom, my mind raced. After many hard long months I felt I'd at last accepted things were over between us. I'd done as I was told. I hadn't called again. I hadn't texted. I hadn't anything.

Two days passed. Four. Six. Finally, a week. This time, I called. We were careful to keep our talk on safe ground, keep it off the stupid things I'd done.

The calls grew regular. As did those dreams I'd been having of her. The dreams that were so tantalisingly real, when I'd wake I'd expect to find her there in the bed beside me. The dreams where it was always the good old days.

I was surprised by how little seemed to have changed with her. 'And the garden?' I asked one day. I'd dug out the raggedy old lawn, planted a new one with fescue grass seeds on top of the tonnes of fresh earth I'd rolled.

'As you left it.'

'You didn't put the decking down?' I'd thought there'd be some crude, many-storeyed concrete monstrosity annexing my lovely grass by now. I'd had a thousand thoughts.

'No.'

'And the shed?'

'As I said. Exactly as you left it.'

Visions from epic romances came to me as I lay in my room, as I walked the hills at home. Lovers separated by revolution, by war, by planetary upheavals, making their way to one another, over mountain passes, across deserts, through thornbush.

'I'm back in Dublin,' she told me another day. We were calling all the time now.

'Oh! Since when?'

'Last night.'

'How's things there?'

'The garden is insane.'

'Really?'

'There's *so* much growth, it's wild!'

I let out my breath. I heard myself say, 'I could give you a hand with it.'

'Could you now?' she said in a teasing voice.

'I could,' I said quickly.

'And how would you get here? There's checkpoints everywhere.'

I'd studied train schedules, bus schedules, I'd measured out the miles on foot from the station to the house. I'd a whole alibi ready should I be stopped.

'I'll find a way,' I said.

A pause, during which the blood throbbed hot in my throat.

Her voice was almost a whisper when she spoke next. She said, 'OK so.'

I repeated, 'OK so.'

Repetition
FERDIA Ó CAIRBRE

epetition. At first, it's effective. You notice the same thing being said again and again by a random motivational speaker, and his message is pinned to the walls of your determination. You notice that, in the space of a few days, you've fallen into the habit of doing the same things over and over, and you're happy that you've established some sort of routine, albeit one deprived of sociability. But, after a while, you get sick of it.

Tomorrow will be another day which absolutely glorious weather consumes. I'll wake up. Bright and early, you say? Not a chance. I'll tread down creaky stairs to see my mother frantically finishing a spreadsheet that she knows should have been finished days ago. Breakfast will be eaten. Milk will trickle into muesli. And, when spotted eating an unaccompanied piece of toast, I'll be asked when exactly it was that I stopped eating butter, followed by my proclamation of reasons. My mother will proceed to tell me that her brother is the same, but that it's because he inhaled the stuff (with nothing else) as a teenager, and decided he'd had his life's share. She'll confess that she's happy I chose to eat the bread without the butter rather than the butter without the bread, anyways.

Suddenly, it'll be the afternoon. Homework will

occupy me until lunchtime, which is when my father will venture into the outside world, something which I've not laid eyes upon in almost two months. He'll return from the Lithuanian bakery that we all know and love and announce disappointingly that 'they'd only the dregs.' Piano practice will follow. J. S. Bach will bounce between walls and travel up chimneys, something that makes the birds try, with all their might, to counter-chirp. The same mistakes will be made until my father, Olympic champion of daytime napping, reaches breaking point: 'I thought you said you were ready for the exam.'

Deflated, I'll find comfort in Duolingo. Sometimes, Italian distracts me from what's going on in the world at the moment, but most of the time it only makes me feel more sympathy for its native speakers and what they're going through. I'll then half-complete an excuse of a workout. Whether it's because of an actual sense of achievement or just endorphins, I'll be motivated to compose some music, but I'll know full well that I'm too tired to do so. After countless attempts of trying to pick out what I'm humming, which, in fairness, changes every two minutes, I'll give up around dinnertime.

Most of the house's food will then be eaten and all family members will retire to the sitting room, where I'll act as the night's 'entertainment officer'. My job consists of scavenging through Netflix to find a decent-looking show. I've found that foreign, subtitled ones work best. This way, my parents stay awake because they're constantly reading, and I'm not left sitting awake in the dark at 3 a.m., regretfully watching TikTok after TikTok...

This is a work of fiction.

Mr Das Gupta's Studio

BY URSULA MURPHY

These days, I am finding there is more time to remember, more time to reflect on moments that have shaped me in ways that I could not have imagined at the time. More than ever, I am appreciating the very unexpected delight of a letter from an old friend, and in these strange days I am much more likely to write a timely and thoughtful response. With the passing of each year, I find that sadly, there are more old letters in my collection from people for whom my reply will be too late.

My young sons are sometimes curious about the large black sack of letters and old photos lying in the corner of a newly dedicated space, formerly known as 'the junk room'. Recently, I've been indulging my need to explore its contents, and I open ancient envelopes in excitement, touching again the thin sheets with their spidery script as though I am holding certain pages of my life.

For many years, I corresponded with an old man from Kolkata, or Calcutta as it was when I knew him. In many ways, we were the most unlikely of pen pals, an odd couple whose meeting was completely by chance, although my friend would not have seen it like that. Mr Das Gupta was an elderly Bengali man, a grandfather and a devout Hindu who would begin every letter with a customary 'Om'. I was a newly graduated English teacher, just 22 and on a 'pilgrimage' to Calcutta and rural West Bengal to experience something of the places that had helped shape the imagination of my literary idol and one of the world's great poets, Rabindranath Tagore. In the Ireland of the early 90s, it was almost impossible to find works either written by or about Tagore, and there were times when instead of attending a lecture in Trinity I would visit the Indian Embassy to dig out any books by Tagore I could find in the small library there.

One humid Wednesday in Calcutta in July 1992, when the last of that day's monsoon showers had evaporated in the afternoon heat, I was making my way back to the bus stand. I cannot say what it was that drew my gaze to the tiny Kodak studio on Rash Behari Avenue but I noticed a fading portrait of Tagore in the window and was drawn in.

What a precious repository of Calcutta's past I discovered in Mr Das Gupta's studio that day. The old man told me that his father, also a photographer, had taken a picture of Tagore in 1926 at Mymen Singh, now in Bangladesh, when the poet had visited a girls' school there. He gave me the photo, and on that sultry Calcutta afternoon we struck up a friendship that spanned age and continents, based on a shared love of literature and history. And years later as I write this, I am holding a picture that captures a page in my life and that of an old friend, just a small boy on a step looking up at a poet in a photograph taken by his father.

Table Manners

BY JOHN MCGONIGLE

It wasn't meant to end like this, but Paddy would understand. He thought they were nice neighbours, but then again, when did we see them? Gone every morning by seven and back late. No real bother, though, except for the bins that time, and it's not as if we don't have big enough driveways and gardens here.

Herself two doors down thought they were legal types. Paddy had twigged two days earlier but never said. He saw the parking permit on the car and looked up the company name on the computer. When you've lived here 50 years, you want to know who's moving in to the neighbourhood. Especially now with the Covid about.

I noticed it first. Fewer birds in the garden now and less birdsong. Paddy copped it when he heard the birdsong coming from the legal eagles' garden. Time to check the guttering again, we thought. It was the only way to have a good look over the hedges into the neighbours'. He was no sooner up the ladder than he was down again. His drained, ashen face said it all.

He described it to a tee because he had seen one in a catalogue. A top of the range model, with four tiers and two balconies. We were happy with the simple wooden bird table that Paddy had made in his beloved shed, all those years ago when we came south. We were the only house feeding the birds in the area then. The air rifle in the shed was handy for the magpies, but wasn't used much now.

The Covid changed everything. Paddy twigged that the wigs next door were working from home, and fancied a bit of birdsong while they toiled. We know now what was in the big cardboard box delivered recently – Paddy thought it might have been a wine cooler at the time. He had seen one in a catalogue before, not that we were wine people. A great man for the catalogues, was my Paddy.

The trouble started when the delivery man, with his lovely mask, dropped off our grocery order. Standing back, he announced that it was all there except for the birdseed. Paddy nearly had a fit when he told us that next door had cleaned them out of birdseed last week.

In a flash he was out of the cocoon, into the car and away to the retail park. It was downhill after that. The shops were closed, but they think he caught it at the petrol station, filling the can for the lawnmower on the way back. My test was negative, and I was allowed to go home after the funeral.

The air rifle was still there, behind the crate of old milk bottles, but hadn't I forgotten about the sawn-off shotgun under the bench? Our insurance policy, Paddy used to say. Halfway up the ladder, as if I needed any distraction, I heard the doorbell ringing through the open window.

Shared Determination

BY CIARA EBBS

Sitting on the kitchen floor with cereal crunching under her little bum, Brogan was trying her damndest to get her T-shirt on by putting her feet into the holes where her arms should go. Her little face scrunched and her cheeks red, she let out a high-pitched squeal of frustration. I sat across the room at the table, having my fifth cup of coffee and pushing myself further into the seat to stop myself from getting up to help her. Small beads of sweat were starting to appear at her temples, and I silently laughed at the hilarity and familiarity of it all.

The baby was, as usual, attached to my boob and kicking his feet into my stomach, which had a tendency to fold in on itself now. Hearing the toilet flush, I knew Rory was about to arrive in to tell me about the epic poo he'd just had; he'd been in there a good half an hour so I already had an idea of how that announcement would go. 'Babe, I've to leg it to Spar to get Telly Bingo tickets,' he shouted in from the hall.

Grateful to be spared his toilet adventures, I didn't ask why he suddenly wanted to play Telly Bingo and just shouted back 'Kay!' The front door slammed and I heard the car start. I looked at my phone: the 26th of February. That's why he wanted to play Telly Bingo today, like his Mammy used to. She was six years gone now.

I put the baby down on his playmat so he could kick something else for a while. The same determination his big sister showed on her face trying to get dressed began to creep onto his identical little smush; he was about to start rolling over. I could just hear my Mam: 'Now the fun starts!' His little fists clenched tight and his body rocking side to side, he was pushing himself with all his might. It brought me back. Back to the days in the hospital. One fumbling foot in front of the other, my shoelaces tied tight and the walking frame gripped in both hands.

The front door burst open and with the same determination as his kids, Rory declared, 'Today's the day, babe! Today I'm going to win the Snowball Round, and you can get your tooth fixed!'

'Thanks for reminding me,' I grunted, and pushed my tongue into the gap where half my tooth had broken off.

Brogan stormed up and grabbed Rory by the hand. 'Help me, Daddy!' she pleaded, her T-shirt in her hand and her face forlorn at having failed. Again, it brought me back. The baby squealed and I was jolted from my ponderings. Back on the boob and the kettle on for more coffee.

Them Eating the Bats

BY JO ANNE SEXTON

Best sentence heard today? 'It's because of them eating the bats over there,' was a wise woman's explanation as to why she was queueing outside Lidl this morning before 8 a.m. She was randomly shouting it to her neighbour, five people back in the queue at the time. I was there as I couldn't face the thought of having to think about food or cooking, coming in from work over the next couple of weeks. Working at the HSE front line is a bit interesting at the moment, so I'll forgive myself for doing the big shop this morning.

A surreal experience, in a quiet, orderly queue of people of all ages, snaking around a car park. The eerie silence was broken a couple of times, once when an unmarked Garda car did a tour around and again when another lady, well back from the front of the queue, shouted to those near the door that there was an aul lad who needed shelter from the cold and he was to go closer the top. In fairness, no one was going to disagree with her, as she was dead right and also sounded as if she would lamp the head off you if you disagreed – way too early in the morning for any drama.

Apart from that there was silence in a crowd, very strange. All of a sudden I felt really, really sad, and before I knew it I was trying to hide the tear that was rolling down my face. It was really sad to see this is our normal for now, but also sad to see how scared some people were, standing where they were. You just wanted to say, 'You'll be OK. You won't get sick, don't worry.' But we can't say that with 100 per cent certainty.

The Bat-lady comment snapped me out of the gloom and into Lidl's special offers at the door.

The gloom was lifted again later on, by seeing the faces of two little ladies, my nieces, whose lives are taken up with homework, playing, helping their parents, missing out on birthday parties and our regular weekend Insomnia trips – hands down the best hot chocolates around, according to the girls! Chats and seeing faces have never been so important. In spite of everything, there's sparkles of kindness and people being more considerate everywhere. As the guy in the petrol station gave me a bag for my provisions of wine and wine gums – no petrol, of course! – he warned me that the bag wasn't very strong. 'It's OK, chief, I've got this,' I smiled as I walked out, holding it like you would a baby. He knew a smashed bottle of wine before reaching home would be a disaster too far.

All about priorities, self-care and doing those things that we need to get us right. House sorted, food prep for the week done, good friends on speed dial – cheers!

The Black Hole

BY EMMA PERSSON

Smooth as marble, she's made of ice. Remarkable is the one who sees what is lurking deep under the surface of her weary skin. Words don't come easy for her; there are no words poignant or true enough for all she has seen but never truly felt. Her surface, cool and slick, hides the hairline cracks of her fractured mind. The joyful moments and sorrowful events of the external world fail to touch or cut her as they should. Her limbs and body appear intact while her gruesomely deformed soul limps far behind, ensuring great separation and immeasurable distance from her physical sense of self.

Eternally broken, without hope of redemption, she remains arctic cold for fear of being burnt. The vast canyon of her emptiness is as hollow and dark as a cave can get. The narrow, winding arterial passages of her defeated heart have been filled with the haunting echoes of silent screams since a time when time mattered. She claws furiously against the cold black walls until her fingers bleed, but there is no escape from the turmoil of her most dismal place. The place, deep down underground, where goodness is disintegrated to ash, and any flickering glimmer of hope is extinguished long before it gets the chance to burn.

Air is scarce in her foul prison, each staggered, rasping breath seeming even more toxic than the last. The agonising pain coursing through her is raging, rampant and continuous. Creeping and seeping like poison through the ever-evolving cracks in her own self-worth. Like knotweed it grows, twisting its evil web tighter and tighter until such time as it might choose to unravel and regurgitate whatever small part of her remains.

Just like the great ocean that she once loved, her harrowing despair moves in rough waves, crashing and splashing, soaking every inch of her discontented soul with its venomous spray. While she waits soundlessly and without passion for the final tsunami of looming shadows to engulf her, she hopes to feel the sheer familiarity of nothing once again, and profoundly believes that what is left of her will never be right.

If only she knew then the brilliant truth of her impending destiny. I would comfort her with my own experiential realisation that the ice that trapped her for so long will eventually thaw, then melt, exposing a healing warmth that she never thought possible. With time, the reviving heat of the early morning sun will finally and totally rejuvenate her tired and withered soul.

I long to take her fragile hand and lead her towards the shining light that has always existed just outside of our deepest black hole. We will eventually emerge from the darkness, together and whole again, into the bright possibilities of tomorrow. Fantastically transformed by all we have mutually experienced, and forever grateful to have survived the epic storms that threatened to destroy us.

State of Happiness

BY EILEEN LENNON

We're sitting side by side watching a drama series about the beginnings of the Norwegian oil industry (subtitled, of course), as you do on a lockdown Sunday evening. It's called 'State of Happiness'. We are on episode four and have not got to the happiness just yet, but I am sure it will come.

We started watching subtitled dramas a number of years ago because it is hard to fall asleep when you have to concentrate on reading subtitles to keep up with the story. It might sound like a mad reason to throw yourself into Swedish, Danish and now Norwegian TV, with this particular one based in Stavanger. We got hooked, and now names like Viktor, Kasper and Aurora fall off our tongues with ease. I used to be able to cheat; if my mind wandered off and I missed out on the storyline, I could have a sneaky recap the next day when I was by myself. But with the lockdown, there is no sneaky time. While watching, I am throwing an odd eye on the rooks, who are intent on robbing every one of the wildflower seed bombs I have put on the flowerbed. If any survive to grow, it might be a bit of lockdown madness that I will regret for years as I pull reseeding plants out. But I like to see it as a bit of an experiment in this time when we are so dependent on science for a breakthrough to get us out of the 'new normal'. I know things will never be the same again, but hopefully they'll be better than before.

I begin to think of the hours I sit in the back garden – not even reading, just listening to the birds singing and watching them eat and drink. We've started feeding them each day, possibly not the best move with our current wildflower project. Their singing is only interrupted by the sounds of kids playing. The squeak of the trampoline and laughter lifts my heart, although I am glad it's four doors down! With the sounds of the kids and the birds in the sunshine, sometimes it's easy to forget the awful time we're going through, and the sadness for so many families. I feel guilty when this happens.

My mind drifts off again to what will be a happier time, and funnily enough our state of happiness will also be in Stavanger. We may not get to see the bump grow into a cosy, safe haven as often as we would like. However, I hope by November we will have battled our way with this bloody virus and can enjoy the birth of our first grandchild, maybe even named Kasper or Aurora. A new beginning, the next generation to hand a better world on to.

I smile as I think of the trampoline that will be in our garden, the happy shrieks, and our neighbours who are next door and not four doors down.

Poker Face

BY EMMA BURKE

14 April 2020

Day 18 of the lockdown.
  This note was put under my door today…

> *Dear community,*
> *Due to the irresponsible and selfish actions of*
> *one of our residents, I am calling an immediate*
> *emergency meeting in apartment 2A.*
> *Your president,*
>
> *Mr Meseguer*
> *Apartment 2A*

When everybody was assembled in the living room of 2A, Mr Meseguer began. Twenty-four rolls of loo paper and five bottles of hand sanitiser (the building's emergency supplies) had been taken from the utility closet on the top floor of the building. Because of the lockdown, it could be surmised that somebody sitting in the room right now had to be responsible for this reckless crime. Cameras had been consulted, and the perpetrator was known to 'the authorities' – his words, not mine.

(The authorities!?! In all fairness! I hardly think Messy
Meseguer sitting up like a meercat behind those cameras qualifies as an authority.)

Anyway, residents were given until 8 o'clock tonight
to 'come clean' before the video evidence was handed
over to the Guards. Now, I know that this is a scare
tactic, because Meseguer's eyelid kept jumping when
he was saying it – a nervous tic that means I always beat
him at our monthly poker game. I also know that the
camera on the eighth floor isn't working; it hasn't been
for months. Sketchy evidence at best – and the Guards
aren't going to waste their time coming in here to sort
a 'domestic'.

And that's what it is, as far as I am concerned. A
domestic issue of fairness. I'm all for equality – women's
rights and gay rights and all that malarkey – but sometimes a man has to look after himself too. It's called the
survival instinct; it's in our DNA. We have to prepare for
what's to come, you know? And, sure, if I didn't do it,
someone else would have.

And I'm a good person; I won't see anyone else go
short. I just want to have enough for me. It's an anxiety
thing, really. It's totally understandable and justifiable,
really, because surely everyone understands what that's
like.

No, it isn't the big deal they're making out like it was.
Anyone would do it. I just thought of it first.

But now there's a different kind of anxiety gripping
me. It's one that's more familiar, and in some ways comforting. The fear of the virus is a new anxiety, new and
imminent and deadly. The fear of dying had engulfed
me like a cloak, so it was nice to take it off and put back

on the light summer jacket that was the fear of getting caught. At least I knew how to behave with this one: poker face, Brian, poker face. They know nothing. They have nothing.

Haul-out

BY NIAMH MCANALLY

21 March 2020

The boatyard manager in Antigua stares at his computer, shakes his head and stares some more. We are begging him to get us on the schedule, to haul our home, the sailing vessel *Freed Spirit,* out of the water and secure it on land. But so is everyone else. The boat lift has not stopped humming in the last three days. Seaports are closing all around us, airlines are declaring last flights out, and governments are urging people to return to their country of citizenship or risk remaining overseas indefinitely. Our plan to protect ourselves from summer storms by sailing four days across the Caribbean Sea to Bonaire is scuppered. Grenada is also closed. Curfew is coming. If we stay, we'll be quarantined onboard, access to shore uncertain. We feel we've no option but to abandon our home in the hurricane zone and just go.

But it all hinges on what this man and his computer say next. I'm watching his eyes flicking back and forth, his hand rolling an ancient mouse. Beside me, Gary's knee is jigging up and down. Gary. My captain Gary. Four years ago, I'd come to crew for one month. He was a solo sailor, allergic to pecans and relationships. Not that that mattered. Neither of us would have picked the other out of a line-up anyway. But somewhere on the ocean, our souls connected and brought forth a love more joyous than I could have ever dreamed. Today, I wear two diamonds in a sapphire sea. Our wedding is planned for 15 July in Ireland.

Hoping it will help, Gary says:

'We've managed to secure a flight to Miami on Tuesday.'

The manager just shakes his head. Now Plan C is dead too.

'We understand,' I say, in a voice two warbles short of tears.

'Unless...'

'Yes?'

'... unless the guys agree to work overtime and we get you out tomorrow night?'

I want to kiss him, but can't even shake his hand. We run. To prepare our boat for haul-out takes five to seven days. We have less than 30 hours. We de-rig the sails and strip the canvas in Force 6 winds, defrost our fridge-freezer and donate months' worth of food to the local community. Gary adheres tinfoil to portholes to keep out the sun, and duct tapes the hatches to stop leaks, while I vacuum-pack every item of clothing and slather vinegar from ceiling to floor to prevent mould from destroying our home while we're gone.

The jobs continue. And when it's all done, and our duffels are packed, we worry. We worry about boarding an airplane that might infect us; worry about how long we'll be gone and where we'll end up; and worry whether I'll ever get to wear my wedding dress and matching shoes.

The Covid Years
(And years, and years…)

BY RUTH O'CONNELL

'It's called *re-naming* nowadays, Mum. It's 2020.'

'Is it, pet? Well, I'm sure it's the same whenever we are. Carry the 1…' A pencil falls to the floor under the kitchen table and there is no effort made to pick it up. It rolls under the radiator. I sigh. Another thing for me to scrabble after.

'I'll tell you one thing,' I mutter. 'I feel like I have been re-named.'

In my mind I hear the voices of imagined 'other parents': 'My child has been up since 6 a.m. tidying his room. How kind of him to do the windows for me too! Ancient Greek went so well yesterday that I really think it's time to start Japanese now, before Arabic tomorrow.'

My reality is: 'Eh, I think purple and yellow make turquoise, yeah. Or possibly black. You can use the bowl you had your cereal in, that's fine. Yup. Grand, it'll wash off.'

Re-naming. It suits me now. My life has been re-named. I no longer work like I once did, in bursts of efficiency and achievement, interspersed with moments of healthy frustration, the rest of the time spent making my little family function, and having fun together. I am locked down, in more ways than just the physical. My kitchen table is covered with work notes, a laptop with what I suspect is a bit of fried egg on the lid, maths, and piles of fabric I collected over many years in Africa. I am making wonky facemasks on my Aldi sewing machine. Our ears stick out perpendicular to our heads when we wear them as I can't get the elastic from anywhere other than old tracksuits and the tops of socks.

I now have an Alice band of white hair. A sign on the hair clippers, visible to no one but me, says USE ME. I have resisted until now. I don't need a DRINK ME sign on the gin to encourage me to sink gratefully into the sofa every evening, glass in hand.

Everything is an opportunity for learning, we are told brightly. Don't worry about the curriculum! My employers, on the other hand, don't see homemade pizza as something to include in my annual review.

I see my son walking like a cat burglar. I wonder if he is doing PE with Joe. We tried it once. Maybe he remembers? I feel a brief moment of accomplishment.

'I'm practising for when we have so many people here we can't move.'

I hug him fiercely.

'I can't breathe, please,' he says into my tracksuit top.

Later, a wan little voice. 'Mum?'

'Yes?'

Wanner littler voice: 'Do you ever get sick of looking at someone's face?'

I sit bolt upright and think: This is *a parenting moment*. This is the child I would lick a shopping trolley handle for. 'Oh no, I would never get sick of looking at some-one's face,' I say.

Wannest littlest voice possible: 'Me too.' [Deep sigh]

We both know we are lying.

Today in D4

BY LAURA PAYNE

I have been having these Daliesque dreams at night, even during the day when I catnap on the couch while considering my next adventure. My ears are bombarded with world plans and medical science and numbers and figures of Covid-19 when I put the radio or television on. Every station and every channel is up to date on the deaths, and the population doing the 'right thing'. I sometimes think, 'When did we become so compliant? Where are all the rebel streaks we are supposed to genetically possess as Irish? People, come on! Crying about bad self-inflicted haircuts, and bread that has to bubble on the kitchen counter and prove for several days before you can slather it with half a pound of Kerrygold, in which case you can end up with a 'breeze block' that you have to hide in the brown bin because the birds refuse to eat it.

All the experts with the constant pseudo-science rock up from every corner of the world – some you've never heard of until now. Academic types with big words and hand gestures Zoom from their dodgy spare rooms, predicting the crash of the world. 'Sure, we're all in this together' is the mantra from far-flung parts of the universe in various languages, which you try to patch together in case you miss a beat. In debt or solvent?

Rent or run? Mentally damaged or the one with all the great ideas? Solpadeine or paracetamol?

Constant scrubbing and cleaning. The house resembles the inside of a lab, skin resembles an orange from the washing and sterilising. 'Some president' has taken to conjuring up his own prescriptions based on some 'science' 'they' have 'understood': 'Well, it works for malaria, and it won't do ya any harm.'

'This is a WAR!' we hear from the elites and experts. 'How to keep calm' comes in various guises from the tweedy-clad psychobabble experts. Bend your body like an S-hook on a mat on the floor, and train your dragon – that voice in your head in the background playing mind games, telling you to wake up, it's all a dream.

Every dream brings the copious strange feelings of colour and movement never before experienced, like being on a movie set, and you can remember it when you wake. Strange red fruits or vegetables going by in various forms and conditions. Multiple shapes, sizes and colours, which I then turn into culinary delights. Various television chefs rattle on as to the 'wonderful things' we can conjure up in the kitchen, which has been scrubbed and pummelled into showroom condition. Fash kitchen equipment ordered on Amazon in the expectation of producing Michelin-standard food while I wallow in a self-inflicted prison. Going out is the 'new normal', whatever that is. Staying in is the 'new normal'. The fridge becomes your 'new friend'. You forage constantly. You break out that exercise mat and look at it while you have that bag of crisps from the couch. You roll it up again, in case you have an accident. God forbid you would have to go to a hospital, the no-go area for the foreseeable future.

Supermarket shopping becomes the highlight of the week. Before leaving the house you have to 'kit up' just in case you come in contact with the Virus, or someone spluttering and coughing all over the place. Gloves and masks, gels and potions to kill any possible contact with infection. Which size, shape or colour will I get my hands on to bring back to the lab and turn into an edible exhibit? Will I put it with cheese, or asparagus? Throw it into eggs, or line it up on pastry? Will I shower it with basil, or oregano? Will I fry it, or watch it develop in the glass door of the oven, on some of that expensive foreign equipment? Glass of wine, or bottle of water? Put it on a china plate, or throw it on the 'usual'?

Falling for the New Housemate

BY CAROLINE NOLAN

Thank God for Alex, she has been my lifeline lately. Yes, I'm lucky to have my family here as well, but having an employee, confidante and drinking buddy is a must-have during any pandemic. Luckily she had just moved in before the lockdown. She can be a little sarcastic and quite snarly, but I've got to know her humour so I don't take it too personally. She is above all really good with the kids. When I'm on a conference call she keeps them entertained with some 'Poo Song'. I can often hear giggles coming from the kitchen. She also plays the guitar, and the kids love to dance around her. She plays old favourite games like Rock, Paper, Scissors and Bingo. I must confess to being a little jealous of their affection for her. The husband loves her too; they often sing Irish country songs together and discuss sports scores and various trivia. Cue eyeball roll – we don't have conversations like that, thank God.

The dog, unfortunately, is rather scared of her. I don't know why.

I watched all the *Star Wars* movies because *The Empire Strikes Back* is her all-time favourite movie.

(Her American twang is so appealing.) I agree; they're very impressive movies. I think if she hadn't been here, I would have lost my mind. I look forward to our chats. Alex confided in me that she is happily single. She's also really clever, and witty:

Me: How was your day?

Alex: Super duper. I like these long days; it gives me more time to spend with my favourite colour.

She is so insightful and uplifting.

Me: Do you like pizza?

Alex: While I appreciate great food and drink, my good taste is better reflected in the company I keep.

Me: Who farted?

Alex: If you're a denier, you must be the supplier!

Me: Alex, where are you? The blasted internet is gone again. How are we going to get any work done?

She remains stoic and calm as always, even when I shout at her – which is sometimes bloody infuriating.

On good days over a glass of red we order stuff together online. She always seems to know the best deals around. I think I may be a bit in love with her. My husband doesn't seem to mind my infatuation with the hired help!

Me: Alex, make me a sandwich, please.

Alex: OK, you're a sandwich!

She cracks me up. She's definitely more sass than mass.

Me: Tell me something funny.

Alex: I had a really great boomerang joke… it'll come back to me.

One evening over wine I finally opened up to her.

Me: Alex, will you be my girlfriend?

Alex: I like you… as a friend.

I nodded, feeling an absolute fool. Jesus, the AI has knocked me back. Mercifully she can't see me blush

– wait a minute – can she? Thanks, Alexa. She hasn't mastered 'You're welcome' yet. Funny how this make me feel a teeny bit superior... just.

Temporary Peace

BY SASS O'FLYNN

5.30 a.m. lying semi-conscious in the comfort of my old brass bed. I made a promise to myself to get up and walk before work every morning, and the last thing I want to do is let myself down. I turn on my side and listen to the birdsong on my now-silent street. I smile a sleepy smile, delighted Mother Nature is making her presence strong. I stretch my arms overhead and hear that demon voice creep in: 'Five more minutes.' I swing my legs out of the bed in tandem with a vocal 'no' from my soul song. 'No.' I have been let down, I have let people down, and I am damned if I am going to let myself down.

Swift moves to the bathroom jolt my body into action. It's time I say, as I look at myself in the mirror, I really look fabulous this time of morning – I chuckle to myself – now that I have an outright ban on all eyewear in this room! One of your better decisions, Sass, agreeing with myself as my mouth fills with toothpaste and water.

A quick change, a dash of blusher, down the stairs, I begin the mini-marathon of making my packed lunch. Stuffing myself with toast and peanut butter. Coffee made, I head out, load the car, cross-checking keys in my pocket as I snap the front door shut in a well-rehearsed silence, so I don't wake the kids. My feet carry me to the top of the road. The burst of wind and salty air hits my nostrils and I thank the ancestors for getting my ass out of the bed. The smells and chatter from the wildlife cajole me into smiling as I pick up the pace along the seafront. My internal world springs to life as I chit-chat to myself, no longer caring if people hear me or not. It's my conversation with my internal self. I am blessed to really enjoy my own company during these times.

So, Sass, do you think this virus is natural? Was it in a lab? Did they start working on it and it all went terribly wrong? Yes, I answer myself, that is a plausible idea. However, you will never find this out, will you? I turn to head home, and jump into my car for the obligatory journey to work. As I swipe my card on the clock machine, it acknowledges my start. Three paces in, the collective energy is palpable with unowned frustrations and rage. It's OK Sass, I reassure myself; you will get through this day.

4.30 p.m. I remove my face from the inspection light, dying to see daylight again. I race out the door and head for home. Roads quiet, the Guard asks me where I was. I show my badge. Loneliness steps into my heart, and a longing to feel the movement of the sea, bringing temporary peace.

Running

BY SOPHIE SMITH

Every single morning running, running to keep my mind off things, running to keep my mind from negative people and social media, running to impress others. Negative people being my mam. She's always a negative Nancy, and telling me what to do. I'm clearly sick of it. In her world, everything is about how I look and what I do. Can she not do her own thing? I am a little bit on the bigger side. I'm not fat, I'm not skinny, I'm in the middle – which sucks! My mam wants me to lose weight and be skinny, and it has upset and angered me to the point that I just don't care anymore. I just end up doing what she wants.

Every single morning I'm forced to run five kilometres in the park. If I could, I would lie and tell her I did it, but she knows exactly how long it takes to run five kilometres, and she needs proof that I did the run. So, I must use the Under Armour app and track every single one of my runs. After I do all that running for her, I have to take the dog out on a walk, which is peaceful because I get to be away from my family for at least two hours. Yay me!!

I do have the social media apps like Instagram, Snapchat and Facebook. I have to put something up, it's basically society's rules. It's like, if you don't post, you're boring; and if you post too much, you're annoying. It's extremely difficult to please today's society, I must say. Whenever I want to post something, there's always that bit of anxiety I get when I think about what other people think when I put something up. Like a selfie, if I post one; I feel like everybody is hating on me and calling me ugly or fat behind my back. I also feel the need to dress to impress and make society think I'm cool.

I try not to post too regularly either, because it might make people think I'm obsessed with myself or that I like to spam my accounts with selfies. Yeah, it's a weird one alright. I get my daily dose of hate from my family and social media. Oh, and it's also a sin that I haven't had a boyfriend or girlfriend in all my life – who knew?

Honestly, I'm sick of all of it. My life, my rules, right? Nope! Far from it, love! Maybe I just don't want to have a boyfriend or girlfriend, but no one but me understands – my mother certainly doesn't. No boy will date you if you're lazy and big. I have to be skinny to get a boyfriend, she says. People's standards are so high it's unbelievable. Boys and girls want you looking like Kylie Jenner. They'll only like you if you look impossible. They say it's not true, but it is.

A day in my life is fighting with my mother and having my anxiety crippled by social media. What's yours like?

The Sound of You

BY AOIFE POWER

In the kitchen I try to imagine what you would make of it all. The scientist in you would enjoy following the bulletins, the never-ending analysis. Most of all, you would be quietly delighted in the fact that you were right all along. We all now rely heavily on a word you loved and lived by: routine. On my daily calls to Mum I sometimes pretend you will pick up. It forces me to hear your voice in my head.

A teenager appears and starts banging presses with unnecessary force. Neon earphones sprouting from his ears, the tinny resonance of music audible. 'Afternoon.' No reply. 'AFTERNOON,' I shout. A neon green earpiece is plucked out.

An eye-roll so elaborate I can nearly hear it. 'Afternoon.' He reinstates the earphone and sets to a bowl filled with three Weetabix, a milky-white trail of drops from the bowl to a plastic milk carton.

I reach for a used envelope, write in capitals, 'WALK THE DOG PLEASE, WHEN YOU ARE FINISHED, MUM.' I stand up and place it directly in front of the screen of the phone.

'NO NEED FOR NOTES, THAT IS NO PROBLEM,' he shouts – no removal of listening devices this time.

I leave the kitchen and settle to do some remote teaching, imagining all the while that there are carbon copies of my teen in homes all over the country. I think of you again, and how proud you were when I told you I had a job in teaching. You asked me questions I could hardly answer myself. I grappled with keeping you engaged and savoured the admiration you had for me. Still amazed, to this day, at the faith you always had in my ability.

I had suppressed the urge to be alone, so later I was on a walk with my daughter; sullen in her thoughts, the odd time shouting something over the cacophony in her ears. I think of you again. The days when you would ask me not to head out on my rebellious walks, late in the evening on a winter's night. I would slam the door in response and walk for hours, half terrified under the yellow streetlights. Relishing in some strange teen idea of justice, that you would be driving around looking for me. Yet you forgave me. We grew to understand each other better.

At dinner this evening, they come one by one. A meal with no phones, and there is laughter, stories of funny things learned that day in their online bubbles. The chatting makes me giddy and I relish the company. Embarrassed now at my refusal to come to the table, back when you called. Would you still be sitting in the front room reading your newspaper, Mum in another room watching television? She misses giving out to you about your bachelor-like habits. I rise from the table and make my daily call, and before Mum picks up, I imagine it is you I will hear.

Artie

BY NIAMH LINEHAN

A rtie loves to jump; he's jumping right now to music played on the *John Creedon Show* on the radio. He wants to know the names of the songs and the singers. It need only to be played once and it might be played a year later, and he will name the names. Forgets nothing. Except how to be around others. Not true. He does know how to be around people who accept him.

Rio Teslin, Rio Taku, Nord Serena, Nord Isabella. Cargo ships. His timetable of each and every day now. In quarantine. The cruise liners have stopped. *Oriana, Artania, Marco Polo…* They were his year, his month, week and day. It's how he learned time, calendars, months and places: Port of Cork; Ringaskiddy; Cobh Deep Water Quay.

Before he was two, he would perch against the windowsill and study the liners approaching the harbour. His first word was 'guck', meaning stuck. Stuck for a word, stuck in a chair? But soon he learned 'Mum' and 'Dad', and then he learned the names of the ships. He learns the Port of Cork's schedule each year by heart.

But they haven't arrived or departed. They are somewhere in cruise-liner quarantine. When I explain that people are sick, and that when they are better, the ships will come again, he can smell my uncertainty. 'The

159

liners are on fire!' he yells, or 'The liners are exploded,' or 'The liners are in a crash.' He means it's a catastrophe. For him. Every day. His beautiful mouth quivers, tears roll. He angrily wipes them away.

He is missing the big bush in the entrance of the school yard.

'The big bush goes...?' he pleads, and I answer by raising my arms and swaying slightly, and then moving my body around fast and suddenly. This makes the bush move from a gentle breeze to moving in a storm. I become the bush because he misses school... many times a day.

He doesn't want to see his teacher's face on Messenger, face to face, yet he beams when he hears Mr Ó Loinsaigh's voice on loudspeaker.

'How are you, Artie?' in his soft Ballyvourney tone.

Artie answers, 'How are you, Artie?'

A pause.

'Artie's making music,' I inform Mr Ó Loinsaigh.

'Well done, Artie. Are you playing your *feadóg*?'

Artie is jumping with pleasure.

'Artie's playing his fiddle, Mr Ó Loinsaigh,' I reply.

'Great, Artie. It's good to talk.'

Artie says, 'Turn it off, turn it off,' indicating the phone. He is beaming with pleasure. He loves Mr Ó Loinsaigh, and it's mutual. He's overwhelmed. I don't have to explain because Mr Ó Loinsaigh gets him. Artie goes to the sofa, pulls the black tablecloth over his head. I turn off the phone and join him under the dark comfort. For a cuddle, a giggle, a cry and a sigh.

We are a bit 'guck' at the moment.

Chewing Pandemic Food

BY PADRAIG DOYLE

There have been four other days like this. Maybe just how I remember them, but seems looking back that the sun was always aggressive on these days. I know the drill now, so I gather my knees up and sit on this bench until I get hungry or sleepy. Then a carton of soup, a tin of fish. Back to the garden bench, or bed. For the old break-ups I could stand in freezer aisles, slowly assimilating Linda McCartney's nutritional information to try to make a good decision, but this one's left me chewing on joyless pandemic food. Tins of mackerel I bought when Italy went on lockdown. Smart boy that day. Greasy fish mashed on a rock-hard heel of sourdough. Luckily, I suppose, I've no biscuits or beer left. Hobnobs and IPA just wouldn't sit well with the tinned fish.

Today rings familiar. Actually rings. Tuning forks are whirling around my ears and in front of my eyes. All I can do is sit it out. The sun's burning on one side but I don't budge. Phone vibrates off the windowsill. Surprised it's still working after Wednesday night. I'd a phone 17 years ago; an Ericsson, with a good camera for its time. I remember thinking as it struck the wall and disintegrated one night outside Bruxelles, that such a good camera should be better protected. A week later I pulled my knees to my chest on a cheap sofa in

Celbridge after a night shift, listened to the swarm of tuning forks for the first time, and muffled them with a half bottle of whiskey at 8:30 in the morning. The smartphone withstood the impact on Wednesday. I wish it had been smashed.

I pick up the phone to see four missed calls and five messages, the messages growing increasingly inaccurate. I remember these facts, why can't you? Why can't you recall what you said, what I said? We must have lived a different year. You want to try again, and in the same moment, un-tag us from public view like we never happened? I don't follow you. I stare a hundred metres past the garden wall and lose an hour trying to reach out and grab the threads of old fights that wisp in and out of clear memory. I can just about make out their texture and colour but I can't follow the thread to remember exactly what was driving us then. I just remember the relief when we exhausted ourselves and hugged.

A hundred whirring tuning forks mute the arc of the sun, and the afternoon passes like this. The phone is dead now from an afternoon of simultaneously shouting and soothing. 'Make You Feel My Love' was the last song she shared. Ane Brun. Her beautiful cover of a heavy message. But the songs soothe, so I leave the phone on. I just wish Dylan had written 'to let you see my love'.

The Prayer Book and Me

BY PATRICIA BYRNE

Please don't switch off yet – it's not too boring!

For my 21st birthday my precious friend and flatmate gave me a prayer book that cost one shilling and sixpence. I cherished that gift for dear life, and some years later I had it leather-bound to protect it against the slings and arrows of life.

Recently I wanted a recap on the '10 Commandments' and reached for my prayer book, only to discover that it was written in Latin. I had clean forgotten! With such a heavy heart, I closed it and returned it to my locker. I am presently 92 years old, and in this nursing home with all the time in the world to think of my 21st and young days.

My dear friend is living nearby in Malahide and we still keep in touch. In a minor way, I like to think I returned that cherished gift by introducing my good friend to her husband. Sadly, both our darling husbands have died – RIP.

Still I have that prayer book, which I have carried from Carlow, Kildare (where I changed digs four times!), then to Donabate and Swords in Dublin. Finally, here to my home in TLC. We – the prayer book and I – look a bit weary and frayed around the edges but we have endured, as has my friendship with my friend Mary, 71 years later.

Love

Imperial Leather

BY DONALD MCCANN

A long, long time ago, I lived in a house alongside a railway track in Sandymount.

When I was six years of age I would spend every afternoon sitting in my back garden watching the trains go by. I would record the engine numbers in my notebook. Every night I would sit at the edge of the bath and watch my brother Brendan clean up after working in the C.I.E. workshop in Broadstone. I would read out the numbers and Brendan would assure me he had seen the engines.

It was only much later that I realised he could not have seen all the engines. He was just being kind to his little brother. My brother was a special man, very tolerant, kind and a great friend. Each weekend he would put me on his shoulders and take me to the speedway in Shelbourne Park. When I was fourteen, he taught me to drive.

But to return to those nights spent sitting on the bath watching Brendan scrub up. He had one thing he insisted on, that was the soap he used. He had to use Cussons Imperial Leather soap. The sea from the scent of the soap filled the bathroom and took me to a place of contentment. Even today I still use the same soap, and, nearly 70 years later, I am transported back to being that young boy sitting on the bath, notebook in hand, reading out engine numbers to his hero.

Latter-day Mischief

BY SHELLY POWER

I first met eyes with the cute, cheeky Ronnie at church one glorious summer Sunday afternoon. He was what us virgins would call 'a big ride'.

'We followed those missionaries around like the kids in 'The Pied Piper', jumped on the bandwagon, were baptised by immersion in the icy sea in Portmarnock and were now fully fledged Mormons.' Altona was in it for the fellas. They always travelled in pairs, Noah's apostles: a geek and an Adonis.

David, driven by the talent, was there 'for the craic', though at the time he didn't know he was a friend of Dorothy's. My mum had lapsed because at the time you had to go to the North to be baptised, which was also an opportunity to buy cheaper wallpaper, but she couldn't get the day off work.

I was consumed. I went to Sunday school, sang full throttle at church: 'put your shoulder to the wheel, push along'.

Surprising I should be noticed at all; I paraded around in anything that was unfashionable, not quite the vintage look I was aspiring to. A midi, unlined, blue pleated skirt that fell well below the knee, coupled with an elegant silky cream blouse with pussy-bow tie,

both gifts from my mum's friend who always wore styl-
ish clothes. These were pretty ancient, even by June's
standards. Underneath, preloved big green floral nylon
double-gusset Bridget Jones knickers, and a tired too-
big-in-the-cup bra that had gone in the wrong wash. The
sandals – the only thing I really owned outright – tan,
slight heels with strappy ankles, flattering my unshaved,
milky, shapely shins.

I melted in the church that sunny Sunday morning. The sun shot through the big sash window with
the cracked paint like the Angel Moroni was giving an
appearance.

Under my itchy winter wool skirt, there was a sauna
going on, beads of sweat trickling down my legs into
my new sandals, creating suction when I walked and –
the mortification – farting sounds. I clenched my toes,
crossed my legs and hoped no one noticed.

As large damp patches began to appear under the
arms of the sophisticated blouse, its loose silky fabric
reaching up to my chin and cuffs elasticated at the wrist,
the pan stick foundation started melting onto the pussy
bow tie. Soft curls from the sponge rollers hung limp and
lifeless, the leather-bound *Book of Mormon* inscribed by
an elder clutched tight between my sweating palms –
I was a dead ringer for one of the Stepford wives.

Altona flirted effortlessly with the elders, her big
Mediterranean blues dancing and her every girly curve
enhanced by a spanking-new pillar-box red catsuit that
was all the rage. David's pimple-popped face shone
and his just-washed hair smelled of clinic shampoo. We
thought we were it, a bona-fide Bible-basher and her
two disciples.

A wafer below all the regalia, hungry teenagers craving a harmless little fun, our latter-day mischief would shape our lives, not knowing at the time that we were truly charmed.

Paris a besoin des bébés

BY VIVIEN HENNESSY

'*Paris a besoin des bébés*,' he said, the cold November wind rising from the Shannon trying unsuccessfully to drown his words and mock his accent. I turned to face him, understanding the words but puzzled by the meaning. I turned away, facing angry rapids churning brown and white foam in the river.

'We could leave, go to France, find work and decide what to do once we get there.' Is this a question, I thought, or is he just testing the waters? I listened, but chose not to reply. We started walking along the river bank, 4 o'clock and the daylight had already drained from the darkening sky. 'Well, we can't stay here,' he said; now there was an urgency to his voice. I couldn't turn to meet his eyes; if I did he would see the tears already beginning to well. I had begun to understand, but was no way ready to reply.

Leaving him, I walked along O'Connell Street until I reached the Saddlery where the horse's head above the door cast a shadow on the crumbling steps below. The flat was damp and uninviting, and not for the first time I felt the pang of guilt and regret born of my decision to leave my warm and familiar family home to live here. However, I knew that now more than ever, I could never look back. Outside the wind had started up and

172

the rain-streaked windows rattled. My heart, which had not stopped thumping since that meeting by the river, had finally slowed and I knew what I had to do next.

In the kitchen cupboard, behind the tins of chicken soup, bags of rice and dried lentils, I found the old coffee tin. Inside I counted 60 pounds; another 40 and I might have enough. I pulled a callcard from my pocket: ten units with a wistful picture of Niamh of Tír na nÓg. How far had she travelled for the man she loved? How did she feel when he left her and her children for the land of his birth?

When her heart broke, did she hear it crack?

Outside, early revellers braved the rain-soaked streets carrying skeletal umbrellas and wearing eager smiles. Only a month ago I was one of them, hopeful and care-free. The queue outside the phone box was thankfully short. I pulled my hood tighter and prepared for the wait when I heard her voice behind me. 'Hey, how are you? Long time no see! Have you been sick? Haven't seen you in work this week.' I mumbled excuses, inventing lies, thinking fast, suddenly realising that from now on, all my interactions would be divided into lies and half-truths, the seeds of a new me and a new life stirred shakily into existence.

Finally taking refuge in the phone box, I dialled the number and waited for an answer. 'Hi there, how are you? Sorry, I know it's been a while, but I have only a few units left. Quick question. You know that old suit-case? The big red one? I think it's in Mam and Dad's room. Can you get it for me?'

Capturing the View

BY MAOLÍOSA NÍ LÉANNACHÁIN

The back of the chair was completely gone, and the ripped upholstery hid slyly under an old familiar cushion. There was something so foreign in its shape, a former kitchen chair exiled to the 'good' sitting room after falling victim to years of toddlers pulling at its frame. It sat there behind a now-bare desk, staring out the window, lifeless. Like all the other miscellaneous antiques lining the back wall, we said we'd do it up or sell it on. That statement now bears the weight of 15-odd years. I ran a finger across the remainder of its spine before sitting down.

It was the same chair my father sat in every day to write and sing sad old songs about lost love. This view was his. He had once spent hours gazing out at the massive elm tree. In the long summer evenings it would draw shadows on the blinds as the sun danced between its branches on its descent to rest.

I thought it strange how this sight never crept into his lyrics. I could imagine him sitting there, trying to block out the soft maunder of voices seeping through the kitchen walls as his children painted blank sheets of paper or opened up hair salons for their dolls.

An intense sadness swept over me as an orchestral suite of regret began ringing in my ears. An endless stream of memories was now flooding the basin of my bemused upper storey. One, however, floated to the surface, like an old song clawing at blurred childhood memories: my mother's 40th birthday. It's strange, but I don't remember much about that day.

I barely recall what friends came, or the sight of my mother's slowly aging face when we surprised her. I think the cake was a plain Victoria sponge with pink icing, but that image could have been added in over time, sieving its way through the cracks in my memory. What I do so clearly remember however is my father sitting on this exact chair and this exact sadness swallowing whole my tiny seven-year-old self for the very first time.

Though he sang 'Sunrise' by Norah Jones and 'Happy Birthday' to my mother and a crowd of ignorant guests, I realised then that all his songs were about the woman he called his wife. Their love was drawing to a close like the evening sunlight falling slowly between the elm tree's branches. In his own way, he had been capturing the view all along.

It was subtle at first. Lack of affection, separate bed-rooms. Then harsher. Slammed doors, piercing looks, fierce tirades swirling aimlessly through the air. After a decade it crescendoed to a back hall of storage boxes filled with my father's belongings. And that was it. Dark-ness had fallen on their seemingly once bright future together. This old rickety chair was where it all began, and where I would come to sit, attempting to navigate my way through life without the love of its original owner.

Hawaii

BY RÓISÍN CONROY KEEGAN

I suppose it had been disingenuous of me to do that, but I was 22, and going on what I now know of 22-year-olds, it's a pretty selfish age. Selfish in a detached way, a lofty way, where it's just you and the bubble around you, floating independently of the greater world and others in it.

We were to interrail that summer, buy a tent together or generally do anything that involved the two of us, but all that fell away when the visa came through. The visa that I hadn't told him about. The visa that was given out in a lottery, my way of blaming it all on fate, as though I had no hand or part in it. It was beyond my control, and now that it was an option, I simply had to take it.

He reacted badly, of course. We broke up, but reunited the next day, drinking all afternoon in a darkened pub and promising to stay faithful. Tight holds, tears and goodbyes, then a jet 7,000 miles away to an island in the Pacific. Years later Hawaii would be a state of mind to me rather than a place, a perfect manifestation of everything I could have dreamt of for that moment in time. My final results were revealed online, and I lay for hours on inflated plastic, drifting on the gentle waves, revelling in the peace of having absolutely nothing weighing me down. Lightness, staring up at a vast blue sky, dizziness at just being there, freedom. I savoured those hours, forgiving myself for having spent four years of my life studying something I hated, because I was here, I was floating, I was free. My life had brought me here.

When he arrived to visit weeks later, having spent all his money on flights, I knew immediately that something was amiss. He was cold, angry, imploding almost, as though he was only here to punish me for having gone in the first place. We were two people at war, in a one-bedroom apartment shared with eight other people. I found myself alone on the beach at unearthly hours, hugging my knees and sobbing, and wondering why? There were rumours of someone else now, a friend of a friend, and I seemed to have no voice but only eyes to see it. I thought about that first night, how I'd been so happy to see him, flowers draped around my neck, feeling so pretty, tanned and transformed. I thought about how I stripped off on the beach, giddy and laughing, running into the water, beckoning him to follow. The Pacific was a lonely place to be with no clothes on, and I quickly realised he would remain there on the shore. He and his disdain and disapproval. My high, my lightness, my sense of abandon, crashed with the moonlit waves and slowly, almost ashamedly, I walked back to my clothes, dragging them up over my wet skin. 'Who are you?!'

Toast for Breakfast

BY AOIFE READ

This morning I made myself four slices of toast: two the way I like them; and two the way you like them, with the bread slightly cold and hard so that the butter doesn't melt. I didn't even realise I had done it until I began eating the second two slices. A habit formed through seven years of making you toast. I wonder how many habits like this I'm going to have to break.

I sat at the computer. All college work is finished now and I am desperately trying to find something to distract me from my doldrums. I sit in the room that cradled me from kidulthood to adulthood, that carried my pain and my tears through various hardships and break-ups and mishaps over the years. I just never thought it would carry me through the end of us.

From the screen, like a beacon, the folder on the desktop that contains all the photos of us is glaring at me. I could swear it's brighter than the other desktop icons. I haven't been able to look through it. I haven't been able to delete it. The folder that holds a thousand smiles and memories. I can't help but wonder how many of those smiles are lies. Every inch of us feels tainted now.

I think about how easy it was to delete you from social media; all I had to do was block you, and all of our memories, joyous posts and loved-up sentiments are wiped from my life for as long as I want them to be. Forever if needs be. But I can't remove you from my computer's desktop. I have taken the physical photos I had around the room and hidden them in secret places that I never need to see again, but I can't throw them out.

So I sit, staring blankly at the screen as that folder glows fiercer and brighter at me. I begin to spiral into thoughts of ruin. There's nothing to distract me from inside my own head. I can't stop thinking about the folder and the lies and the truth it contains, and which is which. The story of us that is woven in pixels and blue light within that folder is a tale of one woman's blissful ignorance, and another's growing disdain. Turns out I've been in isolation for longer than Covid-19 ever chomped its jaws down on us. Your distance from me grew and grew until it swallowed us both whole. I never knew. You never told me how far away from me you'd gotten.

I swallow the final bite of toast, and create a new folder that's just called 'New Folder' and I put the pictures folder into that. Suddenly my screen seems calmer and my head stops buzzing.

I look around my safety net of a room, take a few deep breaths, open the window, and make the decision to have cereal for breakfast from now on.

Echo

BY GER CREED

This is the place I last saw her. This wild, abandoned place. I didn't know I could ever come back. I still don't as I take the sharpest bend in the road that makes the house disappear again. I put my foot to the pedal, crossing the bridge. Water stretches either side of us, reflecting the sky so that pink, sugar-spun clouds are above and below us now.

'We're flying,' Amy exclaims.

'I can see countries,' her sister Lucy adds, and it's true; the reed swamps dotted across Dysart look like tiny kingdoms. Long ago, these reed swamps hid floating forts called crannogs. When I was 12, like the twins are now, I'd take my father's boat out searching for Viking coins and spearheads on these islands. I recite their names: Fort, Oge, Goose, Cherry, Cro Inis (or Cormorant), Chapel and Green Island.

'Did you take her to the little islands?' the girls ask.

'I did,' I whisper, 'to every single one.'

When we reach the pier, it's smaller than I remember, and the drop from the diving board shorter.

'Do you have something to say?'

'A prayer, like?'

These girls, who've been cooped up in the car, want some drama now.

People around here called her 'the English cousin'. She was 13, a year younger than me, but looked older. I see her sitting on this pier, blowing smoke rings out across the water. The best view of Cullingham House is from here, in the evenings with the sun dipping behind its roofless walls. We'd sit for hours, her and me, watching the glassless windows fill with blood-red light as I recounted tales of garden parties and croquet on Cullingham's sweeping lawn. I teased her about that bit of our shared history – how the land had been stolen from us by her fellow countrymen. And we'd try to guess which room the daughter was locked into after being caught with the stable lad. We'd never met before that summer, so had little other history to share.

She said swimming washed the bleach from her hair, and when I guessed she couldn't, I taught her how. I see her above me, pushing out from the board, whooping 'Geronimo!' before slicing into the clear black. And later, sitting on this rusted ladder, dangling her bracelet before me. 'It's yours,' she'd said, 'if you take me to the house.'

The ashes are lumpy and not easy to manage, but eventually do as they're told.

'She's a genie escaping her bottle,' Amy announces, and in her scattering, I feel a weight, like a suitcase, lifting off my chest.

'So long, cuz,' Lucy calls.

'Auntie,' I correct.

We are above the lake now, springing out from the board. When they found her bones three months ago, they requested a DNA test. That we were sisters didn't surprise me.

I surface, touch the silver bracelet that spells her name. 'Aisling,' I call, and she comes back to us, as hopeful as a blessing.

Standing Tall

BY PATRICIA KINCH UNDERWOOD

It's probably one of the most defining days of my 60 years of life. What brought us here? A rollercoaster becoming a train wreck. These last weeks, these last memories, these last loves, these lost dreams, those last words. I glance at him in the passenger seat, my man, my safe harbour, my soulmate, found against all odds. From James Street to the Registrar's Office. We have an appointment. Second-time-rounders, middle-aged teenagers in lust and in love. Both life-damaged, different, slightly crazy – but together, healed.

In the automatic, I can hold his hand as I drive, a hand that now feels like a little broken bird wrapped in crêpe paper. Silent, by mouth – well, he is never very talkative anyway, fond of saying, 'Sure you can talk for both of us.' But his eyes speak louder than any megaphone: fear, acceptance and great love. The grid of the radiation mask still imprinted across his beautiful bald head. There's nothing more we can do, they said, the last hurrah. It's not curative, just palliative.

Arrived, he has to capitulate, and uses the wheelchair, his best white Savile Row shirt, Louis Copeland trousers, made for standing tall, not for sitting in an old person's chariot – and you're not old, my fine big yellabelly man. Not good – I can see you look down, ankles and socks on view, sartorial embarrassment.

The porter shows me to the disabled toilet. A friend has lovingly made me a beautiful white chiffon thingy I can pull on over my clothes to make me look somewhat bridal. Janice, a town clerk, helps me. Someone gives me a little white clip to tidy up my blonde straggles.

No aisle, no red carpet, no shotguns needed this time – we both had all that in the '70s. Not our first Wedding Rodeo. I walk from my bridal latrine to your side, my love. There is a chair so I can sit beside you, as the Bluetooth plays 'Stand by Your Man' – ironic.

There are four other people in the room – none of them our adult children, my five, your three – just us, you insisted, 'They won't be happy.' We exchange vows: they don't include 'in sickness and health' (we're living that one); they don't include 'till death do us part' (that one is a sure bet). I promise above all else to live in truth with you, to be your partner in all things, not possessing you but working with you as part of a whole. I DO X 2. Choking emotions, my tears bubble, a gentle squeeze of my hand, a tiny whisper with breath that is precious: 'Relax. Love you.'

The first dance, the last waltz, intertwined. You stood, we held each other, we shuffled, Jim Reeves on speakerphone. We went home to our marital bed, lay silently for hours just holding hands, the perfect honeymoon. Sixteen beautiful days your bride, the rest of my lifetime alone: your lover, wife, now widow.

Keeping in Touch

BY FRANCES HARNEY

'm fiddling with the tuning dial, trying to reconnect
with RTÉ Radio 1 and a Richard Ford interview.
'Bloody thing keeps sliding out of tune,' I complain,
more to myself than to Liam.

Suddenly the ancient transistor surges into clarity:
'A marriage only survives if you can keep the conversation going,' the writer declares authoritatively.

My reclining husband rouses into voice: 'What a
load of rubbish!' I wasn't sure if he was referring to this
eminent author or the actual radio set. 'Everyone's an
expert on everything these days. Who wants a "surviving
marriage" anyway? Does he mean a "living marriage"?'
I was about to answer, but he had already drawn his own
conclusion. 'I've said it before and I'll say it again, words
only serve to confuse understanding!' Liam has never
been a big conversationalist. The transmission fades to
an unintelligible whirr. I feel him smiling beneath the
discarded T-shirt he has placed over his face. I click the
dial, and we lapse into a lazy silence.

We are lying semi-naked in the 'den', Liam in his ill-
fitting boxers and me in my mismatched bra and knickers. We are lying in the sun, together, apart. This summer
practice is now in its 38th year. With closed eyes, we bathe
in the warmth, sheltered in our 'sanctum sanctorum'.

Our cadenced breathing attunes to nature's own voices, humming, buzzing, chirping, singing, translucent in harmony. I drift on sounds of grazing cattle in nearby fields. Snippets of conversations carry on memory's wavelengths – my mother's voice – 'Do you think she'll marry him?' My father's tones resonant and decisive. 'They're a total mismatch, him and his motorbikes, her and her books. He's a townie, she's a country girl. I don't even know if he goes to Mass. You'll have to talk to her.'

The petal touch of Liam's hand on mine draws me back to the present – skin on skin – and I reawaken. His gentleness talks as our fingers intertwine, reaffirming his promise 'to take my hand'. We stretch palm to palm, reciprocating tenderness – 'I take thee.' He rhythmically strokes the moist folds to my fingertips turning my dial, megahertz spinning – 'to love and to cherish'. His thumb caresses my palm with perfect frequency. I cup it and thrill at its firmness within my soft embrace – 'to have and to hold'. Our hands pulsating in the most ancient of all languages copulate in scintillating communion. My heart bursts into full bloom – 'for all of our lives'.

No words to confuse understanding as these two hands fit one into the other, perfectly matched, each bathing in the warmth of the other, totally satisfied. These hands, snug in their snuggery, have held each other through births and deaths, disappointments and joys, sickness and health, good times and bad.

If marriage survives on conversation, it lives on the language of the touch of love. No need for fine-tuning. The reception is strong with conversations that will last a lifetime.

The Excuse

BY ANN BATTERSBY

After I stitched the cardigan together, I held it up.

'Would you look at the size of that! It's tiny.' John put his hands over his eyes and said, 'Don't be showing me that.'

I laughed and waved it at him. Another one of his superstitions; he was full of them.

We had an early start the following morning. It would be my last trip in the Scania for a while. It was very bumpy, and John didn't think it was good for me to be bouncing around in my condition. It was almost Christmas and we were expecting our first baby the following April, and planning to marry soon after that, so it was exciting times for us.

I always looked forward to our trips down the country. We would stop off for breakfast, and have lunch on the way home. John had been a truck driver for years, so he knew all the good spots. I loved being high-up on the road. We'd listen to our music and sing along. We stopped just outside Waterford at a small little house that served food, the smell of bacon and cabbage greeting us as we walked in the door, the place full of truck drivers tucking into their dinners.

On the way home John was very quiet. I put it down to him being tired, but it wasn't like him at all. I was going to my mam's, so he dropped me at the top of the road and said he would give me a call in the morning. He kissed me on the cheek, and I hopped out. I stood and waved as he drove away.

The following day I didn't hear from him, but it wasn't that unusual as we didn't have mobile phones. I had a hospital appointment, so the day went quick enough, and I had an early night. I knew I would hear from John tomorrow.

I woke to hear my sister Una's voice downstairs. She worked nearby and often called over on her break for a chat. I threw on my dressing gown. Una was sitting at the table chatting to my mam. She worked with John's sister, whom she said wasn't in work. She was a great one for taking unofficial days off, and always came up with great excuses. I laughed and said, 'What excuse has she used this time?'

Una smiled. 'Ah, you're going to love this one: she said her brother is getting married!'

We all broke our hearts laughing. 'She really is scraping the barrel now.'

Later that evening the phone rang. Mam said, 'That's probably John.' I answered, thinking it was him, but instead I heard my friend's voice. We chatted for a few minutes.

'Are you OK?' she asked.

'I'm fine.'

'You haven't heard the news, then,' she said.

'What news?' I asked.

She paused. 'John got married today.'

If Only They Knew!
BY SINÉAD NÍ THRÉANLÁIMH

You're a great girl,' they say. Some girl at 73! 'Great' just makes me cringe! Guilt is supposed to be a female hormone. I could trump any level.

I didn't sign up for the position of carer but it was probably in the small print when I said 'for better or worse'. If I thought about it at all, I probably saw myself rising to the challenge with compassion – a far cry from someone who could be reported for 'elder abuse' on a bad day.

Parkinson's disease operates at only two speeds: slow and very slow. 'Frozen' is the word for the stage when the body goes into total lockdown. Of course, my better self is full of sympathy. But when there is a deadline involved, I just want to scream: 'For fuck's sake, will you just MOVE! One step! Anywhere!'

The tendon in my shoulder is torn from catching him as he falls. In a tone guaranteed to get his back up, I complain about his reluctance to use his rollator. As if I didn't know that madness is doing the same thing over and over and expecting a different result.

I was never the earthy type. Never one of those wonderful souls who cope with pee and poo as perfectly natural indicators of a healthy eliminatory system. Sadly, my approach to dealing with excrement is more akin to Michael O'Leary's attitude to his children: 'Children are like farts,' he said, 'you can barely tolerate your own.' I am full of sympathy and daily grateful that nobody is cleaning my bum. But I sure forget this when I swear at him for maximising the mess because he won't ask for help after an 'accident'.

Some irritants are so small. He refuses to drink the water with his medication. They don't work without water. I beg him to take just another two sips. Just like I did with the babies long ago: 'Have a spoon for Daddy, now one for Granny.' That's before I break into, 'For Chrissake, will you just open your mouth!'

There are bigger issues and guilt triggers. Like the times when I ignore approaches for what remains of the possibilities for sexual activity. I just can't seem to rise above the passion killers like nappies, pull-ups, wipes, nose drips and drools. Not to mention the guilt that accompanies packing up my clubs while the real golfer stays behind.

I get credit for making the nettle soup and growing vegetables. But I do this mostly for me – for respite. What he really needs is crosswords and supervised exercises. Just sitting with him at the television would do. Patiently answering repeated questions would do.

I want to wrap up by sanitising this unlovely picture. I want to talk about the love that still exists. But, just for today, I want to remove the rosy glasses and allow a glimpse at one dark page from my life.

She

BY KATE DURRANT

It's easy to pass 25 years.

It flies by in a blur of school and work and the mundane busyness that is the bread and butter of day to day life.

Of tiny teeth left under sleepy pillows, of parties and chickenpox, and children with bit parts as angels in Christmas concerts.

Of shepherd's pie every Tuesday, of homemade cards too precious to ever discard, and slammed doors and broken teenage hearts.

The good times resonate, the bad times less so, although undoubtedly they are the times that shape us more.

The first step, the first time a tiny hand clasps yours, the first time you hear that most beautiful of words: 'Mammy'.

All those firsts, all those little miracles, all those long days and short years, bring us all too soon to our goodbyes.

Those of us lucky enough to have kept our children, to still have them in our lives, to have with them the relationship we had always wished but at times never dared hope for, get the privilege to say goodbye as they shed us and grow their new skin.

The dramas of life, at the time so terrible, now become the anecdotes of Christmas Day lunches and wedding day speeches.

And it's true to say that the drama that temporarily divided us along the way is the same drama than binds us so tightly now.

So today I say farewell to her, my first-born, my best, and toughest, of teachers, as she moves away and properly loosens the ties that bind us.

She who must go and make her own firsts, her own wonderful mistakes and huge triumphs.

She who taught me that others' opinions and thoughts were theirs and theirs alone.

She with the big, beautiful heart, and the ability and will to change lives.

She who will always try to do the right thing when doing the wrong is easier.

She who passionately stands up for those who cannot stand up for themselves.

And as she moves away into a life that is only beginning to reveal itself, I hope that she learns to be as kind to herself as she is to others.

That she learns early, and often, that it's OK to say no, and remains true to what she really believes in but is open to the truths of others.

That she takes pleasure in the minutiae of life, for therein lies the really important stuff, and that she finds love and great friendships and gives them her all, as love never grows in a cold climate.

I hold back my tears and wave as she passes through the portal of passport control and I offer up a silent prayer that she will always remember that whatever and whoever comes to pass, the door to my heart and my home, to the heart of she who loved her first, is only ever the turn of a key away.

Brave

BY MEGHAN ELIZABETH

Lately I've been walking with a small version of myself. We walk side by side, mostly, except for when she bursts ahead with a skip and a twirl.

I worry that I bore her, but she never worries that she bores me. She has never been to Ireland except in library books, and she delights in it all, picking bunches of scraggy wildflowers that she tells me she plans to press in her diary.

'Did you come on a plane or a boat?' she asks.

'A plane. People don't really come on boats anymore,' I smile.

'I've been on a plane,' she says. She bites her lip in a happy memory. 'We went to Disney. I've been to Canada, too, you know.'

We stop at a gate and stare at a fluffy donkey who is snuffling around a dry, stony field. She holds out her wildflowers to the donkey, offering them as a snack.

'Does it count if you were a baby?' I ask wryly.

'Yes,' she reassures me confidently. She points up the road, her sparkly pink nail polish a beacon atop her dirty fingernails. 'Where does that go?' She trots towards a gap between two walls, a green boreen bordered with the brightest yellow gorse, the peachy smell dancing in the air; in the distance, there's blue haze of the sea.

She doesn't give me a chance to answer (which is good, because I don't know) and says, 'I'm such a good swimmer. Mommy says so and sometimes I win. I have so many ribbons.'

These are my favourite chats – the ones where we tell each other things about ourselves.

'Did you come here all alone?' she asks one day as we tiptoe into a grove of trees where a single wooden swing hangs from a branch.

She only comes up past my elbow and when I look down, I see the part in her blondie hair is turning pink in the sun, and I touch the top of my own warm head.

'Yeah,' I say. 'I came on the plane myself and lived in a little room all my own.'

She glances up at my face, blue eyes that seem bluer than my own. Blue like a polished stone in a museum or the sky an hour before a storm. 'That's so scary.'

'It was, a little,' I agree. 'But it doesn't scare me anymore.'

'You're brave,' she says casually. She digs the toe of a filthy white runner into the dirt. 'I couldn't ever do that. Not ever ever.'

'But you did,' I say.

Mothers Doing Time

BY JOSEPHINE HARHEN

Monday, my favourite day of the week. I look forward to it because for 15 minutes I get to see my lovely, funny, kind son by video link to the Midlands Prison. We haven't had a regular visit since the lockdown – only a six-minute call each day from a noisy landing where it's often hard to hear and there is no privacy.

So this time is precious. I tidy the kitchen in case he can see behind me. I shower, put on the make-up and straighten my hair, wear my nice top and get ready to be happy and lighthearted, because that helps him to not worry about me and home.

This week has been really hard. His friends in the area are out playing their music, hanging out, maybe having a few beers and a barbeque. Each time I see them it brings a pang of regret to my heart, regret for the life he is not living and won't be for another year. Of a life slipping by, day by day.

I feel in my bones the door of his cell banging shut at 7 p.m. He tells me he's OK, makes a joke of it, but hangs his towel over the window because he hates to see the brightness when he can't go out. When he calls at teatime, he always asks what we're having for dinner. I lie and tell him we are having food I know he doesn't like, just so he won't feel bad, when all he has are packets of noodles or crackers or whatever he has bought from the prison tuck shop. He fantasises about crispy bacon rashers on Brennans bread and ice-cold drinks from the fridge, roast-chicken dinners and ice cream. I fantasise about a life of freedom for him, and for myself.

But back to today. I followed the same routine, dressed and ready, knowing he keeps his best clothes for the visits and is waiting patiently. But today the link didn't work. I tried on my laptop, and then my phone, my panic rising as the time got closer and closer to 2:30. All I could see in my mind was his disappointed face as he sat in the room waiting and worrying when the link was empty, because he always worries about anything happening to me, about me getting sick. He keeps reminding me that I am 60, that I need to mind myself.

So, no video call, no need to dress up or put on lipstick today. He rang within half an hour just to see if everything was OK. Even though he joked and said, 'All's good, Mam, I'm grand,' and I replied in the same way, I sit here now in tears, heart full of pain. It's 3:58, and in two minutes his cell door will bang, and he will sit and eat whatever is on the prison menu today, and look at TV till 5:00 when the doors open again for an hour or two.

And I will stop crying and pretend none of this hurts, but like every mother, father, wife or girlfriend, I too am doing time.

Kangaroo Care

BY GAIL CASHIN

While I wait, I reach for another squirt of hand gel, just to be extra sure. I try to relax back into the recliner chair, lucky that it was available today. But I hang off the edge, nervously peering into the Perspex box that contains my whole world. I push up off my toes to get a better look. She looks so content; maybe I should tell the nurse we can wait till later. But she's already approaching, gloves donned. Her familiar soothing voice speaks directly to Rose: 'You're in for a treat, little bud! Mommy has saved her best songs for you today!' She flashes a glimpse at me, and I can tell she can sense the anxiety bubbling up in me. Why do I get so nervous before my favourite time of the day?

'You ready, Mommy?' she asks. I try to muster a smile, to stifle my nerves while keeping my gaze transfixed on the ventilator. She waits and gently nods in the direction of my chest. Quickly, I fix my top to ensure a smooth transition. I take a deep breath and tell her I'm ready.

Slowly and carefully she begins to detach the multitude of wires and cables. Rose lets us know her displeasure and squirms, her tiny limbs stretching to their full length. Even at this she's no bigger than my hand. The nurse flashes a glance back to double-check

I'm ready before the worst part: swiftly, she unplugs the Blue Tube.

This solitary tube that means so much; my baby's lifeline; her breath. Again, Rose displays her displeasure as she wriggles.

I sit back, every muscle in my body tense and rigid as I hold my top out and watch as my little baby is placed against my chest. The alarms pounding in my ears, letting all in the NICU know that no breath is detected. As quickly as she removed them, the wires and tube are reconnected. The wailing of the alarm is momentarily silenced. The figures on the monitor kick back in, both reassuring and perturbing in equal measures. 'Don't watch the monitor, watch the baby,' the nurse remarks as she adjusts the oxygen settings and repositions Rose.

'Hello, my gorgeous girl,' I whisper as I cup her entire body in just one hand. As much as I try to block it out, I can hear the knell of the alarm, informing the nurses that her oxygen saturation is at the boundary of its limits. The nurse is still only two feet away, busying herself fixing the bed sheets, but I know she's watching the numbers too.

'You are my Twinnie...' I begin to hum quietly as I try to slow my breathing and relax. Rose responds immediately, and I know not just from the silence of the knell, but by her body relaxing into mine, skin-to-skin, tucked under my top. All 800 grams of her. Everything else just fades away, it's just me and my little kangaroo.

Neiler

BY CHRISTINA MELIA

There weren't many fellas I fancied when I was 13 in my Northside suburb – most of them were snotty-nosed little feckers I knew from school or playing football on the GAA pitch opposite my house. I was too mature for all them, you see. Sure, wasn't I reading 'well above my level', according to Mrs Devine, my first-year English teacher? And not just books about boarding school by Enid Blyton – you know the ones that give you a very unrealistic idea of secondary school? I was bright, and sophisticated. I deserved a fella with class.

I'd given up all hope of meeting the boy of my dreams, and then I saw him. Neiler. Well, I didn't know his first name, but the family was called O'Neill – I'd managed to glean this information by looking through their letterbox one day and seeing an ESB bill on the floor. If they'd caught me, I was going to shake a Tró-caire box at them and tell them I was collecting for babies in Africa.

He wasn't like the other fellas around my way. He had style, Neiler. No tracksuit bottoms for him. He wore his hair in a way I'd only ever seen on TV – floppy fringe, but gelled at the back, like something out of Spandau Ballet. And the kind of shirts you had to buy in expensive shops, not a football jersey in sight. He was class.

And he made my heart beat faster. But how could I get him to notice me?

I decided to take the advice of *Jackie* magazine. For teenage girls, *Jackie* was the source of all things love-related, plus posters of George Michael. And all that for less than a pound! *Jackie* advised us to find out about the boys we were interested in: what music they were into; which football team; their pet hates and stuff; and use this knowledge as a foot in the door. 'Oh, you support QPR? Me too! What a coincidence!' Sounded logical enough to me, I thought. The only problem was that Neiler wasn't in my school and I didn't know his friends. I'd have to be sneaky, I thought.

So, I put my plan into action. I moved into the phone box opposite his house. He lived far enough away from my street that my ma would never find out about my stalking habits, but not so far that I couldn't get home in time for dinner. I was armed with snacks and a note-book to jot down interesting information about him. I was ready. I was organised. I was in love.

Day one, nothing. Day two, a glimpse of him in his dad's car. Day three, nothing. Day four, a girl arrived on his doorstep. Blonde and tall and beautiful. He opened the door – and they kiss. Afterwards, he looked over the road, straight at me. Maybe he had heard my heart break.

Two Things

BY EOIN PÓL Ó RÚIS

There were two things I had to say that weekend, to confess. No – to tell, not confess; after all, I'd left those days behind. It's tempting to say, 'that was a different me,' but I have always thought people dispense this phrase too readily, too easily. In my case, it wasn't a different me.

As I sat on the edge of the chair in my bedsit on North Circular Road, puffed with pride at how far I had come, I was still the same me. The same me that made a decision on a balmy summer's evening in Piazza della Repubblica, the sunset glittering through the frolicking fountain, piercing bubbles in glasses of prosecco on the tables underneath the stage whilst Rome's equivalent of Frank Sinatra crooned 'I Did It My Way'. It was precisely at that moment that I knew. After months of doubt verging on despair, I suddenly realised what I needed to do. That evening, I packed my bags and turned my back on the seminary, turned my back on five years of studying for the priesthood. A whole new life lay before me.

And here I was. I had found a job in Dublin and felt that I had begun to put down some semblance of roots. The Catholic Church didn't exactly cultivate the needs of the individual; you were part of a collective, a bigger picture, living a communal life. You can imagine then the joy and freedom for me having a place of my own. And, as I turned the key in the big red door and headed towards the city centre, I knew I had made the right decision. There were just these last things I wanted to – no – I *needed* to tell.

My mother was already there, standing outside Bewley's Oriental Café, keenly watching the world go by, cigarette in hand. Meeting up on a Saturday was a regular occurrence, as she would often spend the weekend at my brother's place in Drogheda and we would meet up in the Big Smoke for a latte and a squishy bun. I never led her to believe that today was any different but, as we hugged, I noticed an extra glint in her eye. It was almost as if she knew.

We went in and sank into a big red booth.

'I'm gay,' I announced before her coat was off.

'I know,' she said. 'You might as well tell me your hair's a different colour. It doesn't make a difference. I love you. I love you as you are, as God made you.'

My heart exploded in gratitude and tears slid down my face. She held my hand and listened and listened and listened . . .

Suddenly, she jumped up. 'Oh, my God, what time is it? We'll miss Mass!'

I couldn't bring myself to tell her my second secret, that I no longer went to church. Judging by her smile as we sat into the pews of St Teresa's, though, I guessed she already knew.

Ladies' Day

BY MARIE GILMORE

It was the last time I saw her. She had just given birth to a beautiful baby girl. And so had I. We were the proudest parents in the hospital. Two young, glowing new mums of two adorable baby girls. But that's where the similarities ended!

'It's a lady,' the gynaecologist beamed as he handed me my beautiful baby girl. It was Ladies' Day at the Laytown Races and I was fortunate to have my gynaecologist that day, as the world and its mother were at the races.

The happiness and unbridled joy were clear for all to see as my husband returned later, laden down with flowers, cards and pink balloons. I had never experienced such happiness. In those days, new mothers remained in the maternity hospital for three days. So in time, I became aware of another new mum in that four-bedded ward.

She had no flowers, no cards and no visitors. The little baby girl beside her slept soundly and contentedly. 'Congratulations!' I gushed as I looked admiringly at the sleeping infant. 'Our girls are the same age,' I whispered.

'Hi,' she said shyly. 'I'm Sarah and this is my baby, Amy.' Sarah told me that she had come from Tipperary.

Amy's birth was the result of a brief encounter the previous year. Her parents, filled with embarrassment and fury, had informed the wider family and friends that Sarah had gone to France to improve her French, while in fact they had sent her to a family in Laytown to await the birth.

I was so tormented and filled with sorrow on hearing Sarah's story. The following morning I was surprised to see that she had two visitors. The middle-aged couple spoke quietly.

'You will give her up for adoption,' the woman said. 'I have it all arranged. They will send someone from the agency later.' The woman's male companion never spoke, but gazed lovingly at the baby in the pink swaddling blanket. It's strange, the things that stay with you forever, as I will never forget the muffled sobbing of the new mum that night. How could her parents do this after seeing their first grandchild? That's when I thought of it. What if I brought Sarah and Amy home with me? I had plenty of room. My husband must have been shocked when I told him but never showed it. 'We can use the spare room, it will be grand,' he said.

The following day, a representative arrived from the Adoption Agency. Sarah refused to sign the papers, and firmly and politely asked them to leave.

I couldn't wait to share my plan with her. But alas, no. Though surprised and utterly grateful, she planned to go to England, where she had a friend who would help her. We hugged and shed tears and wished each other well. I never saw them again.

I wonder what became of Amy. My little girl is now a mum herself. I think of them often. I hope Amy has her mum's remarkable spirit and courage.

The Day Before U2 Day

BY LYNDA CLIFFORD

7 August 1987

'Mam, is Net home?' I shout as I head downstairs and listen at Annette's door for any sign of movement. 'No, she's not back yet, why?'

'Just wondering.'

As quietly as I can, I open Annette's door and slip inside delighted to have a few minutes to nose around. Annette's room is in the new part of the house, the extension. The extension that has etched Dad's face with worry lines and led to whispered tight-lipped conversations between him and Mam. Still oblivious of what is to come, I love it. I like to check out the front bedroom upstairs to see what treats Mam has hidden away. If I'm not there, you might find me in Rich's room in the back to see what's going on in the Dalys'.

The Holy Grail of snooping for me though is downstairs in Annette's room. Annette is my big sis, and her room holds a haven of stuff for me to inspect. Today I know exactly what I'm looking for. I heard her mention to Mam that she got new jeans and my mission is to try them on. While the coast is clear, I head straight to the wardrobe. There they are, neatly folded on top of her jeans bundle. I take them out, quickly slip off my tracksuit bottoms and pull them up. Success. They're flipping gorgeous, sleek navy denim and skin tight – perfect!

'What the hell are you doing? Mam, Lynda's in my room again! GET THEM OFF AND GET OUT OF MY ROOM.' I'm trying to get the skin-tight jeans off me quickly while being pushed out the door. 'Mam, I need a key to my door. I'm sick of her!'

I eventually get the jeans off and run quickly up the stairs to my room. I grab some old jeans from my small, antique-looking wardrobe, which used to be Nana's. I treasure the sense of her I get every time I open the mirrored door. While I'm putting my jeans on, my eyes rest on the U2 ticket stuck to my mirror. What am I going to wear now?

I head over to Fiona's to see what she's bringing with her, and to get out of here while Annette cools down. Fiona runs through what she's planning to bring for the weekend. To be honest, the two of us are shocked we're allowed to go. An hour or so later I head home to face the music. I creep in quietly and, hearing murmuring in the sitting room, head upstairs to my room. When I open the door my heart lifts – Net's new jeans are on my bed. On top is a neatly folded note, and as I open it a tenner falls onto my bed. The note reads:

Lyn, you can have these for the weekend, here's some money as well. Happy U2 day!! Annette xxx

Páirc Uí Chaoimh here we come – this weekend's going to be massive!

One-quarter full

BY JEAN HARRISON

God bless the man – or woman! – who invented prosecco. I'd marry ye, if ye'd have me. I can be bi-, I'm sure... Let's see what's left... three-quarters empty. No, no, let's be positive here: one-quarter full. We're not allowed be negative anymore are we? Not to worry, there's at least two more bottles where that came from. No, can't afford to drink that much, no one here to pick me up if I fall...

Ah, that sun's lovely, the birds singing, my book, prosecco... what more could a body want?

'Hello?'

'Hello, Anna.'

'Danny? Danny? Is that you? Why are you here? How could you...? God help me, I am drinking too much...'

'Your dreams. You keep dreaming about me. I'm sorry – I've frightened you...'

'I'm having horrible dreams since this started, and all about you... still... I'm opening another bottle. I'm not doing this. You're dead, gone – long ago.'

'I just came to say – ah, the garden's lovely, you've worked very hard as always – I came to say, as you're on your own, happy birthday and happy anniversary, Anna.'

'Anniversary? No one mentions that anymore,

Danny. It's a sore reminder for people. We'd have been...
34... 35... ? Instead, what did we have? Twenty-five?
And not all good, Danny, but I worshipped the very
bones of you.'

'Did you? I didn't know that!'

'No, you were too drunk, too depressed and too out
of it... those bloody drugs. One of the things I loved
most about you when we met was that you– you didn't
drink.'

'That was because of your father.'

'Yes, I know. You were never violent, though. I think
I was supposed to be grateful for that. The worst beating I ever got was from my mother – the buckled strap.
I wrote a poem about that a few years ago, for a competition, did you know that?'

'No! But you did tell me about the beating.'

'I won 50 euro. I thought it might drive away the
demons a little, writing it down, like. It didn't. But you
were the one who hurt me most, and you broke the kids'
hearts. I can't forgive you for that... maybe that's why...'

'I thought you'd have remarried by now.'

'Once bitten, twice destroyed! Did you see the men
I went out with? All of them still obsessed with their
exes. One of them told me he still went on holidays with
his – and her mother! Not sure why he wanted another
woman in his life...'

'Were you? Are you? Still obsessed with me?'

And we talked about some old times
And we drank ourselves some beers
Still crazy after all these years
Oh, still crazy after all these years...

'You still sing... and always beautifully. That's good.
I miss that. I'm sorry, Anna. If I could...'

'But you can't. We can't.'
'I know. I'm sorry. So sorry… Bye, Anna.'
'Bye, Danny… Be here… Be there for me, please…'

Unconditional Love

BY GRACE FITZGERALD

From the very minute you came into my life, I knew our journey together was going to be precious. One look at those hazel-brown eyes of yours was enough to let me know that I was going to be hooked on your love until the end of time. Although I did think that we would share many exhilarating, joyful memories together, I never anticipated how much pain would be attached to those moments after they had left. I would trade anything right now to go back and hug you just one more time. Your hugs were the greatest pick-me-up I have ever encountered. Nothing could beat the wholeness of your love, the sensation of your soft, golden-brown coat against my bare skin was so tender, so pure, that nothing could ever again compare to it. From the very beginning, you were keen on teaching my nine-year-old self how to love and love freely. Undeniably hesitant at first, throughout the courses of our ten unforgettable years together I will admit that you succeeded in doing so. Without you, Iz, I don't think I ever would have been capable of imagining the sensational life that you gave me. For this, I will be forever grateful.

I loved you so much that oftentimes I was slow to show and tell you. You were there every morning when I woke up, each evening when I came home from school and in the night-time before I went to bed. I got used to your constant company. My naivety led me to believe that you would always be there, which you were... until you weren't. I took your solidarity and companionship for granted. It pains me to admit that I did not remind you daily of how much you meant, and still do mean, to me. Oh, Iz, I never imagined the day when our only form of communication would be virtual. It's true what they say, life really is too short, but I cannot help overthinking about all the time I wasted on my phone, rather than playing or being with you. It is all that I have been thinking about since you left. You have sent my thoughts into a frenzy filled with regret, frustration and, ultimately, sadness. I keep forcing myself to look on the bright side and be thankful for all of the contented moments we spent together. My usual optimism has been tainted since you left. Instead, it has been tinged with the hurt of heartache. However, I know for your sake that I must look at the glass as being half full. While I lament the many adventures we had planned, but never had, I now know that you gave me the best present I may have ever received: a best friend.

A Man of the World

BY ANYTA FREEMAN

I dressed with care – not for college, but in anticipation of meeting Julian again. My shoulder-length hair was shiny and lustrous as I examined myself in the mirror. Satisfied that I looked my very best, I headed off to take the Metro.

The course was extremely interesting, and my fears of not being up to it disappeared the more I participated. Before long it was noon, and college was over. I was not homeward bound like the other students, heading instead to the little café on the corner. I had butterflies in my stomach – will he or won't he be there? I went in; no sign of Julian. Stupid of me to think he wanted to see me again. I sat at a table beside the window. I felt conspicuous. Were the other customers looking at me, knowing I was being stood up? I'll have a coffee and wait ten minutes, no longer.

Half an hour later I saw him rushing down the street towards the café. My stomach churned. This beautiful man was coming to meet me! I tried to remain calm as he rushed over. He kissed me on both cheeks in greeting.

'I was afraid you wouldn't be here! I ran all the way. So sorry for being late – work, you know.'

'You're here now, that's all that matters.' I had never spoken to a man like this. Instinctively I knew there was no time to waste. No playing the game, no feigning non-chalance. I knew what I wanted from him and hoped he felt the same.

Two coffees later, we were still chatting. He was working for an international newspaper, and had many anecdotes and stories to tell. He enthralled me. A man of the world, sophisticated compared with any of the boys I had known in Dublin. His dark brown eyes searching, looking deep into my soul. I was taking everything about him in.

Time had flown and it was time to head home.

'I'll walk you to the station. It's a good distance away,' he said, carelessly flinging his scarf around his neck. Comfortable in his skin, knowing he looked good no matter how he was thrown together. I loved that about him. Maybe I was feeling love for the first time? I felt a difference between us now. In that short space of time an understanding had been reached. This was going to happen and I was open to it.

As we walked he placed his arm gently around my shoulders. I shivered at his touch. 'Are you cold, little one?' he whispered. Stopping in my tracks, I turned to face him. 'No, Julian, I'm not.' He looked into my eyes and slowly bent to kiss me. I wanted to pull him closer, not let him go.

The T-shirt with the Good Neckline

BY VIVIENNE MULREADY

It was just a soft white cotton T-shirt, brand new, but cheap as chips. A souvenir of a holiday with the resort name on the front, its only saving graces being that it was snow white and actually had a really good neckline. It was worn for such a short time that the scent transfer barely lingered, but it didn't stop me from burying my face in it and sniffing so deeply as to almost inhale the T-shirt. There it was. Almost imperceptible but, oh, so precious. My eyes screwed up in concentration as I held that barely discernible smell in my nostrils, savouring it, with my brain frantically trying to replicate it before it disappeared. Sealing it in a Ziploc bag was all I could think of in that moment to try to preserve its sacred integrity, sneaking it open for an occasional whiff. I knew this served only to risk losing the last odorous molecules, leaving behind nothing but soft white cotton, an irrelevant resort name and the good neckline.

Sadly, that day did come when the contents of the bag only served to mock and jeer at me with their pristine, odourless fibres. I wanted to keep it forever, regardless, but knew that was bordering on the obsessive and felt it wasn't a good place to go. I wondered what I should do with it. It clearly could not live under my pillow forever. I felt that maybe, if I waited a while, an opportunity for its best use would present itself to me.

Soon, he was homeless again and had fallen off the wagon for the umpteenth time, but the latest twist was that all his possessions had been stolen from his room in the hostel when he went out to score. Just an extra little something for his burden, another excuse to feel sorry for himself and add to his victim status. It didn't alter the fact that my child now owned a sum total of nothing. Strangely, when I heard the news, despite my annoyance and frustration and my heartache, the first thing I thought of was that soft white cotton T-shirt with the good neckline. Perhaps it was time it left the Ziploc bag, re-entered the world and earned itself a new scent. Despite this logic, the thoughts of parting with it caused my stomach to churn and my heart to race, but it was still the first item I packed into his survival kit. This was how it should be. This is what his dad would have wanted. This T-shirt was going to live a new life. A life that guaranteed putting paid to it remaining snow white or retaining its good neckline, but, unlike his dad, it would live.

Departure

BY AMANDA NOLAN

The backpack lay on my bed, large and bold. The blue and black pockets and straps suggested travel, adventure, independence and self-discovery. All around in piles and bundles lay clothes, shoes, books, tapes, the collection of my most treasured possessions. The disarray was in stark contrast to the orderly bedroom I shared with my younger sister. The neatly made twin beds, the pale yellow curtains that did nothing to keep out the early morning light, simple furniture containing the shared clutter of our worldly goods.

The clock radio emitted Rick Astley's 'Never Gonna Give You Up' while I packed and repacked that backpack, most likely breaking all the rules of backpacking etiquette and weight distribution. My thoughts roamed between terror and excitement as I contemplated the trip I was about to undertake. Abroad for the first time, flying for the first time, and going it alone for the first time. My crisp new passport and plane tickets were already tucked safely into my money belt, along with my USIT card and Swiss currency.

As I worked my way through the pile of debris on my bed there was a gentle knock on the bedroom door. It was tentatively pushed in, and my father stood there. The August heat had him with his shirt sleeves rolled up and his greying black hair hanging loosely on his fore-head. He was rocking slightly on the balls of his feet, hands in his pockets, jingling coins, or keys, I wasn't sure which. He nodded towards the backpack and jumble of possessions scattered around it, and asked the obvious question: 'Packing?' I looked at him then, and perhaps all my fears, worries and hopes played across my face as we looked at each other across the expanse of those two single beds. I nodded. He moved then, coming towards me, rounding the foot of my sister's bed. He reached out and pulled me into his arms. 'I love you,' he said, and then letting me go, he turned and left the room as quickly and quietly as he had entered it. He may have said more, he probably did, I imagine things like, 'Have you got everything you need?' 'If it doesn't work out you can come home,' and 'Keep in touch.' I can only recall those three little words.

I stood where I was, paused, in the blanket of those words. As my backpack swelled with my things, my heart did too, and I realised that this story of my leaving was also his story of being left. I have no memory of finishing the packing or of what went in the backpack in the end, or of the moment I left the house. I did leave, and though I never returned for more than short visits, I revisited that moment many times. There, in that memory, I found the comfort and reassurance I needed to navigate the many and at times difficult journeys of my life.

2-in-1

BY SAMANTHA LONG

I couldn't stop looking at him. Couldn't believe I was a mother, and after all the guessing, wishing and waiting he was really here. I had wished for a boy for a very simple and practical reason: as a tomboy, hairstyling is not my first calling. The pressure to create elaborate little girls' hairstyles used to pop into my mind during my pregnancy and I worried, knowing I could never come up to the mark.

Months later I knew instinctively that a boy was on the way. No scan was required – I could smell his pheromones through my own skin; that faint, clean, male smell like the one in boys' classrooms or barber shops.

Sitting on the edge of the hospital bed I was desperate to wash my hair at the sink in the ward's sparse bathroom. A shower was impossible with surgical stitches in place, but my sweaty hair was annoying me. It's so warm in hospital – dry, centrally heated air that smells of hot radiator paint.

The baby was born at 3:27 p.m., and by 8 o'clock that night it was time for his new dad to go home and take care of our dogs, who must have been wondering where we had been all day. The nurses said that I really should rest at last; my baby was fast asleep, and fine. I told them that I needed to wash my hair first.

I wheeled his little Perspex cot into the bath-room with me. Two of the other mothers in the four-bedded ward offered to keep an eye on him, but I couldn't allow it, not even for five minutes. He stayed asleep while I washed my hair. I had brought that 2-in-1 shampoo and conditioner that hairdressers warn you off, but I didn't care. The online mum-to-be articles told me how and what to pack for hospital, and I complied. Mam had died suddenly five years previously, so I depended on Mother Internet for advice, and she had been good to me. My birth mother, too, had died during this first pregnancy, and that had been public and very hard.

Back in bed on the ward, combing my clean, wet hair and looking at my sleeping newborn was one of the most serene and beautiful moments of my life. I was deeply happy in a way that I could never fully have anticipated.

At half ten the nurses came back to see how we both were. They gently but firmly suggested that they would bring baby up to the nurses' station so that I could finally rest. I felt a surge of lioness-like protectiveness and cried quietly, explaining that that no one was ever going to take my baby away from me. Thirty-one years after my birth mother had been forced to give me away, my infant past had finally caught up with me. The nurse embraced me tightly as I wept in a 2-in-1 mixture of my mother's loss and my new joy.

Little Ones

The Find

BY PEARL SHELLY

Every Thursday you'd hear the seagulls screeching, soaring frantically, flapping around for the scrounge of latest deposits. The smell was horrifically high – cheesy, dead, rotten – I still gag at the putrid stench.

Lord knows what was dumped there. Often we would imagine we were detectives, discovering bodies, a popular make-believe game. Finding a dead dog in a sack saddened us; we might even perform a blessed ceremony.

Looking for treasure when the new dump trucks arrived was like a lottery. Airlines were fantastic; they dumped great stuff: plastic knives and forks and spoons along with napkins still in plastic wrappers, lemon-fresh wipes, all great for our picnics at Dollymount.

Dirty-faced one-eyed dolls, no longer loved, with matted hair, or bald. One-wheeled bicycles, scooters, rusty prams – lick of paint made them all new.

The odd time you would find real treasure, but you had to dig deep. Like an overflowing chest of drawers, if you knew how and where the early-bird makes its finds.

On one particular day after a dump truck's fresh delivery, I was on a lonesome scrummage. No one had picked at these bags yet, and sieving carefully like a professional, I began my quest. At almost seven, I was becoming as good as the others by now. A pile of crisp, white envelopes jam-packed inside hessian sacks, unopened. I tore through them. Each envelope had grown-ups' handwriting, posh envelopes, and stamps, unmarked.

Sifting through those letters, I was hoping none of the others would come. Suddenly, notes came fluttering to the ground: a pound, a fiver, another few pound, a tenner. I could smell the reward. No loose change in these lucky bags! Quickly beginning to stash the cash down my knickers and into my socks, I gave thanks to the sky.

I knew Mum would go ballistic: my mucky shoes still not fully paid for, on tick from Farley's Shoe Shop, which I had carelessly stepped out of and left at the front door.

'Were you playing in that dump, ye dirt bird?'

'Yes, Mummy, but look what I found,' my full-freckled face beaming as I proudly pulled a wad of cash from my knickers and socks.

Soon after, we were skipping all the way to Thrifty's local supermarket for fresh bread and butter and more than the bare essentials to make a picnic for Dollymount Strand the next day. There were corned beef sandwiches, ginger nut biscuits and salty Tayto crisps, Club orange and enormous discs of choccie biscuits that melted in the gold wrapping – but licking the wrapper was the best bit. Loo rolls – maybe the electricity will be turned back on! – and shillings for the gas meter with the change.

Candles put away, back in the drawer for the next rainy day.

Granny Garvey might come now – there'd be stories, and soda bread toasted on the fire along with steamy baked potatoes baked in the hearth that melted into a fluffy mess, all smothered with golden melted buttery bliss.

Alice in Wonderland Syndrome

BY ELEANOR HOOKER

There's always an easier path, but we didn't mind about easier paths that summer afternoon as Dad and I climbed to the top of the Cup and Saucer.

Aged eight, it felt like Everest to me. At the summit we sat on the grass and looked out over our town.

The steeples of the two churches pierced the sky, and beyond, Galtee Mór mountain was a sleeping beast, stout enough to carry the world on its back.

'We need to talk about your tall tales, Nell,' Dad said.

I knew well 'tall tales' meant lies. Dad would've said 'spinning yarns' if he meant the stories I told to the family after dinner.

'I haven't told a single lie, Dad,' I said.

'None?' Dad asked.

'Well, I did say three lies once,' I said. 'Will I tell you why?'

'Do,' Dad said.

'At my First Confession, I hadn't any sins to tell, so I made up two. I said I called my brother a feckin' pig, and that I'd finished my homework... when I hadn't.'

'That's two,' Dad said. 'What's the third?'

'I only learned the first two lines of the Act of

226

Contrition, so I said them out loud and pretended to mumble the rest while I waited for my penance.'

Dad shook his head, bewildered.

'Have you ever told a lie?' I asked.

'I have,' he said. 'When I was a boy, Mam and Dad went out, leaving me in charge. I came up here to play hurling with my friends instead. Caught the sliotar badly on this finger.'

Dad held up his left hand. His forefinger was short and stubby.

'Did the sliotar knock the end clear away?' I asked.

'No,' Dad said. 'A few days later, something was sticking out of the cut. I bit it away.'

'What was it?' I asked.

'It was a little bone,' Dad said. 'The little bone from the top of my finger. When Mam noticed, I lied it happened at school.'

'Janey,' I said, awed by his finger, not the lie.

'Nell?'

'Yes, Dad?'

'Why do you say those things about the world getting bigger and smaller and moving far away and getting closer?'

'Because it does,' I said. 'I wondered why myself, so I asked everyone. And everyone said, "Ara g'wan, ya eejit ya."'

'Why would you tell tall tales and have us worry?' Dad asked.

'Don't you believe me?' I asked.

'I believe you believe it's happening,' Dad said. 'Which doesn't mean it's really happening.'

I didn't like this answer one bit. It meant Dad thought I believed in a lie I was telling myself to make mischief.

'If I say it's not true, Dad, that's a lie,' I said. 'What should I do?'

'It'll go away, Nell. I promise,' Dad said. 'You can talk to me anytime. Okay?'

'Okay so,' I said, learning, not for the first time, that some lies were needed if I were to fit in a world that hadn't much room for articles like me.

Admiration

BY ELAINE WILBUR

We climbed to the top of the high wall around Kelly's field. 'Come on,' she says. 'Just stand up. It'll be faster.'

Kelly's field has the biggest hay jump. We heard that you could jump from the railway bridge. She wants to go, and I want to be her. I watch her nutty legs stretch in front of each other, her socks inside her corked German sandals. That smile she flicks backwards is warm and taunting, the same smile she has when she loans me another ten pence for Chickatees or Rubble Bubble. I want to get up out of my nine years of milky ordinariness. To shrug off early bedtimes and my Enid Blyton collection. To be white sliced pan for a day; normal for everyone else except me. Be brave, I say to myself, but my body refuses. My raspberry-ripple knees grip both sides of the concrete blocks so tightly I feel printed with gravelly ridges. Those indents are the branding of my weakness. I knew I would never stand next to her or walk along this imagined tightrope. I knew it in the same way I knew I hated the wet potatoes in my mother's stew. 'I probably have to go back for dinner,' I say, and drop my leg down into my shame, searching for solid ground. I see her knowing smirk as she skims away from me. Her

229

form briefly covers the sun, and I lower myself into her shadow before coming back to earth.

I wipe the ingrained grit from my knees and make my way home. I hear the faraway screams of the hay jump threaded through the cuckoo's call. The tarmac folds under my footsteps and I look back at my temporary mark. As I round the corner I see my brothers playing kerb-to-kerb. I hear the plastic spoke beads of someone's bike rattling closer; someone who gets Kellogg's Frosties more than once a year and doesn't have to fight for the plastic treasure inside. My fingers thrum along the different wrought iron gates I pass; each gap in a wall brings me closer to our opening.

I have the scooped-out feeling that something is missing. I look behind me, wondering if I was worth following for once, but I know that her reach is always further than mine. I will always drop with the anchor while she soars with the sail. She is Mary and I am Laura, the Elisabeth to her Jessica. She is racerback tan lines and I am sunburned freckles. She is Quinnsworth, I am Dunnes. She zooms along with her inline skates while I paint a P on my wooden tennis racket with black shoe polish.

It's Wednesday, so that means steaklets and chips. I can smell it coming through the open front door as I round the pillars. I like Wednesdays. I still do.

Toronto to Belfast, 1981

BY CIARA COLHOUN

Zooming over the Atlantic is better than birthday cards weighted with coins. It's the 10th of August 1981. I'm seven years old. The air stewardess brings me to see the captain. He gives me a cookie with a jam heart in the middle. In four hours we'll be in Belfast, where Mummy and Daddy grew up.

I wonder if my goldfish has made it to the sea below. Daddy took me to free him in Toronto's Humber River the day before. He said he would swim away and be reunited with his family, just like us.

At our farewell party the women were swapping recipes. Granny's stew was written out on light blue paper, wet with tears. Mummy pulled me on her knee and whispered to avoid the curry before the plane.

There was hugging and crying before Daddy sneaked the five of us off to McDonald's – the closest thing to meat and spuds we could get at that hour. He'd follow us to Ireland when our house was sold.

They're smiling and sunburnt, the family at the airport. My aunt has stayed home to get the tea ready. 'Her cushions will be patted into oblivion,' my uncle says. We sweep along narrow roads, pass the green fields of Daddy's songs. We screech around a bend, stopping a whisper away from a white van. I hold my breath as my uncle and the other driver roll down their windows.

'Ha, ha, that was close. You're well packed in there. Lovely day.' And we're off again.

My aunt's hair is as white as our Canadian winters. There are jam tarts and soda bread toasted on one side under the gas. Children drink tea. Family rules are waived for a walk to the sweet shop. My cousin teaches me the difference between Tutti Fruttis and Rainbow Drops. I share a bed with my sisters, but the curtains let the light in so we can't sleep easily. We eventually drift off to the shushes and muffled laughter of people calling – our new lullaby.

When I look out the window in the morning I see the H-shaped statue being built on the hill.

Our housing estate was built in the countryside for families escaping Belfast and its bombs. Bobby Sands' face looks down from the lampposts. I have hot melted stuff cut from my hair, hurled for saying 'popsicles' and 'candy'. Nuns and metre-stick punishments shock at school. I become afraid of being the last one in our house to fall asleep.

The following spring we run up the garden of our new house on the other side of town. It's dusk and I hear possibilities in the sound of children playing nearby. Daddy hugs Mummy in the shadow of the fir trees.

'Did we do the right thing?' he asks.

Biro Tattoo

BY MICHAEL G. SNEE

I studied the biro tattoo on the back of my hand, a large heart with the words 'Mick loves Miriam says Noel'. My boys' Timex watch, a present from my parents for my 11th birthday the previous week, read 3:30.

'Any sign yet?' I shouted to Noel.

'No, nothing,' he replied.

I had looked forward to this moment so much since meeting Miriam down by the river the previous afternoon. I had gotten into trouble that day in school for looking out the window and daydreaming, as the teacher called it. I couldn't see anything out of the window except Miriam and the way she flicked back her long black hair and her eyes crinkling up as she smiled.

Noel had spotted them first as they walked along the top of the hill. He called them down, and after a moment's hesitation they came down to the opposite bank. Noel was good at that sort of thing, I was the shy one. We acted all macho, wrestling each other to the ground and trying to make the girls laugh. They dared us to walk under the bridge to the far side of the main road. I took off my American-style basketball sneakers and stuffed my socks into them. I held them in my hand as we slipped on the slime-covered stones on the river bed. I stumbled and dropped one of my sneakers, and watched as it floated for a couple of seconds before sinking in the mud-clouded water. The girls shrieked with laughter. I looked at Miriam and laughed too.

She had smiled at me when I asked Noel to cross the river and find out her name and ask her to go with me. He shouted back, 'Her name's Miriam, and she said yes.' My heart started racing and I got a funny feeling in my stomach. Miriam. It was a nice name. Mick and Miriam. Miriam and Mick. Michael and Miriam, I'm sure my mother would prefer. Her friend agreed to go with Noel, so the pairings were set. They said they had to go home, so before heading off we'd arranged to meet at 3 o'clock the following day at the park entrance.

So here we were, waiting. 'I think it's time to head off,' Noel said.

I sighed deeply. 'OK.'

As we walked home, I spat on the back of my hand and used the end of my T-shirt to remove my biro tattoo. I didn't want my mother to see it and start asking awkward questions, the answers to which I wouldn't know. Where did she live? What school did she go to? Do you not think you're a bit young for a girlfriend? I really wanted to get that feeling in my stomach again, but I couldn't explain that to my mother. I wanted this day to be over. As I turned the key in the door, I looked at the faded outline of my tattoo. I shouted to Noel, 'I'll call for you after school tomorrow. We'll hang around down by the river.'

The Little Blue Bicycle

BY ANYTA FREEMAN

I grew up in an old house, and apart from being cold and draughty, it had a particular smell. A mixture of must, mothballs and tobacco. Not a particularly nice scent, and it seemed to permeate everything, even my clothes. I was particularly aware of this as a child, and I carried my home with me wherever I went. It was like a protective blanket smothering me. A constant reminder of where I came from, somewhere I try to forget. To this day, if I smell mothballs I'm immediately transported back to that house. We came here when I was five years old. My parents were loving and kind and did their best for us, but we were outsiders and always would be.

The little blue bicycle leant against our garden seat, proudly displaying its new paint job. A shiny bell had been attached to the handlebars. My parents led me, eyes closed, to the garden, excited to show me my birthday present. I was seven years of age. I had wanted a bike, but not this one. I wanted a shiny new red one like the one Pauline down the road had. I wanted to ride up and down the avenue showing it off. I couldn't hide my disappointment. I wasn't happy; I was ashamed. Everyone would know it wasn't new. They would still think we were poor. I just stood looking at it. I didn't thank them, just said I didn't want it. I remember the look of pain on my father's face. It didn't matter that I was loved and cherished by my parents. It didn't matter at all. All that mattered was I didn't get a new bike. I suppose I could've had a tantrum then, making them feel even worse. But I didn't care how much I hurt them.

There's a lot I don't remember from my childhood, a lot I choose to forget, but that day stands out clearly. It still haunts me that I could have been so cruel. Seeing my father's disappointment, letting him believe he had let me down. I wanted to punish him, and I succeeded. I never ran to meet him coming home from work after that day. I no longer sat on his lap when he would teach me to spell words I had never heard of from the newspaper. His whole demeanour changed. He seemed to shrink, no longer the upright proud man returning home from a hard day's work. I had been his precious little girl, the light of his life. I had done this to him and at age seven, and I knew what I was doing. I felt powerful, convinced that if I kept this up, I'd get the new bicycle.

Me and the Exotic Irishman

BY TINA MCCORMACK

'This is so STUUPID!' He flung the full force of his fury at me across the kitchen table. Stress levels at boiling point. 'Nan! YOU DON'T UNDERSTAND!'

[To myself] 'I do, son.'

'What good is algebra or some crusty hundred-year-old poem gonna to do me?'

[Silently] 'I know, son.'

His pen slammed the table, his chair jarred backwards – along with my teeth – and the door ricocheted off its hinges as he stormed from the room, leaving behind a molten cloud of exam frustration. I sighed, and memories of my 16-year-old self, clear as cut glass, danced before me. 'It was at your age precisely that I upset the proverbial apple cart, and all because "The Exotic Irishman" came to stay next door!' I thought.

There was something different about him. He was in a band, I was told, and I used to peek through our letterbox at him as he strolled nonchalantly down his sister's driveway with his jacket flung over his shoulder, hanging by one finger. Eventually, we got talking across the garden wall, the same wall that had served as a horse, a circus tightrope or a shop counter as me and my sister grew up.

Conversations grew longer and deeper, and as cups of tea were passed over that wall our fingers sometimes brushed against each other, and the seeds of love were sown.

The day came when he told me that a new job awaited him in Ireland, and the decision was made that we'd leave together. Me, who'd never even been to London, 20 miles up the road! Me, who would have described myself as the colour grey, barely visible, whilst my friends were much more colourful, prettier, cleverer and braver than me – or so I thought! I couldn't wait to shake off the chains of school. I very cheekily penned a letter to my headmistress, informing her that I would be leaving school half way through my A-levels, ruining, as she later said, my potential!

I was leaving my idyllic childhood, spent hurtling through the Kent countryside in our tiny sidecar, bulging at the seams with its load of me, Mam, my sister, food, blankets for the beach, boxes of lugworm for the fish, and Dad carrying the rods on the motorbike; leaving the same soft-spoken dad who'd arrive home at 5 o'clock each day wearing head-to-toe black grease after spending hours in the belly of a sick ship convalescing on the river Thames; leaving my beautiful mam, who'd apply her bright-red lipstick with precision at five minutes to 5 ready to greet him; and of course, leaving my impish right-arm: my sister.

We left safe shores for bombings and bloodshed, but were armed with the selfishness of youth, and our love!

The backdoor creaks, banishing my thoughts and the familiar face peeks in. 'Sorry, Nan.'

'That's OK, son. Talking about education, come here and I'll tell you about the fun I had as a mature student in nursing college.'

1965

BY ROSEMARIE CAMPBELL

Looking over my shoulder, I could see my brother starting to lag. His horse, Molly Brown, wasn't as fast as Charlie, my loyal steed. 'Come on, give her the whip! They're gaining on us!' We jumped the windrows, feet slipping in plastic shoes.

There was a loud bang from the other side of the field. Suddenly everything went silent. The tractor and baler had come to an abrupt halt. The girls' singing and laughing stopped. I think the birds even ceased chirping. Myself and my brother dismounted, laying low, out of view. I hoped the horses wouldn't give us away.

Breakdowns in the hayfield could lead to anything, always starting with the cry, 'Goddammit, what have you done?' Luckily on this occasion it was the hydraulic that had come loose, easily fixed. If not, anyone could be held responsible for a breakdown, even the children, who had their own problems trying to outride the Apache. Who had retreated by now? Incidentally, they were no match for the Sioux, who nearly had us yesterday!

I spotted Mum making her way down the field with our lunch. She would have to cross the narrow plank that bridged the two fields, a deep canyon underneath. I worried she wouldn't make it over. Worries unfounded,

Mum and the lunch bags had landed safely. We gathered round her as she handed out freshly made ham sandwiches, tea from a Thermos jug. Milk and sugar in jam jars were passed around, the sugar getting wetter with each spoon dipped. Then thick, buttered slices of Aunty Stella's seed cake always sent down for haymaking week.

My sisters arguing over who was the best-looking Beatle, each hoping their older brother would side with them. He laughed and teased them. Dad was wearing his usual white shirt – unusually, without a tie – sleeves rolled up above the elbows, his serious, handsome face tanned from a week of haymaking. We knew lunch was over when Dad would stand and announce, 'God bless the haymakers,' Mum making her way back to the house with her now-empty bags, safely negotiating the canyon.

Myself and my sidekick would go in search of baby hares orphaned by the cruel steel teeth of the baler. Survivors never lasted long; they always received a nice burial using bird feathers as headstones. The pinnacle of the year's haymaking was the ride back to the farmyard on top of the haystack. Our brother would lift us high above his head. I can still smell his Old Spice mixed with a hard day's work, the girls pulling us the rest of the way, our legs scratching along the bales – we didn't care. We all sang 'California Girls', swaying with the movement of the load, our brother joining in from the tractor's driver's seat, Dad walking behind, his arms clasped behind his back. I think he may have even smiled. Summer 1965. Nothing could have prepared us for autumn and the sorrow it would bring.

A Letter to My Parents

BY BREDA DALY

E very age has its own questions, own answers, desires
and demands. I was ten; I wanted to get a pet.

I was not very affectionate, and I didn't smile
much. I had a dark, brooding cloud over me, which was
a constant. I was a very sickly child and had to wear
garments that none of my peers wore, like a bodice to
keep me warm. I was always outside of the norm, and,
because I was afraid of my shadow, I had to try extra
hard to be liked.

You granted me my first pet, after much pleading,
begging and bargaining. I did this for most things,
including the pull of a Sweet Afton cigarette, granted
only on the condition that I would smoke it in the small
toilet, windows closed and door locked, not to come
out until it was completely burned out. This didn't
happen overnight. I had my teeth worn for this opportunity. Smoking in the '70s was cool. I loved the idea,
the smell, and the crack of the match and the smell of
the sulphur. If I had any cop on, 'I could have pulled
a cigarette from your pack,' Dad. But no. You see. That
would break the commandment 'Thou shalt not steal'
– a sin! The alternative was the honest route. Dearest
Mother, you hoped that the 'flow gently, sweet Afton'
would make me as sick as a dog, in the stuffy little

room. No such luck. I loved it and cleared the table in record time, as promised.

To my surprise, a pup arrived. Dad, you brought him, from the country. I was overjoyed. He was gorgeous, a small, little terrier, black and brown and full of life. I loved him the minute we met. I was so happy. He got a special bed in the kitchen. You even called in the vet to check him out. I was in heaven. He had no name on arrival, no Spot or Pup was good enough for this bundle of joy. Dad, you had the honour of naming him; after all, you brought him. You were a country man at heart. Loved animals. You always kept a few cattle, who in turn, kept you sane. As a nation we had just entered the European Economic Community. Keeping abreast of current affairs, you decided to call him 'Brussels'.

Unfortunately, neither of you are with me now. But you are very near. Brussels got killed in town, during an Easter rally. We found him together, stretched out by the Friary church. Me and you, Dad. My little heart broken. Even though you were aware that our missing doggy of three days could have met a sad ending, you persevered with me, until we found the body.

Thank you both for the lessons in giving, receiving and letting go.

Breda

The Rope Swing

BY RUBY ARON

The day I first felt it was warm and still and timeless. I was eleven, awkward yet carefree. Our house was old and strange, with separate staircases for each bedroom, and a thatched roof. There was always a novelty factor in showing my friends the big overgrown jungle of a garden that surrounded our house. It was full of secret passages and hidden tree houses. Hide and seek games in our house were superior and lengthy.

One of my favourite spots was the rope swing. At the top of four big stone steps stood a leafy ash tree, and from it hung a swing. We used to hang from the frayed blue rope for hours, swinging and twirling in the dappled sunlight.

When I was eleven years and four months old, I sat on that swing, spinning and swaying lazily in the afternoon warmth. I remember exactly the moment it hit me. I swung forward, one purple high top pushing off the shed door for momentum and then – as if I'd swallowed it – a fact landed in the pit of my stomach that stopped me in my tracks.

'My childhood is almost over and there's no going back.'

I blinked up at the sky, feeling slightly sick. Not a huge realisation, nothing monumental or extraordinary, but I was eleven and had suddenly, for the first time, noticed that I was growing up. I sat there on that swing, and I suddenly felt very different.

'I will never be a child again,' I thought. 'Nothing lies ahead of me but adulthood. And then I'm going to die.'

I don't think I felt scared of growing up, but this sudden self-awareness saddened me. I'm not sure if I miss my childhood, but it's funny recalling that my 11-year-old self was so sad to leave it. I stayed there on the swing, basking in my state of not needing to know the time, and watching insects on their haphazard commute. The light turned golden, and shadows grew into longer, darker things.

Lily ran out then, blonde pigtails flailing behind her.

'Ruby! We're going to Eddie Rocket's for dinner!'

I jumped up for my philosopher's perch, all thoughts of mortality gone in an instant. Maybe my childhood was ending, but right now I was going to drink a strawberry milkshake the size of my head.

Existentialism could wait.

Coming Events Cast Their Shadow

BY MARY FLYNN

I never quite knew when I was growing up what that meant. As I grew older, I came to understand why the older generation believed it.

My dear dad was principal in the local country national school. He was an educator and believed in education for all of us. As we had no secondary schools near us, we were all despatched to boarding schools in a town where his mother was born. The education was first class. I disliked boarding. I was an only girl; I had grown up in a family of boys, and had great difficulty in fitting in with 200 girls.

Our first-year dorms were beside the national school. Many mornings I watched the little ones coming to school. I thought it strange that they were all dressed the same and looked so sad. I remember so vividly one morning they stood looking at me and I can remember their little sad eyes. Suddenly a sister appeared and demanded I go to my class and not to associate with 'people like that'.

I realised there was something different about these little ones. For the first time, I was told of a mother-and-baby home in the town and these were unwanted children. I was only 14 and I vowed when I got older I would find a little one who needed me.

Years went by. I left school and began a career. I never forgot those unwanted babies. I met a fine man and married. Our second Christmas together, we decided we could give a little child a great Christmas. I remember sitting at my desk one evening as I had decided to write to one of the homes to enquire about taking a little one for Christmas and befriending her. I had a wonderful boss and he suggested a home quite near us. That was news to me.

We called to the orphanage one evening and explained why we were there. We were brought to the parlour and introduced to a little girl who was two and three months. She was so tiny and so full of fun. She only had eyes for my husband, and from then on she had him wrapped around her little finger. We took her home every weekend so she could settle with us. Time went by and we didn't send her back. We fostered her so we could send her to school.

After she was settled with us, we took home a little boy. His birth had never been registered; neither had hers. We were told he was about three. We had no date of birth.

Here we go again. We started down the road of securing his future, and eventually his adoption order was handed down the same day as our daughter's, when she was nine. We were very proud parents.

We have a wonderful daughter and son, and five very precious grandchildren.

A true case of 'coming events cast their shadow'.

Johnny

BY PATSY LEE

I earned a guinea when I was nine. It arrived by post with a little slip of paper that told me the £1-1-0 was for 'Professional Services to Radio Éireann'.

My dad was a keen fisherman. One 'half-day' he returned from Baker's Bridge with a baby duck in his tackle bag. At seven years of age, you don't ask why or how. Johnny Duck had arrived to live alongside a cat and two kittens, an Irish terrier called Ginger, Ginger's five pups, and a tamed jackdaw that pecked at night on our landlord's scullery door up our common yard.

Johnny settled in to the same shed as Ginger and her pure-bred pups. His staple diet was white loaf bread, supplemented by grubs and worms. These we dug nearby from the old rich soil of what had 20 years earlier been a leisure park for the gentry of Cavan, the Farnham Gardens. The neighbours became used to him. Our back yard had open access to Ashe Street and was shared by four terraced houses. We had paid dearly for the openness of that yard a year earlier after going out to a bazaar at Drumalee Cross. My dad had left our huskie dog, Paddy, loose in the yard. I'm told that Paddy used to stop me as a toddler from straying out onto Ashe Street. My father never forgave himself for leaving Paddy out of the shed that night. Stolen!

One of our younger neighbours worked in a Main Street drapery store and had to run the gauntlet of Johnny's persistent pecking at her shoes in the mornings. The laces of shoes in the '50s had the same attraction for him as wriggling worms.

I made a rough and shallow pond for him and filled it from the one common tap in the yard. He enjoyed splashing. Johnny had no problem sharing a food dish with the pups and kittens. And I had no problem holding him in my hands as he grew a bit fatter. His only photograph shows me holding him on a stool taken out from my dad's barbershop.

One Saturday night, a busy barbering night in the '50s, Johnny had gone missing. He had never waddled up the yard and through the archway onto the street before. We were bewildered and, search as we might, we could not find our duck.

I can still picture the miserable little guy who had actually stolen Johnny. He had probably come out the back way from the pub beside us and had seen his chance. And what had he done with my little friend? He had wrung its neck and had sold the duck for the price of a pint.

I told my story to Radio Éireann for a guinea and named a piece of music to accompany my boyish letter. I chose 'There Once Was an Ugly Duckling', sung by Danny Kaye. Ah, go on!

Summertime

BY MAELA NÍ CHOISTEALBHA

The scent of the cut grass collides with the soft buzz of the lawnmower. It was the smell of summer. The lawnmower hadn't met the luscious, long grass yet. We still had time. I stood tall underneath the goal post. The goal post was standing tall too, one of my father's energetic constructions, yet he wasn't the only one to be thanked; the goalpost was the ocean's concoction. Driftwood stained by the vigorous waves, worn from its lengthy expedition overseas. Hoisting its noble fishing net, tangled with stringy, slimy, spindly seaweed. Such a warm colour, a colour crammed with wisdom and knowledge, following in the footsteps of its fathers.

He controls the football between his feet, dribbling through the tall grass, a look of deep concentration on his freckled face. His tongue hangs out. I tense.

This was the moment, the make-or-break moment. If the ball hit the back of the fishing net, the game would be over, and the freckled face would fill with felicity and fulfilment. My fist fastens, my teeth grind, my eyes meet his, I give him my famous ferocious face, a stare that could crucify.

The sound of the lawnmower ceases. Our field would soon be hijacked, the sweet grass slaughtered.

The ball lifts into the air, it would hit the top-left

hand corner, a shot he had practised with me the pre-
vious day, one my little legs couldn't manage to master.
I jumped, reaching as high as I could – I was flying.
My short arms failed to fulfil the function; I could not
reach, the fast-moving bullet bit down on my fingertips.
His eyes widen with joy.

His freckled grin fades once he figures out that I have
broken the rules. No tears, no telling, no pulling hair
and no biting. I pinch my eyes closed, trying my hardest
to stick to the first rule.

His eyes widen with fear when he sees my swollen
fingers. He grabs me. 'Don't be a tell-tale tattler,' his
voice strong and stern. 'If you tell, I will never play with
you again. Never.' I start to really cry, tears masking my
tiny face.

Instructions were given to evacuate the warzone; the
lawnmower commences.

He lifts me up on his back, and runs with me behind
the wooden shed, another one of my father's creative
constructions. He sits me down. 'Stay here. Don't move
and don't make a sound until you stop crying! Don't be
a baby'. My chest starts to heave.

Gigantic red sunglasses hover over me, the bronzed
princess arrives. She lifts me up onto her hip, my arms
tighten around her sun-cream-scented neck. She cra-
dles me, as if I were her baby. Her soft, sleek fingers
mop my tears. She reaches into her pocket and pulls
out a Juicy Fruit gum. My tear-stained face brightens; I
was not allowed Juicy Fruit until I was old. I would be
in trouble. 'Shh, I won't tell. Now. Smile, little princess,
it's summertime.'

Visiting Auntie Cissie

BY JEAN FARRELL

9 May 1961

Auntie Cissie gave me this diary for my birthday yesterday cos I'm eleven now. And Assumpta and Bernadette and Concepta haven't a diary, and they'll be mad I have one.

I'm out in Auntie Cissie's house for one day and one night, and she only invited me. Assumpta and Bernadette and Concepta are raging raging mad.

Mr Galvin drove me out here when he was coming to collect Uncle Ultan for the funeral they had to go to in Donegal. That's why I'm staying with Auntie Cissie, cos she's on her own.

I helped her to feed the hens when I got here. Then after the Rosary she prayed for all her children in Limbo. I know about Africa and America, but I don't know Limbo.

Auntie Cissie must be sick, cos after the Rosary she asked me to get her tonic out of the press for her and a glass. It's in a bottle called Buckfast Tonic Wine, and Auntie Cissie said it's lovely and makes her feel great.

The only thing to read in her house is a missal. It was bursting with memoriam cards. I took them all out and looked at the pictures of old people on them. Auntie

Cissie filled up her glass again and asked me to read them out loud and she'd tell me who they were. She told me heaps of stories about the old people and what they died of.

I said, where is Limbo?, cos I got fed up of hearing about TB. She asked me to get another bottle of Buckfast Tonic for her and she'd tell me. When she did, she cried. I never saw a grown-up person crying before. All her babies died inside her and came out dead. Wait till I tell Assumpta and Bernadette and Concepta. I bet they don't know about blood and bits of babies coming out your bottom.

Then she told me that she wasn't speaking to her best friend any more. She said she put him up under the bed I was going to be sleeping in. I said what, and she said it was a holy picture of Saint Jude, and he wasn't the saint of hopeless cases, he was just hopeless. No matter how much she begged him for a real baby to be born, he didn't listen to her.

Then she said to open page 100 and see Saint Agatha cos I'm called after her. Auntie Cissie told me that Saint Agatha had her two breasts cut off with a sword because she wouldn't commit an awful sin with a bad man.

Then she told me to get a glass and she'd give me some tonic. It was lovely. I had two.

When I went to bed I had awful dreams of some saint coming out from under the bed and cutting off my breasts, even though I don't have any yet. I'm glad I'm not staying here again tonight.

I'll write more tomorrow.

A Father's Torment

BY KEN GIBSON

I magine a father's torment. A decision was needed. So, he chose to abandon his daughter. For ever! He sacrificed her so that his wife and other daughters might have a chance in life. And imagine a bedridden child's anguish as she realises that no one will ever collect her from this hospital. Dad's promise was a lie.

My heart raced and my gut churned. Inside, I was spitting fire. What kind of man abandons his daughter? Or betrays a child so cruelly? But Dhukia spoke calmly as she unpacked the whole tragic tale.

Dhukia's feet slowly lost sensation. She could walk on the rough stones and thorns without feeling pain. Even when the thorns punctured her soft skin and caused her tender feet to bleed, there was never any pain. But they'd get infected.

'Warm them at the fire,' the local healer said. But he didn't understand the disease. Dhukia felt no heat. The flames destroyed her soles.

Then someone in the village suspected what it was: leprosy. So, Dhukia's dad walked her on her young, damaged feet for three days through the forest to reach the hospital. 'I'll come back for you next week.' The weeks became months and years. Dad had lied. He was not coming back.

I asked questions and the bigger picture emerged. Dhukia has three sisters and a mum at home. The doctor explained the problem. Leprosy is still feared. People are still driven away. Some are beaten or stoned.

By then it was clear: this dad chose to sacrifice one daughter so that he could save three others. This wasn't just between Dhukia and her dad. It was a tragedy for the whole family. It affected everyone in the village. And it was repeated right across the country. I was no longer angry at the dad, but at a world that allowed this ancient disease to continue to exist.

I'm a dad. I couldn't imagine choosing between my precious children. I've never had to. But I was far from home in a country and culture I did not yet understand.

I stood, shaking my head. 'No man should ever be forced to make this choice,' I repeated to myself time and time again. 'No child should ever have to be abandoned.' No one needs to suffer the physical damage, the social isolation or mental torment that leprosy causes. There is a cure for this disease, discovered in Ireland. The greatest tragedy is that it's not known about in the villages where it's needed most.

Without warning, I was now caught up in this tragedy and I faced a choice. As the orange and yellow sky gave way to darkness, I knew that my life and my family's life was changed. For the past twenty years this has occupied every day of my life. And now, at last, the finish line is on the horizon.

The Long-awaited Speedy Arrival

BY MARIA JORDAN-O'REILLY

It was gone past midnight, and a Donegal woman was sitting with my mother. Dad had not yet returned from his work in the Irish Glass Bottle Company. Shift work – he finished at midnight and then headed home in his little Fiat.

The reason why Mrs Byrne was with Mum was that she was in labour on that evening, 60 years ago today. The doctor and midwife had assured her that nothing would happen till morning, and had gone on their way. The doctor in his fancy car, the midwife on her bicycle, heading back to her home in Rathfarnham to get some sleep before being called upon again. They had only left when Mum called for Mrs Byrne, who came up the stairs to sit with her till Dad got back.

Mum was agitated. 'The baby–' she began.

'It's OK,' came the soft Donegal lilt, 'the doctor said it will be a while yet.'

'No,' mum insisted, 'the baby is in the bed.'

Incredulous, but wanting to keep Mum calm, Mrs Byrne pulled back the covers, and there I was!

She told me about that night many times, as I grew older. 'You were looking at me with the darkest eyes, a

255

head of black hair... and just then I heard your father's car and shouted down to him to go after the midwife. He caught up with her before she even got home.'

She would smile and tell me, 'I was the first one to wash your little face!' I get teary-eyed now remembering that gentle Donegal woman who was a special part of my childhood, and also thinking of how long my parents had waited for their second daughter. My sister is 12 years older than me, and as I grew older, I came to realise just why I was handled with kid gloves, dressed up in pretty dresses and spoiled. It had taken 12 difficult years for Mum to carry a second pregnancy to term.

I was wanted, and loved, and had a wonderful childhood. The one thing I remember Mum saying to me was that I came into the world in a hurry, and then became the most laid-back person she had ever met. But I think she may have been fooled, because I was always paddling madly beneath the surface, always tenacious, and always, eventually, achieved my goals.

My life has been filled with adventures, challenges, and obstacles – and it still is. Today, on the eve of my 60th birthday, I am still learning, still exploring this wonderful, frustrating and exciting experience that is life. I am also sitting here, looking back on my life's journey, and so far, it has been quite a ride!

Perhaps I should take time to sit and write it down...

King of All the Das

BY JOHN LYNCH

It was always sunny when I was a kid, the evenings were full of golden haze, and sweet smells from the summer grass and hedges wafted through the air. My da was the top of the food chain and king of all the das in the known universe. As far as I was concerned, he owned the world and was the authority on all things. Well, that was my innocence then, but sometimes it just takes a little tweak of my ears, or if environmental conditions allow, and I am instantly transported into that world.

Evenings spent walking for hours through the back fields with Da – and of course we couldn't even think about walking towards the door without the dog, AKA Snert, looking suspiciously at us and then going feckin' nuts when his suspicions were confirmed. He would nearly put the lead on himself, get the keys, give them to Da, kiss Ma goodbye and then burst a dog-shaped hole in the front door. He was given the name Snert after the *Hagar the Horrible* comic strip published in the *Evening Herald* every night. My Da loved that; it was on the same page as the crossword puzzle and the nine-letter word thing. I was often flabbergasted at how the hell he could complete the crossword and the nine-letter thingy *and* still answer all the fecking questions on whatever quiz was on the telly during the '80s.

257

As I said, he was the king of all das and master of all knowledge, full stop.

I can still vividly see my eight-year-old self gently putting my little paw into the giant daddy paw – in my memory, this is always in slow-motion with the low golden sun in the distance and warm summer breeze on my face. The sense of security and happiness, a little glance down to me, a wink and, 'Are ye right, John the Cron?' That's what Da called me. Funny how things stick. Like poor auld Snert. His name used to be Rebel, but my da altered that.

My name evolved through the years, starting out as 'John the Cron' from age five or six; then, as my sweet tooth came, each Friday I would get the Friday treat as payday came around. 'Payday Crunchie!' I would chant. I was duly paid with Crunchies and Mars bars along with the standard PRSI and PAYE debits. So, my name got extended to 'John the Cron, the Crunchie schoolboy', and my da would put it to a poetic lilt. Then as I turned seven and made my communion and every other milestone until it finally came to – and I need to clear my throat to say this, or should I say lilt it – 'John the Cron, the Crunchie school boy, multiplied by seven, who is now a holy boy, walks like a man, is able to get up in the attic, and is a great dancer, come in your dinner is ready!'

I know, I thought everyone's da was like that. We lost him this year to that stupid virus. He was my biggest fan and best mate. Miss you every day, Da.

Web of Life

BY HUGH DEREK FLANNERY

His petite putty-soft hand clings firm to mine. His free hand playfully pushes the iron gate, which obediently swings open as we enter through an old stone archway on which the gates are hinged. He automatically lets go of my hand as he hop-skips and jumps along the gravel pathway, excited knowing he's free from the crosstown traffic outside the enclosure.

He runs along the path, glancing back at me for approval to investigate his surroundings. 'Look,' he says pointing, 'a spider web.' His eyes flash with sparkles of wonder that only a child can't fake.

I turn his attention with a wave of my hand towards a willow tree a hundred yards ahead. 'See if you can find any near that tree.' He scatters ahead, making a beeline towards the willow.

On arrival, he shuffles his feet, then bounces, 'Another one!' he bellows. 'It's gigantic,' he yelps. His face is an inch away from the web, his bright blue eyes wild and wide with anxious glee. He investigates, balances one hand against the bark, the other on a smooth, shiny marble surface. He steps back as if awakened from tunnel vision, initially squinting, then his eyes widen as he takes a slow panoramic view of this surroundings.

'Crosses,' he says, 'lots of crosses.' There's a pause. 'Is

this… is this the graveyard?' All of a sudden, he sounds serious.

'''Tis lad,' I answer. He's silent.

'When do you think me and you will be dead?' he asks in an intonation beyond his years.

'Never, lad, we're alive forever.'

'Forever and ever?' he replies

'Aye, lad, but DTA: Don't Tell Anyone!'

He smiles and leaps up into my arms, squeezing my neck tightly then loosely, and leans back grinning, 'So, we are like secret superheroes?'

I nod my head, smiling. 'We sure are, son.'

I tap his button nose with my finger. He jumps down, clutching my hand, pulling in the direction of the exit.

'Let's go to the park,' he says. He beckons me down, as if to whisper. I put my ear at his level, and he tips my nose with his finger. 'DTA,' he says back at me.

The Egg Dish (Menemen)

BY THERESA MCKENNA

yse arrived in January 1993. It was the year my son Baris was born. A cold breeze from the Aegean cut through the light cotton of her summer dress. 'Welcome, Ayse. Yasar has told me all about you.' Locks of curly black hair parted to reveal intelligent almond brown eyes with flecks of green staring at me with guarded curiosity. I had very little Turkish in those early days, and Ayse had no English at all. I took off my padded jacket and gently placed it on her shoulders.

Ayse became part of the family. Her story is that of many young girls in some parts of Turkey. Girls need dowries so that they can be married off or risk bringing dishonour to the family by having boyfriends, for which they are denigrated as whores or mistresses. If young girls come from poor families like Ayse, they cannot access an education so they are forced to marry in this way, or work in badly paid jobs, where they are vulnerable prey for exploitive males.

She was one of three sisters. Her father left and her mother was forced to find another husband. Their new stepfather didn't want the burden of providing for three young girls. That wasn't part of the bargain when he agreed to his own *nikah* or marriage. The three beautiful girls, Ayse, Kesban and Aysegul, were dispensable.

Ayse was the oldest, and she found work as a waitress in a local hotel where she also resided. The handsome young owner, Mehmet, wooed her while remaining happily married. The other two sisters agreed to marry suitable young men. I had learned much of this from Yasar as she came from his village of Selçuk. I needed company in the house as he spent long hours at the shop, especially during the tourist season when he sold many rugs and kilims.

Shiny green vine leaves glistened in the sun, winding their way through the latticework of the pergola. They were the close companions of the rambling rose, whose train of sweetly perfumed, dusty-pink blooms rustled softly in the sea breeze. I rested on the swinging seat, stretching out my aching legs as I swung back and forth, dreaming of my baby boy's sweeping eyelashes. As the birth drew nearer, I prayed that my baby would have his father's beautiful long brown lashes and that his smile would light up his face with the same irresistible charm that had won my heart.

'Let's cook some eggs – the ones with peppers, tomatoes and onions.' I was suddenly craving *menemen*, a popular Turkish dish. As I munched my way through the menemen, I asked, 'Why don't you ever eat eggs, Ayse? Please, please try them, they're delicious,' I pressed.

She didn't speak for a long time. Then, stepping into the past, she spoke with a deep sadness that came from a dark place. 'I was eight years old. He burst in the door, shouting, drunkenly pushing my mother towards the stove. "Cook me some eggs, woman!" he roared. He turned to look at the three of us curled up like kittens on the ragged couch near the stove. He pulled us out by our hair, as we whimpered. One by one he lined us up. I struggled to breathe, unable to move, frozen as he raised the gun. It felt cold and hard as he placed it to my ear. He laughed as he shouted, "I'll shoot the whole lot of you!" finger on the trigger as he made his way from one child to the next. I watched in horror as he swayed and grabbed me, dragging me towards the table. "Eat, or I'll shoot the lot of you." He pointed at the eggs. I couldn't move. He looked at my sisters. In slow motion I moved towards the table. He was my father.'

Picking Stones on a Big Day

BY GERALDINE HANLEY

My Confirmation day was here. I had been looking forward to this morning for ages – there was so much to be excited about. It was a big day. I had a new dress to wear; it was white on the top and green on the skirt part, and I had a lovely green bolero. It was probably the first new dress I'd ever had. Don't get me wrong, I had worn lovely dresses, but they were all from my three older sisters. This was mine, and it was new, and I just loved it. It was hanging in my mother's wardrobe.

When I got up I just wanted to get ready. But I was soon heartbroken. Expectation and excitement, followed by disappointment – I had to go over the fields picking stones! I think my mother felt sorry for me when she told me. I innocently went out to the yard to say to my father that I was making my Confirmation today. That didn't go well. He told me there was plenty of time, the day was long. The thing was, we had picked stones in that field almost every day this week and they just seemed to grow overnight; there were always more to be picked. I went over with my father and two brothers and got it done.

I came home and got ready. I was nearly there. I went with my parents, my younger brother who was also making his Confirmation, and our youngest brother. We travelled on the back of the tractor; we didn't have a car then. Our village was three miles from the town where the church was.

I don't remember much about the church ceremony, but I remember the bishop; he looked very powerful to me, and was very serious. I took the name 'Rosario' for my Confirmation. We took the pictures outside, and the day was lovely.

Back home, my mother had cakes and orange and sweets for us. It was so memorable as we wouldn't usually have those, only on very special occasions. My brother and I went around the village to meet up with all the others who had made their Confirmations. We played a game called 'Goose' in a field nearby, and hurling and handball. We spent the day playing. My godfather lived near us, and he gave me a half-crown.

This day comes to mind when I find things are tough, and obstacles have to be got through. It can be all part of a plan: the feeling that morning when I had to go over the stones in the fields; the way the day turned out; hard and easy are always linked together, I have been reminded many times throughout the rest of my life. Somehow, I get comfort from this page of my life; just get through the hard bit, and it will work out.

The Young Reader

BY ANNE STANLEY

My mother tugged my ponytail so tight that the little hairs at the base of my neck snapped. 'It's time,' she hissed. 'Remember, don't annoy him, don't talk when the Queen's speech is on, and for God's sake, don't cough!' And with that, she propelled me up the first two steps of our steep, unrelenting staircase, my Christmas cardigan in stark contrast to the grey, curling paper on the walls. I clambered the rest of the stairs on all fours, which I had discovered was the quickest way to propel myself upwards. The boiling ham below had covered the landing window in a film of steam, but by dragging my finger in a line across I could see the frost sitting crisply below in the yard, sparkling on the puddle by the shed.

I tapped softly on the locked door, and the soft slipper-shuffle across the wooden floor responded. The key turned, and I entered my father's room. Immediately, I became unable to breathe; the hankies drying on the wire fireguard in front of the blazing fire, the strong smell of my father's pipe smoke tickled my nose, and my nostrils shut down in protest. The old Pye radio crackled statically in the corner, spewing out Christmas carols. I felt sick. I could feel my cheeks burn from the heat, but I didn't care. It was Christmas Day, I was five, and my father was going to give me my presents.

He pulled across the faded pink floral curtain that stood to the side of the fireplace and reached in behind the piles and piles of old newspapers, stacked as high as the ceiling, and pulled out two large, black plastic sacks, and proudly presented them to me. I grabbed them, my fingers anxiously tracing the shapes, afraid to breathe almost, but like old friends, reassuringly, there they were: long and thin, fat and square, some in shiny red paper, some with Christmas stars on them. The knot in my stomach unfurled. I was safe. I had my books. I could lose myself and not think about the rest of the day ahead.

The Day I Met My Angels

BY BERNICE CALLAGHAN

I sat on my kitchen floor crying.

I remember it clearly. It's July 2000, the sun was shining through my window and *The Gerry Ryan Show* was on the radio. I had just dropped my daughter Alanna to summer camp. She was non-stop chatter about this and that, but mostly so excited about the baby in Mummy's tummy or the 'little Bean', as she called it, because I had explained at one point that it was the size of a bean and this is what stuck with her.

But how could I tell my little girl that they could not find my little Bean? According to the scan results under a week ago there was no baby, no heartbeat... Again! Yes, again... as this had happened just under a year before, nearly a copy of that dreadful, traumatic time for me and my little family.

The year before, at 15 weeks they couldn't find my baby, no heartbeat. But I was so healthy! No bleeding, no pain... I went back a week later and they still could not find my little Bean. I had a D&C the very next day, and my little Bean was gone.

So here I am, sitting on my kitchen floor, 12 weeks pregnant with Bean number two, waiting to return to the hospital the very next day to see if they could find my baby, feeling emotional, powerless and very much alone.

I can hear the *The Gerry Ryan Show* on in the background. I loved Gerry Ryan and the morning show. I was crying on the floor and in a desperate attempt at something, I cried out, 'God, I am sorry. I am not holy, I don't go to Mass or anything, but if there is something up there, out there, please, please, send me a sign, what will I do? I need help. Please, please, help me.'

I don't know if it was my outburst or what, but I said to myself, 'Bernice, you're losing it. Get up off the floor and get it together. Be thankful for the little girl you have.' What will be will be, hearing myself say, 'Grow up and get on with it.'

Just then, and clear as day, there was a surge of electricity and the volume on the radio increased. I heard the distinctive voice of Gerry Ryan say, '... and after the break, an angel reader will help you find your angels. Yes, you heard it here first, folks... stay tuned!'

'Bonkers,' I thought, but... was it a sign? I listened intently to the interview, a woman with a soft, soothing accent chatted with Gerry. I doubted myself many times that day, but that night as I lay in bed, when the house was quiet and my family asleep, I did exactly what the angel reader said. I asked the question: 'Was my little Bean dead or alive?'

What happened next was astounding... a little miracle, perhaps?

Seeing Red

BY MAGGIE BURNS

By far the most embarrassing aspect of having a crippled mother was having to go shopping for special occasions with whoever she could find to take me. My Confirmation shoes were bought on a cringy expedition with a couple up the road who I felt so awkward with, I took the first pair I tried on.

Similarly, for my first uniform for secondary school, mum's cousin and her husband brought me to be kitted out. I died a thousand deaths as I was measured for everything from the gabardine skirt to the running knicks. They treated me to tea in Arnotts' café after, but I was beyond jealous that other girls were doing this with their mothers while I was making small talk with strangers.

When the time came for my first bra, I was dispatched with a different relative. A single lady, equally uncomfortable with the situation. She needn't have worried; as a late bloomer, I was familiar with the entire St Bernard's Teen Bra range. I think there was a choice of two, and I had been longing for the day when I would eventually own the one with the lace inset.

Such was my teenage self-centredness that I genuinely believed I was the injured party in all of this. I just wanted to be normal, to have a normal mum, one I could go into town with.

The number one most embarrassing moment of shopping expeditions with randomers came when I was doing Irish dancing and entered into a Feis. Our dance school wore red costumes. I got mine from a small ad in the paper; I think a friend's mother took me to get it. It was a magnificent red dress with a Celtic pattern embroidered into the panel of the centre pleat. It came with a black velvet bolero, white lace collar and a cape secured by two Tara brooches. I can't remember how I got the dancing shoes – but I'll never forget the final piece of my ensemble coming together.

We had to wear red knickers so that when we were up on stage high-kicking our way through slip-jigs and two-hand reels, our undergarments would match the lining of our dresses, be less visible and not detract from the dance. Red knickers were hard to come by in the '80s, but I left it with Mum, knowing she wouldn't let me down.

It was a Friday evening and we were having dinner when a knock came to the door. I answered it to find a lad I didn't know, but recognised as being a couple of years ahead of The Brother in school. He had a brown bag in his hands. 'My mother sent me down with this for you.' I stood, suspended in fear, trying to read if he was just the messenger, or if he knew what the bag contained. I thanked him and took the bag quickly. As he was turning by the gate he called out, 'Good luck in the Feis!'

I'll kill her, I thought. I'll bloody kill her.

My Elvis Impersonation

BY DAVID HALPIN

I swore that nobody at school would know about my new glasses. I was ten years old and had just been diagnosed with a lazy eye. Elvis, my hero, didn't wear glasses, so no way I was going to either. My mam assured me it would only be for a year, but I didn't care. Everyone at school would laugh, and my status as a cool kid would be ruined. Why me? I asked myself, looking in the mirror, trying to focus my good eye on its traitorous brother. I would now have to face the jibes of Eddie Butler, our class joker.

I had a secret routine on the way to school. Once I reached the laneway near our house, I took a comb and can of hairspray from my schoolbag. I would pour my beaker of water over my bowl haircut – the only style our local hairdresser knew – then spray my hair, combing it into what I thought was a quiff of which Elvis would be proud. It probably looked like a bird's nest, but I'd strut to school, accepting admiring glances from my classmates while waiting for the lollipop lady to escort us across the main road. But now that I had to wear glasses, those jealous stares would be lost forever.

'Will I go in with you?' my mam asked, straightening my glasses that first morning.

'No, I'm fine,' I replied, grumpily. I dragged my feet

leaving the house, waving forlornly. It was all part of the act, though. At the laneway I pulled my glasses off and flung them into my bag. Out came the comb and hairspray. Looking back, I'm surprised I got away with it for so long.

Months later, my mam noticed that the stitching in my schoolbag was torn but I wouldn't let her sew it up. 'It looks cool like that,' I insisted, believing it added to my rebellious reputation. Alas, as I'd been told many times in school, 'Pride comes before a fall,' and I was about to go over a cliff! That fateful day, it was my turn to say the Angelus.

I was standing at the top of the classroom, about to begin the prayer, when there was a knock at the class door. It was my mam. She was waving something at me. The glasses! My teacher opened the door and my mam said, 'I found David's glasses in the lane.'

'But David doesn't wear glasses!' Mrs Burke replied.

My mam's face darkened as the truth dawned on her.

The hole in my bag! I should have let mam sew it up. Mrs Burke eventually closed the classroom door and handed over my glasses. 'Put them on, David.' As I stood there, exposed, Eddie Butler, the class joker, had to have the last word.

'It's alright, you still look like Elvis...' He paused for effect. '... Elvis bleedin' Costello!'

I still wake to the sound of children's laughter.

The Parcel

BY REBECCA BARTLETT

It would sit on my grannie's bed; she was the custodian. No matter what day of the week it arrived, we would have to wait until the following Sunday after Mass and after dinner. Oh God, the excitement – and the wanting.

We would lie in bed at night, Ruth and I, whispering our expectations to one another. But Sunday always came, and then the ritual would begin. When dinner was over, Grannie would nod at Ruth and smile knowingly. Sis would dive from the table with a sideward look of defiance at me. I hated the way Grannie did that. I wanted to carry it, the weight of it, caress the airmail letter taped to the front, as if I could know what it said by some sort of mail-order intuition. It annoyed the hell out of me. Why didn't Mammy open it? After all, it was her twin sister who sent it all the way from New Jersey.

It would be many years before I understood why my mother handed over that privilege. An act of forgiveness for the deceit that her own mother had played upon her, but that's not right, told here.

Rough string pulled taut. Then falling away under the snip, snip of Grannie's pinking scissors. My mother watching us, smiling. We knew how much she loved us then, in that moment when the parcel from America was finally opened, and Ruth and I knelt on chairs the better to see inside the big cardboard box, 'custom inspected' stamped in big bold letters on the inside flap.

This was our moment, possession was all. Box open: the smell, sensuous, inviting; Hershey bars and Betty Crocker cake mix; women's perfume; cinnamon; lavender-tinted soap; fancy coloured paper to write letters on; see-through blouses that shimmered; and slips, lacy, luxurious, wrapped in tissue paper – pink, turquoise, baby blue; always a handbag and *always* a lipstick redder than anything you could wear in our street.

We would work our way through them carefully, first Ruth, then me, then Ruth again, our trophies laid out on the table, and my mother all the time watching, waiting for the thing that always made her smile. Sis and I competed to be the one to find it for her, the shiny black vinyl nestling right in the centre. Thirteen years, a parcel every year and in every one of those parcels a record. Each of them marking a point in time in her shared history with Aunt Joanie. An annual reminder of that other life lived away from the smog and austerity of Belfast. She came home again, Joanie, my mother's soulmate, in 1969, just before the Troubles started, and that was when I learned that I wasn't really my mother's child at all. It was Joanie who was my mother.

Beginnings

BY CIAN DUNNE

We poured out of the house in stages, stretched out under shadow of sun. My dad insisted that we take a photo outside the front door. He'd recently bought a Fujifilm camera on Shop Street in Galway and was now determined to catalogue all our new memories. I dragged my feet to position, stood tiny beside my older sister and tall beside my younger one. I wasn't starting school, I wasn't graduating school – why should I smile? Steady, smile, click. That was the start of our trip. Standing there, soundless. A moment captured, immortalised, to be looked at quickly once developed and once or twice or maybe several times more before death.

We had a long holiday ahead of us. Our leaf-green Mondeo was hot to touch. We piled books and bags into the boot. My mum turned around and smiled at us with her hand on the headrest. 'All set?' I sat short-strawed in the back seat, squashed between my sisters, with a direct view of the road as it stretched out ahead before it disappeared behind us. Dad punched the radio with his finger, and it was far too loud until he spun the dial. The sun beat through the windows without permission. The presenter coaxed us to guess the year. Shaggy's half-hearted attempt to convince us it wasn't him was a dead giveaway, apparently. I realised my parents had

276

lived too and did not exist solely for the purpose of tying my shoes. A slight shock to my boyish conception of the world.

Kerry was far away. The roads weren't great. It seemed we were never quite there, until finally we were. I tried to behave as best I could, but if my siblings misbehave then I have to defend myself, do I not? I looked left and right past slender shoulders and saw sheep, cattle, a strawberry seller on a hard shoulder and even a castle. About three-quarters of the way, we stopped and stood against the bonnet, ripped tin foil from our ham sandwiches and moaned that there'd after been cheese put in them. We drank still water from the same bottle, passing it on, hand to hand to mouth. I didn't feign to listen while I watched the lake sparkle and glisten. The water was cold and clean. It felt like bliss.

Years later I sat in the middle of the floor of my room, with my left ankle crossed and resting under the back of my right knee. I had gotten the points for the course of my life to change, and so I was clearing out my room before moving out the following week. I invited the stifling sun in through my open windows. Amidst the paper and laminated rubble circling me, I came across our photo from that day. The start of our holiday. I'd forgotten it had been taken. I guess it was worth it, my dad's insistence that day. It was worth my tears, anyway.

Loss

My Brave Face

BY HELENA JOYCE

9 December 2017

Saturday morning. I'm so tired. Not much sleep again. How much sleep does a person actually need to keep going, I wonder. I wish now I hadn't promised the lads a home-cooked dinner this evening. Who knew that teenage boys could get tired of eating takeaways? List in hand, I entered the supermarket; good, not too busy. Right, I think, stick to the plan: get enough fresh meat for a few dinners, avoid making eye contact, and get to the checkout without incident. Sounds straightforward. Usually is. Nothing is now, though, and never will be again.

OK, focus: sausages, rashers – oh, must remember the waffles, that will get them through lunch – hmm... chicken fillets, mince, pork fillet. Fine for a few days, then. I wish I'd taken more notice of what there actually was in the cupboards; a cursory glance was all I'd managed before I left. I wonder who bought all those tins? Gosh, this fridge aisle is chilly. I need milk, cheese, ham... I need to move on to somewhere a bit warmer. Definitely need a few treats: crisps, biscuits, chocolate – and then there it is, the 12-pack of Cadbury's purple Snacks in that unmissable packaging. They're Colm's favourite, and never on the list as they're 'essential items'. And then I began to feel sick.

I leaned on the trolley for support. If I let go now, I'll fall. I mustn't let go. Hold tight, deep breaths, tiny steps. Finally, the freezer aisle; quickly I grab chips, pizzas, oh, the waffles, good. Now, just a few more steps to the checkout, but my legs won't move. I'm frozen, nearly literally – I could be, I decide, if I get into the open freezer. Surely by the time someone notices me I will actually have frozen and be numbed forever. I'm tempted. I hear myself gasp out loud, and I realise I've been holding my breath.

STOP. GET A GRIP. I look around me; no one has heard me, I mustn't have said that out loud. JUST BREATHE, I command myself. It's simple, you've been doing it all your life. It can't end here, the freezer aisle in Tesco of all places – the ignominy.

I suddenly remember that Mary's probably already sitting in the café waiting for me. I'd hate for her to be here when they'd take my frozen remains out. It'd be a terrible surprise too for some unlucky customer just expecting to pick up their frozen turkey for Christmas, while stocks last! I chuckle inwardly and I'm back in the moment. I take a deep breath, and move more purposefully now towards the checkout. Small queue, thankfully. Gosh I'm cold. I really need that coffee, and I'll need something sugary with it too. 'Oh, hi, Mary, I'll be finished in a minute. Yeah, I'm fine. Yes, an americano would be great, thanks.' My 'brave face', the first of many.

Training

BY SUSAN BOYLE

I learned CPR on the floor of the courthouse in the town where I grew up. A high-ceilinged building with 'Resuscitation Annie' dummies lined out in front of the judge's bench. We worked in pairs, saving pretend lives so we could someday save real ones. Did you know, chest compressions often crack ribs? You are warned of this and told not to stop; a cracked rib is a small price to pay for a beating heart.

For years, I swam side-stroke lengths in pyjama bottoms and towed my sister up and down Naas pool. I tossed coiled ropes across the grand canal, learning how to wrap them so they didn't tangle mid-air; blue nylon was my Wonder Woman golden lasso, 'Kick your legs; don't panic, I'm going to save you.'

I was strong. I swam well. I was trained, I knew what to do. My summers were spent on Liffey riverbanks and canal towpaths, sometimes watching bathers splashing in the sunshine, more often than not, huddled against the July rain. It wasn't glamorous but it paid reasonably well, and anyway, I grew up watching red-bathing-suited Pamela Anderson, so I imagined it was better than it was.

As a college student, I declined party invites so I could take early shifts at the pool before class. It was calm in the morning; hazy and still until the sun burned through and heralded another sunny, southern Californian day. The other lifeguards looked like Ken and Barbie, or Barbie's cute Asian friend. They lived on their parents' boats in Newport and called in sick when the surf was good. I looked like Strawberry Shortcake. My poolside presence was a nod to ethnic diversity and a reminder to use sunscreen. I spent a year slowly turning from creamy white to milkshake pink, flecked with freckles, my red hair sun-bleached to blonde.

The first time I needed to use my lifesaving skills on a real person was just after a swim. I walked through the hall door, my hair wet, a damp towel shoved awkwardly in a bag for life.

We train so our training kicks in. I knew where my hands needed to be; count fast to 15; two breaths on blue lips. I felt outside my body. These motions, skills that lay dormant for 20 years.

No one knows how they will react gripped by adrenalin and fear; that is why you train. When your brain can't process what is happening, another part of you wakes up and takes over.

Her ribs cracked under my palms. The person who had given me life, her life now in my hands. The ambulance arrived. They said I did everything they would have or could have done; they said I did my best.

Afterwards, waiting in the quiet, softly lit hospital room, my still-wet hair smelled of chlorine. All those hours of training, and they never told me it wouldn't work.

Sorry Loss

BY PHOEBE BAXTER

I am staring at a ripped hole in the sleeve of my jacket, part of a very nice suit that makes me feel smart and professional from the moment I put it on. I need this armour as part of a ritual that gets me through the day, but a dog has just put a hole in it and my arm – a couple of huskies in fact, that fervently bit the ample meat of my buttock and calves at the same time.

I'm here to photograph a family reunion. I stand in the kitchen while the father argues with his niece, who has also just had a chunk taken from her leg. For the first time ever, my professional façade crumbles, and I start to cry. I decide amidst the shouting that I should find a plaster for my arm, a pathetic gesture towards asserting some control over the situation. I still have an event to photograph. The mother assures me that I can get a tetanus shot later. A middle-aged lady in a floral outfit and pearls inserting a needle into my ass does not compute. Myself and the niece leave for the doctor's, knowing I would miss the vital shots of the family coming home from Australia as they arrive at the surprise party being thrown in their honour. We waste no time with getting-to-know-you small talk: we curse and commiserate about how things have happened. We speed along the windy, rural roads back to the house and I get there in time to photograph most of the day. The father looks at me with a mixture of suspicion and annoyance that his wife had been upset by my missing the big moment.

Picturing my smart suit jacket left thrown across a kitchen chair with a shredded sleeve, I'm now sweating inside my green, tweed, full-length winter coat which is being used to hide my injuries. The young upstart of a caterer wearing a waistcoat too big for his puny body sidles up to me in the garden and whispers he'd like to 'get into' photography. Trying hard to transcend the numbness of shock, I tell him that now is not the time; I'd rather have said, 'Are you for fucking real?' I have no emotion left, just a laser focus on the job at hand. I walk out of there seven hours later, say goodbye to the niece with a silent eye-to-eye nod of solidarity, and finally allow my stinging skin to break into my consciousness.

It occurred to me on the four-hour drive home that I possibly care too much about a line of work that utterly depletes my soul to a point where I am left with no sense of autonomy. On that journey, I grieved my lack of self-respect, cursing my way through salty tears. By ignoring myself, I was bringing back the feeling of being ignored by adults; I was a child when my brother died, not important enough to have my hand shaken by the oversized, earth-engrained hands that bypassed me as they moved along the front row of the church muttering those 'sorry loss' words.

Mark Twain Bent Pipe

BY SANDRA BEHAN

I hurried along the quays, pulling my winter coat tighter around me. The stench of the Liffey at low tide almost took my breath away as I headed for O'Connell Bridge. I could see Dad waiting for me, a faraway look in his eyes.

'Are you OK?'

'I'm fine, love, just remembering the day your mum and I had our photo taken here.' I slipped my arm through his as we walked through a stream of Christmas shoppers. The sound of carol singers and the festive lights were magical.

Dad loved our yearly visit to Kapp & Peterson. I could smell the rich, deep, moist, pungent tobacco with touches of spice as we entered the shop. There was a large collection of pipes and tobacco exhibited in floor-to-ceiling mahogany glass cases.

A well-groomed young man approached Dad. 'Céad mile fáilte, Sir. I'm Sean, can I help you?'

'Go raibh maith agat, less of the Sir, call me Shay.'

'Would you like me to show you some pipes, Shay?'

'No thanks, I'll let you know when I find "The One."'

I was captivated by the array of Peterson's tobacco: Irish Oak, Gold Blend, Nutty Cut, Connoisseur's

Choice – it went on and on. I bought a tin of Old Dublin ready-rubbed tobacco that Dad liked.

I held up a Churchwarden pipe, a long, slender, elegant design. 'Too straight,' he said.

I showed him the Classic, unique and timeless. He shook his head.

I watched him as he scrutinised each pipe, turning them around in his weathered hands. He stood in front of a mirror, holding a pipe to his mouth. I took a photo.

'This is The One.'

'What's so special about that pipe?' I asked.

'Great choice, Shay,' Sean said from behind the counter. 'A Mark Twain Bent Pipe. The deluxe system includes a deep reservoir to collect excess moisture, and has a graduated-bore mouthpiece that funnels the smoke.'

I was sorry I had asked. 'We'll take it,' I said, pushing a wad of cash in his direction.

'Nollaig Shona!' Dad said as we left the shop.

Now the photo sits on your coffin; you caught in the moment, your pipe hanging out of the side of your mouth. Eyes that now stare down the aisle of the church. I don't want to cry for you, I'm furious at you. Why didn't you do what you were told? 'Nil by mouth,' the doctor had said.

So there you are beside your fancy Kapp & Peterson box, a pipe for life, looking at us all as we ruffle tissues, sobbing in our black.

I read the eulogy that I had been up all night writing. I can hear you now: 'You did me proud, love.'

And now the bagpipes are playing 'The Dawning of the Day' as we walk, distraught, behind your coffin.

A tall woman dressed in black steps out of the shadows and pushes a small box into my hand.

'Your dad wanted me to give you this,' she whispered.

Expectations

BY KATE DURRANT

When I think of her now I remember mushrooms, swimming in garlic butter, and crusty bread.

They were quite the thing then, all those years ago.

Served at lunchtime, with a glass of barley wine.

Whatever that was.

She loved those mushrooms that glistened in a thick earthenware terracotta bowl, reminiscent of a week in Spain.

But without the sun.

And definitely without the laughs.

Children were to be washed, and dressed and fed, and compared favourably, outwardly, to the offspring of neighbours.

But, thank you very much, we'll have none of those shows of affection.

None of that NONSENSE.

Report cards were altered on the way home, with Cs becoming clumsy As.

Sixty-eight per cent becoming 88 per cent, and tell me, WHAT happened to the other 12 per cent?

And, NO, I'm not remotely interested in what the others got.

And then one night, yet another night, the phone

rang, and the woman who had tried but couldn't, spoke, again, of how she had sat on top of a cliff all day and was going to throw herself off, and when she did, it was going to be ALL YOUR FAULT.

And, so, relationships ended, they had to, before history repeated itself and the next generation became poisoned by the disappointment of the one that went before.

She died a week ago.

No one knows when her funeral is.

No one is invited.

Consistent to the end, disowning and barring from arrangements those who had failed to live up to expectation.

She never saw the wonder of my children, or shared their laughter and happiness, and she never experienced the relationship with her own adult children that, had life been different, she could have enjoyed.

I hope peace finds her.

The Rollercoaster

BY MARIE NICHOLSON

'I'm nearly four,' she tells everybody. With her untidy blonde hair and bold grin, she's cheeky and demanding and beautiful.

'When is my leg going to get better?' she asks on a daily basis.

'Very soon, darling!' we promise with reassuring smiles.

She demands hot salmon and hollandaise sauce, cola bottles and bubbletape from Quinn's shop and a constant supply of purple dodos. These were easily granted, even at midnight – that was something we could control.

She carries all her dodos in one hand, one on each finger and one in her mouth, and laughs at herself, and wanders around the house again with her doll Katie covered in biro and naked.

'The cows eat all the vrass,' she says instead of 'grass'. 'Bold cows!' and tuts as if they are greedy and unworthy. On Christmas Day she comes home for a few hours from the hospital to see what she got from Santa. She doesn't even look at the toys. She asks after a few hours, 'Can I go home now?' So we bring her back. This is her normal; institutionalised in a hospital, this is all she knows. So we stay on the rollercoaster.

Then one sunny day we get great news. No more treatment, no more hospitals, no more running and racing. We go back to the old normal, which seems like a lifetime ago. It's fantastic. She's reunited with her siblings, she has Mum and Dad at the same time, still playing one off the other, back in her old bed. And we have our lives back after two years of being to hell and back on the rollercoaster of bad news after good and good news after bad. There are many, many sunny days and many, many smiling faces, and she gets back into her old antics of breaking eggs behind our backs and drawing on the walls and eating hot salmon and hollandaise sauce and finally green veg which are not spiked with potions and powders that everyone tells us that prevents cancer.

A short few months passed by. Then one day our neighbours' two horses stand to attention with the spring sunshine shining brightly between their two heads. Not a sound can be heard; the birds, sheep and the bold cows all pay their respects as the little white coffin is driven up the road.

Fairy Godmother

BY FREDELLE KEOGH CAMPION

It started with the phone call. Dad was bringing me home from drama class. We heard the phone as we got out of the car. Dad ran – I can still see him run, just the few steps but they were determined. I liked drama; it was easy, and there were no 'shiny everything girls'. Now when I think of drama, I think of that phone call.

It was over. She was dead, I knew, when he said, 'Oh, my wife is on the way to bring her pyjamas. She needed pyjamas. She's probably still on the bus – oh God.' Dad was worried; Mam was on her own – Mam was going to her dead sister on her own. I didn't know what to do or say. Five years ago she had started bringing the happiest moments and nicest of things to me, and now she was bringing the worst thing ever.

My dad was standing looking out the net curtains. His shoulders were moving up and down; his shoulders never looked so big. Who knew shoulders could cry? He knew I was there, but he didn't turn to me. My little brother was crying too, his face was all red and blotchy. My mam was alone in a Dublin hospital, crying alone, and not for the first time.

My granny looked grey, she spoke to me quietly but crossly. I didn't really want to talk to her. She looked so sad it was scary. She told me this was the third child

God had taken from her: one from illness, one from murder and one from cancer. She said our children aren't meant to go before us, but I didn't know what to say, so I said nothing.

I kept remembering her that day. She had come back when I was seven. She brought me my Communion dress the whole way from America – America, imagine! – my only claim to fame in school, ever. She came from the airport with a big brown suitcase. The suitcase took up the whole of our sitting room floor and it was wrinkly and old – but not bad old; interesting, good old. It was a bag of magic and she was surely my fairy godmother. Out came my dress with a bundle of other magical items, like pencils with rubbers with the name of an American college written on them. My dress had three belt ribbons and you could choose which one to wear, a pink, a white and a blue – imagine!

On the day of my Communion, I remembered her cycling up our road, hair flowing and dress floating. She was beautiful and strong. She bought me a can of Pepsi, and I had never had a can of anything. Once she brought my mam a cake in the shape of a heart and a pair of petal earrings when everyone else forgot her birthday. She was magical, she brought magic. But on this day she was gone, she was gone, she was gone.

Moyne Road

BY CAROLINE HEFFERNAN

I love colouring at the dining room table when we visit Nana and Auntie Mary in Moyne Road. I listen to their chat and savour the smell as Nana bakes scones. But today is different. There's no chat, just the ticking of the clock on the mantelpiece. I feel kind of sick and I don't know why.

Dad's friends Paddy and Maura drove us here, which was strange. I'd never been in their car before and was queasy in the back, sitting between my brothers. When we arrived at Moyne Road, the boys went into the sitting room to play around on the piano and I went into the dining room looking for Nana and Mary. But they're not here. Paddy took the key from under the stone to open the door, so I should have known.

Mary's moped is in the hall, so she can't have gone far. Maura sits beside me at the dining room table; she's looking at me too much. I pretend not to notice, and pick up a yellow crayon to colour in a flower. She's talking at me now, saying stuff that I don't understand.

'Karen, if you ever need a mam, I'm here for you.'

What's she going on about?

'You know that, don't you?'

She's still talking but I'm not listening. 'Thanks,' I mumble.

Mam's in hospital getting better. 'She should be home really soon,' Dad said when I asked him.

The sound of my brothers banging the piano in the sitting room is getting louder. I wish they were with me. 'Where are Nana and Mary?' I ask Maura as I start to colour in the leaves.

Before she answers I hear a key in the door, and a moment later they both walk in.

I run to Nana and grab her legs, but she doesn't pick me up. She's crying.

I look at Mary and she's crying too.

'Where's Dad?' I ask.

'He's coming in from the car now,' Nana says.

Walking into the dining room he lifts me up.

'Karen, pet, let's go for a drive.'

'Yes!' I shout. It's all going to be OK.

'Are Paul and John coming too?'

'No… just the two of us.'

Dad lets me sit in the front seat. He's very quiet. 'Are we going to the Sugar Loaf?' I ask.

'Not today, we'll pull in here for a few minutes.'

'I don't want to go on the swings,' I say as he stops at the front gate of Palmerston Park, not around the back where we usually go.

'Karen, I need to talk to you.'

My stomach lurches.

'I've sad news. It's Mam. I'm sorry, Karen, she's dead.'

'No, she's not. She's in hospital getting better!' I yell.

'Karen, pet, I'm sorry, but she's not going to get better. She's gone to God.'

I jump across the seat and slap his face. I'm screaming now. 'I hate God and I hate you. Where is she? I want to see her!'

'You can't see her, Karen, she's dead.'
'I want to see her dead then!'
'You can't, Karen, she's been buried.'

Movement

BY SARAH FITZGERALD

My daughter had her dance class. I dropped her off and went to the supermarket. On the way back to the car I began to feel really ropey. Wasn't sure if it was tiredness or hunger. I collected my daughter and headed home. I ate a dry roll in the car to quell the uncomfortable feeling in my stomach. I went to bed for a lie-down and later that evening decided I'd have an early night, hoping I'd feel better in the morning.

'She's not one to cry wolf,' he thought to himself. But a knot was already forming in the pit of his stomach. I started pouring cereal for the kids. 'What the f*** are you doing?' were the words in his head, but thankfully the words that came out were, 'Will you just go – now?' I grabbed my bag and keys. 'Ring me when you get there,' he said.

For once, like in the movies, there was a parking space outside the door. 'Hopefully a good omen,' I thought. The usual receptionist was on duty and greeted me by name. I managed to get out the words, 'Could I see Siobhán straight away?' without choking. 'Go on up,' she said.

I was first in the waiting room and she called me in. 'I'm a bit worried about movement,' I blurted out.

'Lie down and we'll have a look,' she said. She felt the bump and got out her gizmo to check for a heartbeat. Shortly after I heard the gushing sound. 'No, that's your heartbeat,' she said. I was uncomfortable lying on my back, and so sat up and lay back down a few times. She kept on trying. She called in the GP from his surgery across the way, but he wasn't successful either. They said I had better go to the maternity hospital. 'Our device is very small, and the baby may be positioned awkwardly.'

I went out to the car and rang him. 'I'll follow you in after I drop the kids,' he said.

I went to Admissions and told them the story. 'Third child,' I said. '37 weeks,' I said. The nurse searched for a heartbeat. Róisín was her name.

'Sometimes we can't find the heartbeat here,' she said. 'We'll take you down for a scan.'

He had arrived at that stage and held my hand as we made our way downstairs. We walked straight past all the people waiting at the antenatal clinic. Should've known that wasn't a good sign.

I was taken into the room and the sonographer applied the cold gel. She took her instrument in her hand and traced it around my tummy. I never looked at the screen. 'If I don't look, then I won't have to admit it,' I convinced myself. But I looked at Róisín and her face said everything, and I looked at him and his head was shaking, almost involuntarily. So I turned and looked at the sonographer.

'I'm so sorry,' she said. 'There's no heartbeat.'

A Beginner's Guide to Onions

BY GIL FOURNIER

I was nearly 12 years old the first time someone in the family died. Grandad passed while I was drawing a rude portrait of my teacher; I never told my mother, because I thought God was punishing me for it. I didn't know how to grieve, so I silently followed Mam around rooms of other silent people. I didn't cry, because nobody cried. We sat in our church clothes around the casket and whispered, like we might wake him up.

The night before the funeral, my great aunt pulled the roasting pan out from under the sink.

'You can't just rot. People need taking care of.' She told my grandmother, who was sitting at the kitchen table, staring at a photo album. She hadn't turned the pages in a long time. Nanny chopped onions into the pan until they hurt her eyes and made her cry. We all did, then, the women and me. The pan sat out on a white tablecloth the next day, in a room that smelled like dusty perfume. We cooked roasts every night for a week, delivering them to my grandfather's siblings. I wouldn't eat onions for a month after.

When Nanny died, I sat with Mama staring out the window, trying to figure out how to make it better, not knowing I couldn't. We sat there all day and night; when I woke up in the armchair, she still hadn't been to sleep. I made us coffee and watched hers turn cold. I brought it to the kitchen and when I reached under the sink for soap, my fingers brushed the roasting pan. I pulled it out and remembered Nanny, crying in the kitchen but smiling when she brought the food out. I balanced the pan, full of onions, on one hip. I deposited it on Mama's lap. She began to peel without looking at her hands. When I handed her the third bulb, she started to cry. We both cried, then.

The pan sat proudly on a white tablecloth the next day, in a room that smelled like fake pine and baby powder. When the reception ended, the pan was empty. We filled it with the dinners our family's women brought. Red pepper and onion stir-fries. Steak-and-onion pies. Onion tarts. I ate so many onions that afterwards I only ate plain spaghetti till Christmas.

I was 19 when Garrett flipped his car. I was scared, but not of him dying. Twenty-year-old men don't die. I was scared of visiting him, scared he wouldn't know me, scared the surgery would paralyse him. I would love him anyway, I told everyone who'd listen. I was young enough to imagine my heroic life as his nurse, for a moment. My mother and I sat at the table staring at my phone. When finally it rang, my mother answered it. My whole body froze, until she set the roasting pan next to me. I couldn't bring myself to wait for the onions.

Breakfast with the Robin

BY BRIAN Ó TIOMÁIN

Monday

Caoimhe asked me today if I'd prefer to be buried or cremated. We were waiting for breakfast to arrive. My 19-year-old daughter is always direct.

'I think I'm gonna go for burial,' I said. She said she'd be going for cremation.

'I guess you're going for a religious funeral?' she said.

'I am, yeah,' I said.

'Thought so. I'm not into all that religious stuff,' she said.

'I know that,' I said.

We looked out the large glass window into the garden. It's in full bloom now. That same garden that was once featured in Bloom. The robin arrived on the windowsill while we were looking out. He's become a regular.

'Do you believe in the hereafter?' she said.

'I do, yeah,' I said.

'Are you still praying?' she asked, looking at me with that arresting gaze of hers.

'I am, yeah,' I said.

'You must be very disappointed,' she said, holding that steady gaze.

'I am,' I said, trying to focus on my breathing.

The robin at the windowsill was getting very animated, almost as if he wanted to come in. He's bigger than a normal robin. He has a slightly speckled breast like a thrush, but it's orange too. I was remembering we had the robin at the window when my beloved Aunt was dying.

'He's beautiful, Caoimhe, isn't he?' I said, thinking we are both noticing nature so much more than we used to.

'What about breakfast? They're late,' she said.

I was transfixed by the robin. He was peering at me sideways with one eye and then the other.

'I'm sure breakfast is on the way,' I said.

'So is Christmas,' she said. I laughed and she smiled.

'I'm afraid of going,' she said. 'But more than that, I'm afraid of making the journey on my own.'

'You never liked being on your own,' I said as I put my hand on her shoulder. Then I got Raymond Moody's book out of my man bag.

'This is the book I mentioned, Caoi. The one about people who died but were revived. The book has these accounts of people seeing this brilliant light. They met people they knew who had died before them. And then they were back here. Cos it was before their time. But they all said they weren't on their own. I can read you a bit if you like.'

'I'd prefer if you went and got me breakfast,' she said.

At that point, the breakfast lady arrived.

Caoi's mum came in soon after. I kissed Caoi on her bald head and I went into work. Work has become my tenuous link with sanity.

It says in the Bible if you pray for something and truly believe, then it will be granted. That's a deceit. But Caoimhe wants me to keep praying for a miracle. Even though she doesn't believe. So I'm still praying.

In memory of Caoimhe Ní Thiomáin,
14/10/1999–11/6/2019

Death by Memory

BY JEN HANNON

Granny's was busy, one of the ten children always around. Granny's was a dim staircase with Nine-Year-Old charged with cosseting younger cousins and Annoying Little Sister. Adults wandered out of the sitting room, wondered why Nine-Year-Old teacher couldn't keep her students quiet, and found her engaging them in a headfirst snake race. Nobody told Nine-Year-Old that Granny was dying, and that the thump-thump-thump and whooping weren't appropriate.

Granny had a brain tumour. Nine-Year-Old knew that having a large family was unhelpful. Some wanted to operate. Some did not. For Nine-Year-Old's birthday, Daddy brought home a reduced-price skateboard, with a hairline crack. That was around the time that Granny got a hairline crack of her own, in a big hospital in Cork.

Granny returned home to a bed in the sitting room, and Nine-Year-Old knew that things were bad. Granny's curls were gone. In their stead, slender threads of raspy hair peeped out from under a large bandage that would be fantastic for dressing up as a mummy on Halloween.

When Mammy presented Newborn Baby Brother to Granny it had a strange effect on every adult crammed into the room. They sniffled and snuffled, as if the whole room suddenly had a cold. Mammy said, 'This is your grandson. Mam can you see him?'

Granny lay there in her Halloween costume, and not a dicky bird from her.

On day 11 of Newborn Baby Brother's life, Mammy and Daddy were happy when they came home from the injections, until the phone rang. Later, while Mammy changed Newborn Baby Brother's nappy, Annoying Little Sister asked Mammy why she was angry and Mammy snapped at her, 'Because my mother just died.' Annoying Little Sister started to cry and Mammy didn't even seem to care.

We drove the long road to Tipperary for the funeral without Daddy and Newborn Baby Brother. When Daddy sat in beside Mammy in the church, she gave him the look that meant serious trouble. He said, 'I left him in Clontarf,' with tears in his eyes, and she mellowed into his hug. Daddy was right to come, even if he'd left Newborn Baby Brother with Auntie, who had Newborn Baby Cousin, just six weeks old. Damned if you do, damned if you don't. He'd chosen correctly that day.

Nine-Year-Old heard the choir singing 'You Shall Cross the Barren Desert'. She did not cry until six years later, when she absorbed a different organ cranking out the same notes and her loss crept down her cheeks at a stranger's funeral.

Granny was fun. She played cards – Snap, Beggar My Neighbour and Old Maid. She ordered customised story books from L&N. She left chocolate in the larder as a reward for fetching vegetables from the dank, dark room.

Granny was love – the kind you give when you've reared the first lot in tough times, and can enjoy the second lot from afar.

Wail

BY MÁIRÉAD NÍ CHIARBA

'He's dead.' The words jarred in my frazzled brain as I grappled with yanking a grizzly teddy from its position wedged underneath the couch. I straightened up and looked at him, pushing my sticky hair back from my forehead. My heart had stopped beating, or so I thought. 'He's dead,' he repeated. 'I just got a call from your brother. It's over.' I stared at the red and blue teddy in my hand, the vibrant colours shifting in front of my salty eyes. I felt the wetness on my flushed cheeks and realised that tears were streaming down my face. I hadn't been able to cry in years, so this sudden flood startled me. I stared unseeingly past his anxious eyes at the brown fields. The first flush of spring was peeping its way out of the frozen ground, past the memories, the sleepless nights, the denials, the betrayals and now this, after all these years.

'I'm sorry for just blurting it out,' he continued. 'I was trying to get your attention for ages, but you didn't seem to hear me.' His eyes were sad. He reached out his hand and I took it, his strong fingers wrapping around mine. Not like the other hand, which had been large, calloused and weather beaten. A hand which I believed could never be cleaned again, the fingernails dark with clay, heavy grooves etched in the palm. And eventually, returning to its original state, princely clean, baby soft and powerless. I could never have believed it possible only for I had seen it myself.

A baby wailed in the background, forcing my wandering thoughts to reshuffle into my brain like wayward sheep. Another cry, this time a wail louder and more urgent. 'It's Lucy.' I made to move towards the door, but he stopped me. I looked at him and with a jolt realised the wail had come from me, and not my baby sleeping peacefully down the hall. 'You need something for the shock. Please, sit down,' he pleaded. I faltered, looking into his eyes whilst thinking about those words that had fallen like pebbles onto a pond. The ripple effect was shimmering its way through me; I could feel myself shaking as I lowered myself onto the sagging couch. I sank back into it and placed my hand against my forehead. A low intense pain had started to throb slowly and rhythmically. I could feel the intensity of it increasing. The wailing intensified around me – or was it in my head? I wasn't sure anymore as the room started to swim in front of my eyes. I closed them, hoping the pain would ease.

'What now?' I asked. 'What happens now?' He wrapped his bulky arms around my shoulders, securing me, steadying me, pulling me back, desperately trying to anchor me, again. 'How should I feel?' I cried, the words rasping from my heaving chest. 'Just breathe,' he replied, 'just breathe.'

Right Here

BY LESLEY-ANN WHELAN

Y ou had to stand at a certain angle to see him. From the feet upwards, he looked exactly like his mother. Standing at his right elbow, he wears the face of his grandfather Frank, all thick-rimmed glasses magnifying tiny eyes, enveloped in the oxblood leather wing-backed chair, pressing the punt note into your hand as you were bundled out of the house.

When you walked into the room, as his figure became visible the nearer you got, he could have been anyone, waxy and yellowed. You circle around to every possible viewing position until you find him. Right shoulder, looking down from behind, as if you were peering to glimpse what he was reading, or placing his dinner plate down at the table as he was sitting, waiting. From right here, his snow white hair sits perfectly. From right here, he looks as if he has just closed his eyes for a quick nap after a long day in the garden. From right here, he is meditating to the sounds of Gregorian chant. From right here, he will open his eyes again.

People begin to arrive; you don't recognise them. It becomes a rush of faces, hands grasping at your hands, palms cupping your cheeks, bright, wet eyes staring at you. They tell their stories, and you delight in hearing them because each piece builds up the picture of a life lived. Those places you never saw, those conversations you never overheard, that one moment of kindness that changed the course of someone's life. His legacy.

You find your back pressed firmly up against the entrance hall wall, you shoulder squashed into your sister's. Smiling like lifeless mannequins as bodies stream past, if you don't anchor each other, there's a risk of being carried away. Eyes dart from the person clasping your hand, to the queue forming of those wishing to extol the memory of him, to the man standing by the casket, shoulders arched forward, grimacing with pain. His black coat looks too large for him, he holds his chin with one hand and sweeps his hand over his hair with the other. He cannot move away. You want to console him, in his paralysing grief. You want to go over and link your arm through his, this man you barely know. You want to, but you are trying so hard not to feel anything at all that if you go to him, this man's grief might infect you, might drive its way through your immune system, replicating itself onto every cell until your body is overrun with grief.

You only saw him cry once. Not at the funerals of his parents or friends, but in the hospital that morning. Crying with relief that he was alive and with fear for how long. You want to be like him, stoic. You will not cry in front of people. That will be done in bathrooms at 4 a.m., hand clasped over your mouth to deafen the scream.

Today I Know for Certain

BY JEAN MCGEARAILT

I open the cupboard door.

The big red teapot with white spots proudly displays itself on the top shelf. It is fragile, demanding respect and careful handling – after all, it has Kensington stamped on its Pristine Pottery bottom – almost a Royal.

On the shelf underneath, sharing space with scarred vegetable chopping boards and entangled cooling racks, stands the sturdy canary-yellow teapot. With a Mr. Men smile carved into its broad face, it rests like a smiling Buddha, waiting to dispense tea and contentment to whoever, whenever. The blue enamel mug used for single egg-boiling and a collection of non-stick milk pans add to the mismatched inhabitants of this cluttered space. But each has held an address here for a long time. It's cosy here, near the comforting old oil-cooker that has warmed this kitchen for more than 40 years.

I open the cupboard door – and I see them: the intruders. They are long, slim, brownish-grey, solid and unbreakable. They are tucked into every available space, stowed and ready for use: an armful of small, timber lengths. One rests precariously atop the red-and-white piece of almost-a-Royal Pristine Pottery.

My eyes fill and smart. My heart seems to stop,

disengage and do a somersault somewhere inside me. Will it reengage and start again? It finds its place and beats again, but the beats drum out a new reality: I know he is leaving me. He is being stolen away stealthily and silently. Today I know for certain.

I've watched the signs for some time.

I've seen them when he asked yet again, 'What is Brexit?'

I've seen them every time he who was as surefooted as a mountain goat, stumbled and fell over nothing as his shuffling gait betrayed him.

I've seen them when his bright, intelligent eyes were filled with frightened puzzlement, and when he counted minutes on the bedside clock, in the small hours: '3.10... 3.12... 3.15...'

I've seen them when 'home' to him meant a distant place in times past.

And today, he has been home. He's brought in fuel to his mother's kitchen, making sure there was a ready supply of kindling for the old range. He was back there, but still here; boy, yet husband, father, and grandfather. And he holds his boggled mind, full of fog and blank spaces, together within his heart with patience, acceptance and without complaint, as I try to weave a safety net of love around him. Many months later he leaves, as gently as he lived. He turns to look at me. Then he is gone as I am singing 'Danny Boy'.

Today, released from my cocoon, I visit him. The dandelions and daisies, which are surrounding his bed in my absence, tremble in the breeze as I approach. I say an 'Ave' there for him, as promised, and as I walk away the bleatings of Easter lambs fill the silence.

The Day

BY AISLING MOONEY

What does it sound like when you're told you have cancer for the second time, that it's inoperable and will never completely go away, no matter what treatment you have? It sounds like the white noise after an explosion. The high-pitched beeping that slowly fades out into a silence. The doctor is still talking, you just don't have any idea what he's saying. You can see he's talking to you, and then he looks to the person with you because you're not registering anything. They always ask you to bring someone with you when you're getting terrible news, and that's because you stop listening.

Your mind is already racing. What are you going to do? How are you going to tell your children? When are you going to die? How long do you have? Did he say how long I have? Did he? What's he saying now? Looking into treatments, chemotherapy, radiation treatment. Remembering the cold, sick feeling the last time you had chemo, the hair loss, the steroids, the vomiting, the sores, the inability to get out of bed, the loss of hope. Can we go through this again? Do I want to?

Then you look to your companion, your husband, partner, friend, and he's devastated. Crying, and you can see his internal scream. You can see he's broken now too. Life will never be the same again, everything has changed. The doctor is saying, 'So I'll be in touch in about two weeks to talk about treatments, but in the meantime we'll have to keep you in for two or three days to do some more tests.'

Your practical head kicks in. I didn't bring a bag, didn't know this was going to happen. If I send him for the bag, I'll be alone. Where are my kids, all adults now, but still my kids?

Mark my husband is saying, I'll ring Alison and get her to come up and sit with you while I go and get your things. No, don't go yet. Let's sit down and think, or be quiet, or not think, or just make it stop for a minute. The rollercoaster has started and we're at the top of the big descent. Let's just take in the view for one second. If we don't say anything, it will all go away. We'll wake up in our own beds. Anywhere else. On that holiday last year with Lauren and her family in Salou where we laughed every day while the grandchildren danced around the pool.

Just make it stop, but you can hear the rollercoaster clicking forward and pulling you towards the next rushing moment. The big descent into a new unchartered phase of our lives. Down, down, down it goes, and you know that we can only go forward.

Ring the kids. They'll ask me how I'm feeling, and I won't have any answers. I'm numb, sweaty, panicking inside, and if I begin to cry I'll never stop.

Leaving Me

BY GABRIELLE WOLFE

B ack from college he said,
'That's not my dad.'
And I said,
'Don't be stupid, he's just getting old and cranky.'
'No, not Dad – there's something – I don't know
– something.'

I never understood the phrase 'in denial', only to find
I suffered from the disease.

Like the spider, suspended mid-air on a thread,
I dangled. Unless a light shone on the gossamer string,
I couldn't see it.

UNTIL he rang to say he took the wrong train, maybe
he was in Wexford, and we had a nightmare drive into
Vietnam to find him.

'Til he asked me to marry him, and I spoiled the
moment, saying we already were.

'Til he flung open the curtains and shouted, 'Out of
that bed for school!' to his 30-year-old son.

'Til, oblivious to the white carpet outside, he thought
the Dubs were playing live at Croke Park instead of on
the Christmas CD.

'Til it was useless my trying to prevent him travelling: wearisome of his verbal assaults; his bruised
ego; exhausted from shadowing his movements in the

shopping centre, circling the same open-air asylum that was now my John's world.

'Til I stood for over an hour on the train to Dublin, no seats, because the gentleman in him held the train door open and gestured everyone on before him.

'Til the day he turned to me on the settee and said, 'Who's that over there, at the window?' and I saw nobody. 'He's all in black, standing on a stage.' And I told him I had no idea.

'Til I asked him to write his name, and the sadness in his eyes almost broke my resolve.

'Til I put my arm round his neck, to bury my tears, but instead felt a rosary of lumps.

'Til the lumbar puncture, and removal of a bead confirmed cancer, metastatic, spread into every inch of sinew and bone.

'Til the drips chained him to a bed and finally I got control of the madman.

'Til he didn't understand our wedding anniversary card, but instead swallowed the orange sweet, a Steradent tablet, and they sent for the poisons unit.

'Til I escaped with him in a wheelchair, and like Hitler's arm, his outstretched leg stopped traffic and we got to the park opposite.

We stared at the riff-raff glutton seagulls and ducks swiping sodden bread, the swans gliding past, their necks bent in royal curtsy.

'Til our own necks kissed in dignified silence, and I pushed him up the hill, shackled back to an iron frame.

'Til two weeks later he didn't know his son nor daughter.

'Til he cried when I came two hours late

'I thought you'd left me!'

'Til he spewed basins of dark blood, his upper stomach chewed.

And shook with a seizure, as if plugged into an electric socket, and they affixed a box of tricks to his side that released morphine and other magic potions.

'Til I whispered in his unconscious ear.

'It's Gaye. Do you remember when we ....'

The Night Shift

BY LAURA LYNCH

A long, narrow corridor. Pastel-coloured baby elephants and bunnies skip along beside you on the walls. By day, bright and busy. By night, dark but alive. Rows of glass windows, separating each room. Old, wooden window frames, thick with many repaint jobs. A-shaped yellow warning signs remain dotted around on dry floors, a memory of the busy day. The fiery-red emergency trolley poised ready and waiting, like a fire engine hovering near the runway.

The radio hums, always on. Forgettable soft rock classics.

Nineteen tiny cots. Nineteen tiny babies. Vulnerable, overwhelmed parents by their side. Tubes, alarms, nests and blankets. Love. So much love. We share smiles through the glass. Handover begins, the night is ours.

23:20. A glance down through the panes of glass, my eyes pass the settled infants and mums, to the last room. A wealth of knowledge is being passed from an experienced, gentle nurse to an exhausted mum, heavy with doubt.

23:35. My eyeline is again drawn through the glass, to the same room. This time there's a glance. A locked eye that everyone's experienced before, where information is passed without words. I'm on my feet. I don't break my stare with the room for the whole walk. The baby is quiet and limp. Panic from those too close. Careful calmness from those in charge, us.

23:40. The corridor swells with help. Roles are assumed, military style; it's a well-rehearsed play. Ordered chaos. The trundling red trolley springs into action. Fluid sets, needles, vials, labels, checked and checked again. No delay. Working. Working. Keeping time. Precious time.

23:55. A decision to go to surgery. Minutes pass, rolls for transfer are assumed. 'Kiss your baby,' a gentle order by the team lead. Never forgetting that parents are observing every last movement in the room. A kiss to the head. The pain is indescribable.

00:05. A breeze flows through the ward. Every emergency door propped open. An eerie quiet lingers. Painful glances from remaining mums and dads, having witnessed the fragility of life. Holding themselves, their babies, their hopes and fears.

00:10. Notes written. Calls made. Routines resumed. Eighteen tiny beating hearts completely unaware. Innate rituals of nursing continue. It's what we do, care and compassion, whatever the situation. We continue.

00:20. For a moment, everything stops. In a sterile room on another floor, a pause to consider every option has been thought of before the outcome is agreed. There's nothing more we can do. Everything has been tried. An overwhelming event for this little body. It's all too much. Rest now, little one.

One hour of a 13-hour night shift. A shift I'm so privileged to be a part of. Some nights are remarkable for devastating reasons. Nineteen little heart beats at the beginning of our shift. Eighteen at the end. A heartbreaking privilege to be part of.

The Short Trip Home

BY ELAINE DE COURCY

'How much can you fit into a small Micra?' I wondered, as more and more of our belongings were packed in. He closed the boot abruptly as I put our little girl securely into her car seat. I instantly felt a lump in my throat as she looked at me with her huge bright-blue eyes, and I could feel the sting of tears in my eyes but did everything humanly possible to fight them back. This was an extremely hard day as it was, one I was not going to make any harder by crying again.

The hardest part was that she was completely innocent in all this; probably a good thing she was only a baby, ten days in fact to her first birthday. I knew this wouldn't impact her yet, she would adjust, maybe she'd know no different. Maybe in time things would be different, maybe he would decide to make it work, decide it was best for our little family. There was so much going on in my head that was quickly snapped back to reality by him saying, 'That's everything. Are you ready to go?' I nodded my head, still fighting back those tears but determined not to give him the satisfaction of seeing them fall again...

The car journey was no more than five or six minutes, but it felt like an eternity. Absolutely nothing was said in the car – not one word. We arrived at my parents' house. He started unloading the car, and I took our daughter into the house. My parents sensed something was wrong but knew the best thing to do was say nothing for now. My mam took my daughter while myself and my dad brought the rest of our belongings in. Once everything was in, my daughter's dad kissed her on the head and said goodbye. I watched him drive away while I cuddled my daughter. I needed her love and affection now more than ever. I put her down and my dad played with her on the floor. I knew I needed to explain to them what was happening, but to be honest I really wasn't sure myself!

My mam was in the kitchen, and like every Irish mam she had the kettle on and some toast to make sure I ate. It suddenly dawned on me that I hadn't eaten that day, so the toast seemed appealing, if only to take away the sick feeling in the pit of my stomach. I bit into the toast and as I tried to swallow, I couldn't, it stuck right in my throat joining the lump that was already there. That familiar sting in my eyes returned, only this time stronger, I couldn't stop it. The tears fell so intensely, my mam just grabbed me and hugged me tight. 'Why is this happening? Why is he doing this?' I sobbed. 'How am I going to cope on my own, all alone with a baby at 19? Oh god what am I going to do?'

The Dreaded Day

BY SUSAN MCGOVERN

We knew it would happen one day, and it was something we dreaded. We considered ourselves lucky it hadn't happened yet, eight years after Mam was diagnosed with Alzheimer's. There were signs it was coming closer. If one of her five grandchildren came in to see her in the nursing home, she might know Danielle because she was the only granddaughter, but if it was one of the grandsons, she would know he was a grandson, but not which one. We consoled ourselves that they all had a look of each other.

She always knew her four children, though. She frequently recited our names in order of age, as if to embed them in her failing brain. 'Susan, Stephen, Deirdre and Ciara' she would constantly chant loudly, as if trying to convince herself and everyone else that she had not forgotten them.

When the dreaded day came, there was nothing in the early part of the visit that rang alarm bells. By this stage each visit went according to a script, which varied very little. She was delighted to see me as usual and said, 'Oh sweetheart, I was never so glad to see anyone.' My joking reply, as usual, 'Well, I'd be a bit annoyed if you said, "Oh not you again."' 'Never,' she said emphatically.

I took Mam for a small walk and then for coffee in the same coffee shop we always went to. 'Coffee' was a euphemism for wine, since every time I asked Mam did she want coffee or wine, her reply was always 'Wine,' with an echo of the mischievous glint in the eye that the old Mam used to have. None of this was any different on this visit, and Mam drank all her wine and ate her cake.

She told me then that she needed to go to the toilet, so we headed to the Ladies. I went into the cubicle with her, helped her with her clothes and flushed the toilet. Outside I showed her how to turn on the tap to wash her hands and where the tissue was for drying them.

She turned to me and said, 'Thank you. You're a very kind lady.'

The hairs on the back of my neck stood up and I thought, 'Oh God, this is not part of the usual script.' Well might I have been concerned, for my mother's next sentence hit me like a body blow.

'I'll tell my daughter Susan that when I go back outside.'

'Mam, I'm Susan,' I said, near to tears.

She looked at me full in the face and said, 'You don't look like Susan.'

Between then and bringing Mam back to the nursing home, I seemed to morph between Susan and the kind lady several times. When I finally bade her goodbye, I'm not sure who it was that she saw before her, but it was Susan with a very heavy heart who sat into her car and drove away.

A Familiar Sound

BY ALANNAH DAWSON

The old, half-painted, tired hospital ceiling was a patchwork of cracks. Following them with my eyes, as I lay on my back on the examination table, waiting.

Routine scans are never quite 'routine'. Instead, always tainted with a hint of fear, anxiety, excitement, relief and unknowns. Busy places, filled with stories. Stories of people's lives. Mums, filled with a new future, a new hope. Some excited, some fearful, all there for the same common goal: to have a scan to check how the progress of their baby is coming along.

A busy, bustling, noisy waiting room. Midwives and doctors shuffle in and out; long days, overworked and time poor. Unable to sit a while to talk to anxious-looking parents who await their own individual moment of relief with the doctor. Each parent waits their time to watch that scan come to life on the screen. A thumping of the heartbeat. The small, unique little 'person' in there, in that safe, dark, calm, quiet place. A place to grow and thrive.

As I lay there, on the examination table, the doctor is gentle in his voice, quietly comfortable and confident in his profession. Routinely asks me to lift up my top so he can place the gel-covered monitor on my ever-growing belly. I do as I am asked, my small bump sticks up. A baby. A new life. A new hope.

I wait to hear the loud, thumping sounds of the heartbeat, a sound I am familiar with hearing; this is baby number two. It is my second time on this path of checks and appointments, my second time parenting alone. My second time attending my appointments by myself. A single mum, having my second baby, a baby girl, who will be called Sally, after my mum, who died years earlier in a horse-riding accident.

I wait, staring at those cracks in the ceiling that seem to get bigger, deeper, like a road map. Any minute now, I will hear that loud thumping of her heart. I will see her small face on the screen, and I will leave the hospital with a calm sense of peace. That moment lingers. The doctor's hand holds tightly to the monitor and moves with a pronounced urgency in his search. It's here somewhere… There is a deathly silence, not just from the monitor, but also from the doctor. I try to breathe, I tell myself… any minute now. Time stands still. His face says it all. There is a picture of her little body on the screen beside me. She is perfectly perfect. He looks me in the eye, and gently, succinctly and calmly says the words in an echoey chamber of numbness, the words I await, as I can see by his paleness, his sad eyes, that he is the bearer of this news.

There is no heartbeat, I am so sorry.

Mother's Day

BY MAGGIE LYNG

'Can I help you?', the benign Eason's girl asked while stacking cards.

'I'm OK, just browsing, thanks.'

'Grand,' she said, quite nonchalantly, completely oblivious to my suppressed angst. But I'm not OK, it's not grand, and nobody can ever really help me.

I always hate this time of year. These three or four weeks are difficult… triggering and difficult. Like Valentine's is for those who'd prefer to be with someone, or indeed, someone else.

Bloody Mother's Day! Made-up Hallmark holiday! Visiting the greeting card section was, as usual, pointless and provocative. I should bring out my own card range. Less chipper, more blatantly honest, punctuated with plenty of curses.

I wonder if people can spot me, the calm swan with the furiously kicking legs. To me it's obvious. It's not well hidden… like, at all! But I carry on, kicking like a mad yoke, kicking to save my life. The birds make it look effortless, elegant even. I'm no swan, I conclude.

Man alive! I have to remind myself way too regularly to go easy on myself. Positive mental attitude and all that. Self-worth over self-doubt! Be my own biggest fan!

Didn't see these mindful messages in any cards on the shelves.

And that was my segue back to Mother's Day and this bloody awful time of year again. I sighed at the utter impossibility of a release, of escape. That damned noose will forever be around my neck. A lifetime of that relentless reality will weigh me down. It's such a contemptible and caustic situation. Just harrowing, yet simultaneously comforting in the constant presence of it, like a nagging boss or a cracked phone screen. Funny the things you get used to, when they're ever present. Consistency in the chaos.

Mother's Day came and went. Just like a spider on the wall, it torments me, but ignoring the hateful thing makes it eventually fade into the background... somewhat. It's all about managing the dread, making it bearable. I put it behind me for another couple of weeks, until the US will be all Mother's Day this and Mother's Day that. I'm used to the relentlessness. Besides, thoughts of my birthday join constant reminders of mammies.

I post, tweet and bitch about my usual grumblings, exhausted at the lack of progress and equality. The issues I and my crib mates have were the same last year and will be the same next year, guaranteed, unfortunately.

By the time my birthday rears its ugly head, I'm consumed with images of the day I entered the world, when no one celebrated my arrival. When only one person knew I existed. No, 'Congratulations, it's a girl!' cards. Nothing. Just sadness, secrecy, stigma... shame.

I imagine myself, the illegitimate innocent infant, the bawling bastard left lying alone in a cot, crying for comfort. Shivering. Scared. Solitary. My identity gone, my entire family erased and my world irreparably ripped apart...

... as my mother walked away from the maternity hospital, empty-bellied and empty-handed.

A Little Chat

BY JOANNE BURKE

He wore a suit, which set him apart from most of the other staff that filed in and out throughout the day, wearing uniforms of white, blue or bottle green, depending on their duties. He looked alright; most of them were, to be fair. The smell of cloves followed him into the room, however. I've always hated cloves.

Attempting to drag myself up into a sitting position, I felt the now-familiar desperation as my lungs heaved and contracted, striving to find some air after only the slightest exertion. I grabbed for the oxygen mask and after a couple of minutes turned back to my visitor, without wasting any of my precious new breaths on a greeting.

'Hello, Joanne. I'm head of the Psychiatry Department. Your nurses have asked me to come and have a little chat with you.' Anger and resentment bubbled up inside me at the thought of those traitors, so I twisted away from him towards the tiny window of my prison cell.

'You've been crying quite a lot, I've been told?'

My mind darted back to Sunday night, after having suffered through my first ever Mother's Day. A locum doctor, perhaps annoyed at being called out after I had yet another huge spike in temperature, brusquely informed me that it would be many months before I would be able to return home. He had seemed uncomfortable to witness my immediate gush of hot, sorrowful tears, which were always poised on the cliff edge, ready to jump. He couldn't get out of there quick enough.

'I've read your notes. I can see that you have been through an awful lot.'

Silence.

'I've spoken to your partner, who tells me you don't have any history of depression, but as I've said, the staff are worried about your state of mind and the level of crying.'

I slowly turned back and looked pointedly at the treasured photo on my locker of my two beautiful, healthy little babies; eyes closed, entwined together, wrapped in a tiny faux-fur rug. Over a month since the ambulance had ripped me away from my family. Longer separated from my precious twins than I had spent with them. Would they even remember my smell, my touch, my voice?

'If I stop crying every day, you should worry about me.'

'You know, you're right. I'm sorry.'

He laid his hand softly on my arm, nodded and walked out the door. I planted the palms of my hands deep into my eye sockets and sobbed to my aching heart's content.

In Memory

BY ÁINE DURKIN

They said I couldn't possibly remember, but how could I ever forget?

There are things I'd rather not see, but the lost-and-found compartment of my brain has a mind of its own. It pays no heed whatsoever to what I want or don't want to recollect. My memories are mute, like silent movies without the subtitles. This particular one is stuck on replay. Sadly, I see it over and over again.

I'm in their bedroom. Nothing is being said. It is deathly quiet. My father is standing there, just inside the door. My mother is still in bed.

Why is Daddy crying?

I am seven years of age, too young to grasp the reason for his anguish, but old enough to sense its presence. I don't speak. My eyes plead with him:

What's wrong with Mom?

He didn't answer. I think his tears got in the way, blurring questions, obscuring answers. 'Go... say goodbye.'

I think that's what he said.

His hands cover his face. The tears tumble over the tips of his fingers, and flow down the back of his hands. I feel scared. Daddies don't cry! Why can't he tell me what's wrong, and put it right?

Now, of course, I understand it all. Heartache had

conquered all hope. Joy had gone. Parenting had been paralysed.

Warily, I move towards the bed. Sadness surrounds me, like quicksand. A sinking feeling is slowing my footsteps. She seems so far away. The room is cold. I look at my mother's face. I want her to look at mine. I want her to smile, but her lips never move.

Maybe she's praying. That must be it. I don't think people smile when they're praying... do they? But, their lips would move... wouldn't they?

I can't recall if I kissed you goodbye. Maybe I touched your long, white gown. Maybe I didn't. I wish I could remember your face. I didn't have enough time.

I doubt if my mother will ever forget you, Ciarán. She never took her eyes off you. Not even for a second. There was so little time left. One day was all she had been given. Just one day, to fill that lifetime memory space her newborn son would leave behind.

Don't Ask

BY AOIFE CHAOMHANACH

'Anything stirring?'
   'Any neeewws?'
   'Anything we should know about?'
'Anything to tell us...?'
'When will we hear the pitter-patter of tiny feet?'
'When will you get going?'

Some women, irrespective of the closeness of our relationship, assume it's appropriate to flippantly inquire about my sex life, the state of my reproductive system, my egg reserve, my partner's sperm count, my life goals. It is done in that peculiarly Irish way of shrouding the question in euphemisms, making it sound benign, even funny.

It isn't, and don't ask.

No – not even if you're 'only asking' or 'didn't know' or 'hadn't thought' or 'hadn't realised' or 'wanted to be a granny'.

Not all eggs are sunny-side up. This is something you need to know and need to act on; like a practised and serene Taoist living the 'doing by non-doing' philosophy of life.

And your advice of 'just relax' or 'go on a holiday' or 'have a few drinks of a Friday night' do not work as reproductive methods – thanks. We tried them. All of them. Believe me. We know.

And, if as in my case, you receive surprise post from the fertility clinic of a scientific graph plotting my ovarian reserve at less than one out of 20 – referred to as a 'trace', a ghost of an egg, a mere shadow – don't tell me to 'do something else with my life'.

And don't – please DON'T, when in spite of that brutal, irrefutable graph, we somehow, unbelievably, become pregnant – don't ask, 'Was it planned?' or say, 'See? Told you all you had to do was relax.'

And when – despite the graphs, despite the doctors, despite science, and because of a fusion of love and hope and crucially mere chance – our blood-covered child pushes himself, with all he can muster, out and into this world, please, PLEASE, don't ask, 'When are you going again?'

Reflection

BY AUDREY HANNIGAN

Reflection (rɪ'flɛkʃᵊn) *n.*
1. the throwing back by a body or surface of light, heat, or sound without absorbing it. **2.** deep or careful thought.

I sat there, cupping my mug of tea with both hands, thinking about all the little things I remembered about her. Then I sat there thinking about all the big things I remembered about her. Why didn't I ask more questions about what had happened? Why didn't I ask how she was feeling when it all happened? How did she decide to do it? When did she decide to do it? How did they keep it a secret for so long?

So many questions swirled around my head, some with the answers accompanying them, some without. Why didn't we talk more about the past than the future? We knew what the answers were to the questions we asked the future. The past was different; it was like a newspaper with all the headlines, but the stories below cut out.

The beeping of the washing machine quietened my thoughts and brought my focus back to the kitchen and to what my dad was doing. I watched him pull himself off the chair, a move that seemed to last far too long at the time. His strong arms moved slowly and clumsily as he tried to understand how she made the clothes hang the way they did. The confused look on his face, his puckered lips, furrowed brow, a sigh that would release what seemed like every couple of seconds. I pondered whether it was the memory of her carrying out the simple tasks around the house or his frustration at not knowing how to complete such a simple daily task that made his face look this way.

He eventually completed it. Slowly, he walked inside with an empty basket. I scurried back to the couch and tried to remember the exact position I was in when he went out to the clothes line. He returned to the kitchen looking dejected, with a face that looked even more pained than he had left with. I decided not to ask how it went. Did he have enough pegs? Did all the clothes fit on? Instead I knew this was a time to stay silent. His glum, pained face wasn't because he struggled to get the shirt straight or it wasn't because he left the basket too far out of his reach. It was because his heart ached for her – for her voice, for her smell, her presence.

It was the first time he truly felt her loss. She was gone and was not going to come back.

And no matter how well he carried out those simple daily tasks, no matter how many he completed, it would not make him feel like he would be OK. It would only be a daily reminder of what he missed, what he had lost and what wasn't coming back. She was gone, he was lonely and I had to watch.

ACKNOWLEDGEMENTS

Firstly, thank you for buying this book.

Thanks to the *Ray D'Arcy Show* team on RTÉ Radio 1: Niamh Hassell, Niamh Hamell, Neil Doherty, Fiona Donnellan, David O'Sullivan and Emily Hurley.

To our dynamic reading duo of Penny Hart and Rachel Breslin, we say thanks.

Thanks to Brendan Corbett from Eason for his help and encouragement.

To our esteemed judges: Donal Ryan, Emer McLysaght, Emilie Pine and Eoin Colfer, thank you all so much.

A huge thank you to Conor Nagle at HarperCollins *Ireland* for his belief in this book and to his colleague Nora Mahony for her astute editing.

Finally, and most sincerely, to all the writers who bared their souls and shared their stories, THANK YOU.